HANDBOOK
FOR THE
CRIMINALLY
INSANE

CODEX OF THE DEMON KING - BOOK I

A novel by

B. K. BRAIN

Also by B. K. BRAIN

SUPERNATURAL THRILLERS:

DEAD YET DYING

NEPHILIM PUSH

HANDBOOK FOR THE FESTIVE SOCIOPATH

———

YOUNG ADULT FANTASY:

DORIS AND THE ANKH

———

SCIENCE FICTION:

COLLAPSE AT HIDDEN VERSE 3-3-2

———

SHORTS:

HARVEY & ETHEL

A PLAGUE OF STEVE

JEREMY'S POTENTIAL

THE HIDDEN

This book is a work of fiction. Names, characters, places and incidents
either are products of the author's imagination or are used fictitiously.
Any resemblance to actual events or locals or persons, living, dead or undead,
is entirely coincidental.

HANDBOOK FOR THE CRIMINALLY INSANE

© Copyright 2015, B. K. Brain, Brian Holtz

All rights reserved
No part of this book may be reproduced,
stored in a retrieval system,
or transmitted by any means, electronic,
mechanical, photocopying, recording, or otherwise,
without written permission from the author.

Cover design and layout by Miroslava Sobot

Published by
Brian Holtz
Canon City, Colorado
nephilimpush@yahoo.com

Printed in the United States of America
by CreateSpace, Charleston, SC

ISBN-13: 978-1522854876
ISBN-10: 1522854878

First Edition, 2015

For Darren

CONTENTS

——

——

1

A NOT SO FRESH START

The sunrise on October second found Thomas Able belly-down in the mud, wearing a rented tuxedo. His face, submerged in opaque brown water, had not the benefit of air for more than five hours. He remained where he was, silent and alone, until twelve-year-old Rodney Pinkerton discovered him in the backyard while searching for a baseball. The boy did not try to help Mr. Able to his feet, nor were there any words exchanged. It was assumed the man was in no condition to be sociable due to the axe implanted in his back. Rodney took a moment to scream, then rushed inside to inform his mother.

Sheriff Deputies Leonard Simms and Stanley Ackerman arrived ten minutes later. They walked across the yard with weapons drawn, each taking a different side of the house as an ambulance rounded a corner three blocks away. They scanned the area with caution. Nothing out of the ordinary caught their attention until they reached the back porch. The deputies met at a wooden staircase and stood side by side.

They looked across a large square of overgrown land. The previous night's rain had left behind glistening wild flowers, cold pools of dark water, and mud. It had also left behind Thomas Able. He remained immobile under a battered swing set, with a long axe tucked in his spine like a fallen elm. A briefcase sat ajar in a patch of wet grass. One shoe was missing. The men kept their distance as if an impaled back was an infectious disease.

Simms holstered his pistol, then unhooked a police radio from his belt and spoke into it. "Sheriff Shane, you copy?"

A static voice came back. "This is Shane, go ahead."

"We've got a victim over here with an axe stuck in his back."

Silence, the kind one might expect after such a statement, lingered over static airwaves. Sheriff Shane pulled the microphone close, considering his response. He then asked, "Are they dead?"

The deputy looked over the corpse, the weapon, and the yard.

"Yes, sir. He looks pretty dead."

An ambulance duo rushed into the yard with cases of medical supplies. They pulled the submerged face out of the dirty water, tilting the body away from the ground. One man felt for a pulse. He found nothing but raw, pallid skin.

Interference crackled over the radio. "An axe you say?"

The deputy wiped cool sweat from his brow with a wrinkled sleeve. "Yup."

The sheriff paused for a moment to admire a photo of him and his wife, Barbara, which sat in front of him on a cluttered desk. It had been taken at the little league championship game in Ryerton. His grandson's team had just been awarded first place. Barbara clapped, spilling popcorn on a woman in front of her. The sheriff stood smiling with hands on his hips, as any proud grandpa would. The picture was a clipping from the front page of the *Redmondsburg Daily News*, July 24.

He reached for a tin of chewing tobacco, loaded his cheek, and then pulled the radio close. "It sounds like a traffic accident to me."

A paramedic yanked at the wooden handle, attempting to extricate the blade from Tom's vertebrae. It wouldn't budge.

"Okay," Simms replied, shrugging his shoulders and exchanging confusion with the other deputy. "A traffic accident. That sounds reasonable...I suppose."

With mud in his mouth and eyes, the man on the ground complained. Naturally they couldn't hear him; he was dead.

Are you people insane? I wasn't hit by a car! There's an axe in my back!

The EMT tried again. Pulling on the axe only served to lift the corpse off the ground. "Can I get some help here?"

Ackerman stepped on the back of the head while another paramedic held the shoulders down. "Okay. Try it again."

With a heave, the weapon cracked loose.

Ouch! Newly-dead Tom thought. *Watch it; that hurts!*

With the axe tossed aside, the EMT rolled the body over. Mud slid down pale cheeks, away from unfocused eyes. It gurgled down an open esophagus.

I'm not really dead, am I?

The men stood with arms crossed, looking death in the muddy eye. An icy squall abused nearby wind chimes. Loose papers tumbled across the yard.

I haven't been here that long! Try mouth-to-mouth or something!

"He's gone," one EMT said to the other. "What a shame. He was my lawyer."

No! Tom screamed. *Hit me with one of those electrode things. My heart will start right up!*

Deputy Simms turned to a woman and son at the back door. The boy sobbed with his face buried in his mother's side.

"Is this your axe?"

"No," the woman said in a wobbly voice, inches away from tears. "I've never seen it before."

The deputy smiled. "Do you want it?"

She scowled. "Good Lord, no. Don't you need it for the criminal investigation or something?"

"Mmm...not really, no."

Please, Tom cried. *Help! I can't be dead.*

"You're listening to your local WKAZ radio. I'm your host with the most, your station sensation, Bruce Bradley. I'm accompanied as usual by the lovely, the beautiful, the smart as a tart, Katrina Webber. Good morning, Kat."

"Thanks, Bruce...I think. Good morning, everyone. Here are your top stories. A car accident at the corner of Oak and Pennsylvania has left one man dead. The vehicle went out of control early this morning and hit a telephone pole. The sheriff has not indicated if alcohol or drugs were involved.

———

"Vandalism struck Pheasant Park last night. A statue of the founder of the town, Hank Redmond, was found covered in toilet paper. Also a pair of red women's panties had been stretched over his stone head."

"Kids will do anything these days."

"Apparently, Bruce. There were no witnesses to the crime, although local officials say that a full investigation is underway."

"That's nice for old Hank. It's got to be the first women's delicates he's seen in more than a hundred years. Good for him."

"I suppose so, Bruce. On a lighter note, the city council is gearing up for the third annual Halloween celebration. It will kick off Thursday the twenty-second with the Spooks and Specters carnival and run through Halloween day. The parade will take place on Saturday the twenty-fourth and run from one till three p.m., starting at Second Street and ending at Twelfth Street, on Main, in downtown Redmondsburg."

"It sounds like a lot of spooky fun."

"Sounds like it, Bruce. And now on to your local weather. It will be breezy and cold today, with a high of forty-two degrees. Winds are currently out of the northwest at twenty miles per hour. Expect your low tonight to be fifteen degrees."

"Ooh. Chilly. My nipples are getting hard just thinking about it... Check it out, Kat."

"No thanks, Bruce."

A small sign at the eastern city limit read "Welcome to Redmondsburg." It was hidden behind a gathering of trees showing the sparse symptoms of a coming winter. Monica barely noticed it as she sped by. Her mind was fixed on her ex-husband, five years of failed marriage, and an uneasy fear of change.

She'd known that she wanted to move for months now, ever since the divorce was final, but it hadn't solidified in her mind until she'd seen

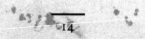

the house. It was beautiful, reminding her of the home she'd grown up in. There was a winding staircase, a huge kitchen and dining room, and an attic for storage. Sure, it needed some serious work, mostly paint and carpet, but it would be perfect.

The most important thing was that she was getting out of the city. She'd only moved there for him, because of his job. She never liked Woodard. Everything was always too crowded and too rushed. She wouldn't miss the malls or nightclubs.

Monica liked small towns and small-town people. They brought back memories of her own hometown, a place she hadn't been since her parents moved to Florida. She was looking for a slow pace, friendly neighbors, and an atmosphere where she could relax. Redmondsburg seemed to be all of those things and it didn't hurt a bit that it was three hundred miles from the city, and him. She hoped the painful memories would stay behind as she made an attempt at a new beginning. Her only regret was that she was moving away from Suzanne.

They'd known each other since kindergarten. She still remembered the very first time they met. It had been on a Thursday afternoon during recess. Monica was on the floor playing with a large mound of snap-together blocks. She hummed to herself, building a structurally unsound, yet colorful wall.

Suzanne, sporting short red hair and a runny nose, arrived without warning. She grabbed for an armload of blocks and began her own project. Sharing was not one of Monica's strong points so she told the redhead to get lost. Suzanne paid little attention as she sat happy and grinning, helping herself to more supplies. Without further hesitation, Monica leaned back on her elbows, cocked her leg, and then proceeded to kick the happy off the offending girl's snotty little face.

Good times, Monica thought, smiling.

With the bliss successfully pruned from Suzanne's tread-printed expression, screaming filled the air. It was a great and pitiful wail that could bloody eardrums and inspire migraines. The teacher, Mrs. Bleachman, crossed the room like fire on dry grass. Monica would never forget how it felt to be lifted off the carpet by the back of the neck, with long, manicured fingernails piercing tender skin.

Two combative six-year-olds were dragged to the principal's office, blubbering with the enthusiasm of the mortally wounded.

The next afternoon they became friends, because that's how childhood operates sometimes. Not to say their friendship was perfect. Even more than twenty years later, Suzanne hadn't fully forgiven Monica for kicking her in the forehead.

She moved to the city a few months after Monica and Ben, almost five years ago. The women were nearly inseparable, especially after the marriage went sour. They spent most evenings at Suzanne's apartment downtown. They reminisced about carefree grade school days and prom dates. They drank margaritas and watched old movies. Those nights kept Monica sane during the divorce. She felt lucky to have such a good friend.

Highway 28 cut through a residential neighborhood before reaching downtown. She slowed the truck when the speed limit dropped to thirty. Once in the business district, the road became Rocky Creek Way. She liked the sound of that. Everything about Redmondsburg screamed small town, from the historic buildings and little shops to the tall statue of Hank Redmond, the founder of the town, in Pheasant Park.

Monica drove by, watching people stand on street corners as they talked with one another. She saw a group of children on skateboards zipping down the sidewalk. Another child on a bicycle pedaled, carrying a gas can in one hand.

It's Monday, she thought. *Why aren't you in school?*

Her trek led her past Johnson's grocery, two antique shops, and a store called Unusual Finds. The Sheriff's Office was smaller than the gas station, which struck her as odd. There was a public library, a post office, and a restaurant called the Redmondsburg Diner.

Monica soon found herself in another neighborhood. She passed through, studying the houses. Most were Victorian homes with trimmed yards and picket fences. As the highway continued west of town, she saw a dry cornfield and then a thick forest. Miller Drive was labeled with a weathered, almost illegible sign. The dirt road led past her house and Lakeshore Cemetery.

Monica liked the idea of having a graveyard across the road. Everything was quiet. The only traffic she expected would be during funeral services. It would be a nice place to clear her head.

She pulled into the driveway and got out. The breeze was sharp, chilling her face and arms. She rubbed at exposed shoulders, evaluating her property. The porch would need new paint. The yard was full of weeds. There was a cracked window upstairs. Monica knew there was work to be done but it didn't hinder her love of the house. In fact, now that she was there with keys in hand, she was ready to get started. There was just the annoying business of unloading the pickup and trailer, which needed to be done first.

She ascended creaky steps. A wooden bench hung from the porch ceiling with corroded chains. A row of three flowerpots, each containing parched soil and a crumbling plant, occupied a shadow below the window. The screen door protested with a raspy whine as she pulled it open. A pause in the doorway; a deep, calming breath. Monica's new life waited for her inside.

She managed a smile, unlocking the deadbolt.

Monica carried in the last box at six o'clock that evening. The entire dining room was stacked full, with only a narrow path between. With beads of sweat rolling down her brow, she flopped into a chair. The two recliners and mattress had been quite a challenge by herself, but she'd handled them better than expected. She was glad she didn't own a couch. With closed eyes Monica tried to catch her breath.

A noise startled her. It sounded like a slammed door, upstairs.

What was that?

From somewhere above a child called out. It sounded like they said "meggo" or perhaps "leggo," as in "let go." The voice was forceful and distressed.

Monica leapt from the chair and dashed up the steps, taking two at a time. With a pause at the summit, she listened. A powerful wind creaked chains on the porch swing. A loose shutter slapped a window frame downstairs. Dust from the yard abused chipped paint on the west side of the house. A distant dog barked.

"Where are you?"

A scratching sounded, like a cat sharpening its claws. It came from the back bedroom. Monica raced. Other than a mattress and box spring leaning against the far wall, the room was empty.

Boards creaked right above her. She sped into the hallway and up the ladder. The sun was down and the attic was dark.

"Hello? Is somebody there?" The scratching stopped.

She wiped at sweat in her eyes with clammy fingers. A frantic heartbeat thumped in her chest, echoing in her throat.

"I heard you. Come on out. Don't be afraid."

She clicked a pull chain and a bulb lit up. A coating of dust shrouded every surface. There was an old trunk, some broken chairs, and a couple of boxes. Insulation dangled like torn cobwebs. The floor was littered with bent nails. Monica opened the trunk nervously. She saw old magazines, newspapers, and a leather-bound notebook. The boxes were stained and torn. One was empty. The other held a pile of musty clothing.

"Hello?" she said once more.

Little droplets of rain tapped on the window in a random percussion. A flash of lightning blurred the glass.

It wasn't my imagination. I heard it.

Monica went down the ladder to search the rest of the house.

The two days inside the body bag were excruciating for dead Tom. He couldn't move, see, or breathe. It was unbelievably boring.

Finally, on the evening of the second day, a mortician unzipped the bag. Fluids drained as the corpse gazed into a florescent light. He was lowered into the soft, silk padding of a shiny coffin. A new suit, sliced up the back, was fitted over him. The mortician stuffed the loose ends of clothing under Tom's body, as if he were tucking him in for a good night's sleep. Then he applied makeup to cover pale skin and combed Tom's hair.

After two hours of preparation, Thomas Able was ready for viewing. The lid closed down, once again enveloping him in darkness.

Many nice things were said about Tom at the funeral. His older brother Bob gave the eulogy, at one point describing him as a "hell of a good guy." People sobbed and prayed. After the service they approached one after another, talking as if he were listening. Little did they know, he was.

His wife was the first. "Oh, Thomas, why did you leave me like this? I'm so sorry for cheating on you with Will."

Will? Tom fumed. *William Barker? The insurance salesman?*

His brother was next. "I'm gonna miss you, man," he said. "It was me who stole the twenty dollars from you that time when we were kids. Sorry."

It was you? I was saving up for a new bike. You knew how bad I wanted it.

As the procession continued, Tom found out that a wallet he'd lost two years ago really was found, just not returned. He was told that his grocer had also slept with his wife, and his best friend. His poker buddies were cheaters and he'd been charged for a tune-up his car didn't receive.

You people are a bunch of jerks. Screw you all!

By eight o'clock Monica had given up the search. She decided the voice must have come from outside. It was likely some kids messing around in the cemetery. She went to the kitchen to unpack dishes.

Monica thought about the last time she'd seen Suzanne. Strangely enough, it was also the last time she'd seen her ex-husband, Ben. She and Suzanne were having dinner at her favorite restaurant, Luigi's. Their fettuccini Alfredo was the best in the city; everyone said so, but it wasn't cheap. Two people could easily drop eighty to a hundred bucks on dinner and drinks. Fortunately, the tab was on Suzanne that night.

She'd said it was a going-away dinner, but what it turned out to be was a try-to-talk-Monica-out-of-leaving dinner. Which was exactly what Monica had expected. Her friend didn't handle change well, nor would she give up without a fight. In the end her agenda was unsuccessful, in spite of an emotional outburst preceded by three rum and Cokes consumed in less than an hour.

Monica did not join in the drinking, as she planned to get up early. She wanted to leave no later than eight. It was a five-hour drive to her new home and she was anxious to be done with it.

Thirty minutes after they'd finished eating and one of three rum and Cokes down Suzanne's throat, something unexpected happened. Some folks might've described it as ironic, although Monica wasn't one of them. She was too angry to recognize irony.

Out the window and across the street, she spotted Ben and his new girlfriend walking hand in hand. They were laughing when she first noticed them. He then pulled her close and kissed her.

"Asshole," Monica spat, and then, "That little tramp."

Suzanne turned to look. "Oh shit."

Out of all the people in the Metropolitan area that could've been walking down that particular sidewalk at that particular time, it was him. The son of a bitch that cheated on her. The jackass that had single-handedly destroyed three years of marriage and commitment. The one she now referred to as "that fucker."

"That fucker," she said. "And that little tramp." Her face went beet red.

"I'm sorry," Suzanne said. "If I'd known he was going to be sleazing around here, I'd have taken you to McDonald's."

Ben and his date disappeared into a bar. Monica watched them go, more determined than ever to get out of the city. And when she was gone, with all the pain and bad memories behind, she'd have her fresh start. Her new beginning. Her do-over. Small-town America was calling her name and she would not be looking back. Bad things happen when you look back.

The window above the sink provided a view of the graveyard across the road. Tall trees rustled against powerful winds as leaves spiraled above the grass. Occasional flashes of lightning illuminated the grounds and headstones. A stern bolt split the sky in half, and for a moment the cemetery lit up as bright as day. The strobe illuminated a man standing rigid across the road.

Monica gasped. A cup slipped from her fingers and hit the sink. She strained to see into the darkness, as heavy rain blasted over the windowpane, blurring the view. She went to the living room around stacks of boxes, and made her way to the light switch. With the overhead light off, she squinted out the front window. Another flash of lightning. The man was still there and had taken to waving arms in the air. His mouth was agape, like he was yelling something. The storm's howl nullified his voice, refusing to let the sound cross the road.

"What is he doing?" she said to herself.

Maybe he needs help. But if he does, he can walk over here and tell me so.

She realized her hands were trembling and clamped them together. The dark silhouette punched at the air with clenched fists, stumbling backward.

"That guy is drunk."

She considered calling the sheriff, but then remembered the phone wouldn't be hooked up until next week. She didn't have a cell.

Maybe he'll get bored and go away.

"Get lost, loser. Go sleep it off."

A light came alive from somewhere above. At first Monica thought it was lightning. But after a few seconds she realized the glow hadn't faded away. Close to the glass, she looked upward to try to find the source. The light blazed on from somewhere above, perhaps an upstairs bedroom. Monica looked back at the man and saw that he was limping into the shadows.

She set out to investigate. Up the steps she went, afraid of what she would find. There was a light shining from the attic.

"Who's there?" she said.

Her body trembled with fear.

"I've phoned the police," she called out. "They'll be here any minute."

Slowly, she climbed the ladder. The higher she went, the brighter it got. And then it went out. Monica's pulse raced.

"Answer me," she said into the shadows.

Nothing.

"I've got a gun!" she yelled.

That wasn't a lie. It was a single-pump BB gun packed at the bottom of a box downstairs.

Gripped by full-on panic, her stuttering hand reached for the pull chain. The attic lit up and she quickly scanned her surroundings. There was no one else. The room was silent.

She stepped onto the trunk and reached for the bulb at the ceiling. With an index finger she tapped the rounded glass. It went dark. Another tap coaxed it back to life.

"The wiring in this place sucks."

After the funeral a burial took place in the northeast corner of Lakeshore Cemetery. Covered over with six feet of soil, Tom remained in the lonely pitch-blackness for more than seven hours.

At the stroke of midnight he realized he could move. His body convulsed to life as he heaved for air. A horrible scream filled the coffin. His fists pounded against the dark confinement. "Let me out!"

He heard banging from somewhere below, and voices.

A quake startled him.

Then another.

Tom's body fell. He descended fifteen feet, and in a collision of earth and wood, hit a hard stone floor. He scrambled away from the broken coffin and torn silk. In a panic, he stood in a dim passageway.

Walking, moaning corpses closed in. Again, Thomas screamed. A tall one lurched forward on a good foot, with the other leg trailing behind like an exhausted fish. The dead man's skin was like worn leather, dry and wrinkled. His eyes were milky white and drooling. Only one tooth remained in his rotten mouth; it was chipped and yellow. Phlegm gurgled in his throat as he spoke.

"You are one of us now. We are the king's army." His breath was potent.

Audibly, the message came out as "Mmmffyahll grrahhm phfft."

Tom understood every word and was amazed that he knew what it meant.

"Moo garr umm he yahhll," said another, which translated to "He is good and strong."

They all joined in, and Tom found himself surrounded by dead speak.

"You people are dead!" he wailed.

The gathering laughed, which sounded very much like moaning.

"I don't belong here!"

"Glub in panu," said a man with a torn scalp and an extreme under bite.

Tom looked over. "I am *not* a pussy."

"Then feed," the rotten man said in gurgling gibberish.

A large plate was passed along from one to another. It was set down at Tom's feet. An entire human brain sat on its dusty surface.

"My god," he said. "I can't eat that."

The aroma wafted up to his pale face. His stomach rumbled.

"I can't..." He was famished, and the smell was enticing. "I...uh... maybe just a bite."

The undead crowd cheered as he dropped to his knees to feast. The taste was better than anything he'd experienced before. The sensation was explosive.

I can't stop, he thought. *I've got to have more. More. MORE.*

"Welcome, brother," the tall one moaned. "Welcome to the crypt of the demon king."

Newly-dead Tom, on his knees and feasting on a surprisingly chewy brain, watched the tall, leathery man approach. He put a cold hand on Tom's head and held the other toward the sky. A strange flow of incomprehensible words began. As the magical speech continued, Tom felt his humanity and compassion, his very soul, slip. A pure animal instinct danced in his mind. A hatred for the living grew. Only two things defined him: rage and hunger. Thomas Able growled like a starving beast.

Then voices down a connecting corridor distracted the tall one's dehumanizing ritual. He stopped in midphrase as another announced the arrival of their master. The final incantation was forgotten as the group rushed to the central chamber. With the unfinished ritual's power fading, humanity took over Tom's thoughts once again. He stood and followed the group.

"I don't think it worked."

The dead limped and lurched down the corridor, moaning. No one cared that his mind was still human. The only thing that mattered was getting to their master.

He said, "I wanted to kill the living for a second, but I...uh...I don't really want to anymore."

They ignored him.

"The evil didn't take, guys."

He joined the gathering in the central chamber as a man spoke, explaining a dark agenda. The dead all around cheered at each terrible point made. He tried to join in but enthusiasm was lacking. He had to admit that brains were delicious, but he just didn't get the whole hatred of the living thing. No one around him seemed to notice or care.

2

THE SPOILS
OF DEATH

At seven a.m., Monica sat sleeping in a recliner with a BB gun resting across her lap. The sunlight shining through windows with no curtains was warm on her skin. A swift breeze scattered leaves outside. She shook awake and glanced around, making sure she was alone. It was impossible to know when she'd fallen asleep, although it had to have been sometime after three. She rubbed weary eyes and set the gun on the floor.

What a night.

She stood and went to the kitchen in search of caffeine. A package of filters sat at the bottom of a milk crate. The coffee can was next to the carafe in the sink.

The cemetery, bright and quiet, sat in direct contrast to the previous night's events. Monica looked out over the grounds, thinking about the voice in the attic. Her stomach rumbled. There wasn't any food in the house yet, so it seemed a trip to the market was in order.

After I take a shower, she thought, *I'll go into town.*

She'd stop at the Sheriff's Office also, to inform them of the drunk in the graveyard. Maybe she could get a patrol to check in on her tonight, just in case.

Dead Tom wandered the dark corridors of the underground mausoleum, wishing he were still alive. His stomach rumbled as he limped along, exploring. A dark figure approached. It had been a woman in life, but having been dead more than ten years, its features were unrecognizable. It spoke a high-pitched, gritty tone, laughing. One drippy eyeball hung loose from a dark socket, while the other remained in place.

"Tommy?" she moaned, "Is that really you?"

"Mom?" he said in shock.

"Yes, dear!"

She waddled up and hugged him. "I wondered when you'd be joining us."

"I can't believe it," he said. "I missed you, Mom."

She took a step back. "Did you have a heart attack? Was it all that fatty food that killed you? You know I told you not to eat so much bacon."

"No, Mom. Someone killed me with an axe."

"Oh," she said with a smile. "Glad to hear it. That's wonderful, dear."

Tom looked toward the floor. "I'm so glad I found you. I've been having second thoughts about this whole brain-eating thing."

"Sit down, son," she said, motioning him to a pile of broken headstones.

The two of them sat in the dim passageway.

"Tommy, remember all that stuff I taught you about treating others with kindness and respect?"

He grinned. "Yes, Mom. I remember."

"Well, it was all crap. Every last word." She took his cold hand. "All that matters now is killing the living."

"But Mom—"

"No buts," she said in a stern voice. "They hate us. We hate them. So, we kill and eat them. It's what we do. We're dead."

"I just don't know if I can do it..."

"You'll do fine, dear. Just fine. Now tell me again about that wonderful axe. I want to hear everything."

Gary Tuttlebaulm stood rigid at the spinning grinder with axe in hand. He sharpened the weapon, readying it and himself for the next outing. His eyes followed along the curvature of its thick blade. With it pressed against the rotating wheel an arc of brilliant sparks shot into the darkness. He smiled at the thinning metal.

The shadowy basement had a cool bite to the air. Goose bumps covered his thick, muscled arms. The chill was soothing; it calmed his jittery nerves. His eye twitched over and over again. The memory of the kill always amused him awhile, but it never took long for the thought of it to yank at his mind like tangled fishing line. It was the fear that did it, the idea of getting caught.

Once satisfied with his project, he lowered the axe and looked into a nearby dusty mirror. The twitch, apparently, had subsided. He headed for the stairs, sucking in a deep breath. Up he went, out of the cold darkness. Wood creaked under his boots as he ascended into daylight.

Given the choice, Gary would've remained in the basement, but he needed to know whom the next victim would be. The only way to find out was to ask Elton.

Elton always knew; he was God.

God was Elton.

And Elton was a hamster.

"There's just got to be more to death than this," Tom said to Wayne McMillan, the dead man sitting next to him. "I mean—eating brains? Plots to kill the living and take over the world? It all just seems so pointless."

"Look," Wayne said, "when I was alive, I was a motivational speaker and an author. I had three published books on success in the workplace, so I know a bit about setting goals and improving self-esteem."

Three published books? Tom was impressed, in spite of the man's missing nose and ear.

Wayne continued. "You gotta embrace your evil, man. Let it flow. I mean—you hate the living, right?"

Tom's smile was half-hearted. "Yeah...I guess so."

"You *guess* so? Come on, man. On the road of death, there are passengers and there are drivers. Which one are you?"

Tom wasn't sure he understood the question. "Um...a driver?"

"That's right, Bob."

"The name's Tom."

"Whatever. All I'm saying is, you gotta take death by the horns, man. You like brains dontcha?"

That was one thing they could agree on. Tom liked brains. Oh yes, he did. "Yeah."

"Of course you do. Who doesn't, right? If you want brains on a daily basis, what has to happen?"

"Umm...we have to sacrifice an innocent on Halloween?"

"Precisely. So what are you gonna do?"

Tom mulled over the question. He knew the answer Wayne wanted to hear, so that's what he gave him. "I'm going to do whatever I can to help capture the innocent."

The motivational speaker's eyes lit up. "Now you've got it. Live death like you mean it!"

"Okay," Tom said, thinking this guy was like a slurring advertisement for sneakers.

"Carpe corpus!" Wayne called out in a battle cry.

"Seize the corpse?"

"Is that what that means?" Wayne asked, his enthusiasm fading.

"I think so."

"Oh...well, I meant to say seize the day."

Tom repeated, "Seize the day."

Wayne smiled big and put an arm around his new pal's shoulder. "That's right, Bob."

"It's Tom."

"Whatever."

With the trailer unhitched from the truck, Monica pulled out of the driveway and onto Miller Drive. The previous night's rain had frozen randomly over the road and in the ditch. She drove carefully over the bright, slick surface. A right turn onto the highway and she would be in downtown Redmondsburg in just a few minutes.

Once through the residential neighborhood and in the business district, Monica saw a farm tractor pulling a flatbed trailer down the middle of the street. A large, colorful banner hung on the side. It read VOTE EDDIE GORDON. A man stood on the trailer with rosy cheeks shining in the brisk air. He wore a brown corduroy suit jacket and sky-blue slacks. A fuzzy hunter's cap protected his ears from the cold. A little dog, a Chihuahua, stood at the edge of the trailer at Gordon's feet.

As Monica drove past, she rolled down the window. His voice boomed from large speakers on each side of the vehicle. It prompted images of a car salesman announcing an insane markdown on preowned automotive beauties. They were deals you couldn't get anywhere else because he was obviously "crazy," just released from the state hospital and given a car lot.

"Vote for me, Eddie Gordon, on election day, and you can be sure that you've voted for someone you can trust!"

People stood gathered on the sidewalks, waving and cheering. Many sported red buttons that said, *Mayor Gordon Rules.*

Monica pulled into a space in front of the Sheriff's Office.

Elton had brown and white fur. He ran on a yellow plastic wheel as Gary walked in. The hamster's living environment was large, taking up the entire surface of a dresser. It was a homemade cage, with a plywood floor and chicken wire fencing for walls and ceiling. Twist ties held it together at the corners and seams.

Elton seemed very happy in his confinement, as he stopped running to eat some sunflower seeds. Grinning, Gary hovered above. He looked at the bottom of the cage, which was lined with squares of newspaper clippings. Each small piece had been glued down to the plywood and was a black-and-white photograph.

Elton scurried over Mayor Gordon's photo, across Deputy Ackerman and Betty Jones, and then stopped to inspect some crumbles of dry food on Daniel Beemer's forehead. He looked up to the one above, sniffing at the air.

Gary's eyes scanned the photos, one by one. The mayor's face was clean, as was Henry Johnson's. Sam Feldon was unsoiled too. The local radio station DJ, Bruce Bradley, smiled in black and white, holding the excellence in broadcasting award he'd received. The city council had presented it to him last May. His photo was in pristine condition.

Then Gary saw what he'd been looking for. It was a picture that had been taken at the Independence Day festival the previous summer. It showed the mayor's wife, Georgette Gordon, receiving a blue ribbon for the pie-baking contest. The entire lower half of the newsprint was stained with hamster urine. Gary's brow slid upward as he clamped hands together. A grin stretched his mouth, inflating reddened cheeks.

"Georgette, hmm?" he said. "Good choice, my Lord. It will be done."

Gary opened the wire lid, carefully sliding in a calendar page. Elton scurried out of the way as October was set down over the plywood. Gary relatched the cage, and the hamster sniffed at the edge of the paper. He walked slowly across the second week, then over the third. He seemed fond of Friday the thirtieth for a moment, but then abruptly backed up to Thursday, defecating in the center of the square.

"The twenty-ninth," Gary said with glee. "Perfect."

When Elton was finished, he scurried across the cage in search of more seeds.

An elderly woman sat crocheting at the front desk. She turned to Monica and lowered the colorful doily into her lap.

"Hello."

"Hi. Could I speak to someone about a disturbance last night, please?"

"A disturbance? Oh my, yes."

The yellow-and-orange project was set on the counter, and the woman retreated into a small office. After a moment, the sheriff appeared at the doorway. His uniform was stained and wrinkled. He was at least seventy years old. His gruff face hadn't seen a razor for days.

"Hello," he said with a thick chaw of tobacco in his cheek. "I'm Sheriff Shane. Come in and have a seat, young lady."

"Thank you," she said, following him in, and they both sat.

"I'm Monica Green. I just moved into a house on Miller Drive, across from the cemetery."

The man's eyes brightened. "Oh, the old Bishop place. That's a fine house."

He paused to spit a glob of brown juice into a five-gallon bucket. Monica wrinkled her nose.

"Yeah, it's great."

"So, sweetie pie, what's the problem?"

"Well, there was somebody creeping around the graveyard last night. I'm pretty sure they were drunk."

"It's a popular spot with the kids," he remarked, as if it were nothing out of the ordinary.

Unsatisfied with his reaction, she said, "It was a bit frightening."

"Yeah." He rubbed an unshaven chin. "The cemetery is open to visitors, you know."

"At midnight?"

"There is no curfew at that location...none that I'm aware of. Were they on your property at any time?"

"Well no, but—"

"Then I'm afraid there's not much I can do."

Monica's frustration flushed her face. "I was hoping that you could send a patrol by tonight. It would make me feel better."

He spit into the bucket again.

"Oh sure, sure. No problem. It was just some kids out having fun. There's not a lot to do around here, you know."

"So thanks, I guess," she said, standing up.

"You betcha, honey muffin. Anything for a lady so pretty as yourself."

Honey muffin? What a creep.

"I'll be going, then. Good-bye."

"Good day to ya, and welcome to town. I'm sure you'll just love it here. We all do."

Monica walked out.

Oh, I love it already, you worthless, old loser. What a waste of time.

Monica climbed into the pickup cab and slammed the door hard.

"Is this Mayberry or something? Do they actually enforce the law, or what?"

She backed the truck out of the space and then headed for the market.

Monica entered the corner grocery store and a little bell above the door announced her arrival. She rubbed her hands together to warm them and looked up at a solitary cash register and the man behind it. He was in his seventies with a head full of wavy gray hair. His eyebrows were unruly and dark. They seemed to move with their own motivations as his forehead flexed. His mouth pinched together tightly, creating rows of small wrinkles just above his upper lip. He had the look of a man who wanted to say something, but for whatever reason, couldn't. He stood with aged hands flat on the glass countertop, watching Monica.

It was the most dimly lit market she'd ever seen, and no amount of canned corn or colorful lottery scratch tickets could brighten her first impression.

"Hello," she said.

The man stayed quiet. He only nodded in her direction as his bushy brow lowered.

She walked toward the deli counter, having a look around. The store was small compared to the supermarkets she was accustomed to in the city, but it would meet her needs until she could get to the Albertson's in Ryerton.

A gathering of five shopping carts sat in a row next to the candy machines. Monica set her purse in the nearest and pushed it toward aisle six. The cart's wheels spun and crunched over a rough concrete floor. It pulled hard to the left as she struggled to keep a straight, forward momentum. She considered going back for another, but the bushy-eyed grocer watched her every move. She found herself wanting out of his line of sight as soon as possible. She retreated into the pop and potato chip aisle, yanking the back of the cart over every couple of steps.

An elderly woman stood reading the ingredients on the back of a corn chip bag. She looked up at Monica maneuvering the broken cart with some frustration.

"That cart doesn't like you, I'd say," she said in a raspy tone.

"Well, that would make us even."

The old lady frowned, "I haven't seen you before. Who are you?"

Who am I? Monica thought, considering the blunt question.

She jerked the cart once more, forcing it to conform to her will. She smiled and looked the woman in the face. "I'm Monica Green. I just moved here from Woodard."

"Woodard?" the woman said, stuffing the bag back onto the shelf. "That's an awful place. The crime rate is terrible."

"Yes, I know."

"This town," she said with a piercing gaze, "is even worse."

The words caught Monica by surprise. "Worse?"

The woman's wrinkly face scowled, cinched by an invisible drawstring. She leaned close and whispered. "Around every corner. Inside every shadow. Behind every door."

Monica backed away from the crazy old lady. "Oh?"

"Yes, dear. Move back to the city…if you want to live."

Another cart rounded the corner, driven by a professional-looking woman in a dark gray business suit. Her stare seemed to burn into the older woman's nerves.

"Oh, hello," she said in a very welcoming voice. "Wanda, who's your friend?"

The wrinkled face pinched in disgust, and she gripped her cart tight. "This is Monica. She's from the city."

"The city? How nice." She turned to offer a hand to Monica. It was icy cold.

"Nice to meet you," Monica said.

"Yes. I'm Georgette Gordon, the mayor's wife."

"The mayor? Great," Monica said, trying to sound enthusiastic.

"Are you the one who bought the Bishop property?"

"Yes, I moved in yesterday."

"That's just wonderful. It's a great old house. Just beautiful."

Monica watched the older woman walk away. Georgette looked over too.

"I hope Wanda wasn't trying to scare you. She's a bit daft."

Wanda, still within hearing range, turned and said, "Yes, I'm daft all right."

Georgette smiled bigger. "And completely deaf. She can't hear a word anyone says."

The old woman kept walking away. "Oh yes. I'm deaf too. I forgot."

Monica said, "Um, well...I've got some shopping to do so—"

"Of course you do," the mayor's wife said. "Don't let me stop you. And welcome. We'll look for your support on election day."

"I just moved here. I don't think I'd be eligible to vote."

"We'll let you, as long as you vote for Eddie." Georgette laughed. "He's going for his third term. Everyone just loves him."

"Okay then, I'll see you later."

Monica shoved her rebel cart around the corner, toward the next aisle. Georgette watched with intensity as she walked away.

"Bye now."

Monica looked down into a cooler full of ground meat. *What a bunch of weirdos.*

She looked up from the hamburger. Through a window she saw a fat butcher, dressed all in white and stained with fresh blood. With a dripping cleaver, he chopped into a hanging side of beef with great force. Monica wrinkled her nose.

That's appetizing.

She strolled, looking over the pork chops. She then saw something she'd never seen in a market before, on a thin slab of Styrofoam and wrapped in cellophane.

Squirrel brains.

"What the hell?"

A woman startled her from behind. "Some folks say that eating squirrel brains will make you smarter."

Monica looked into another elderly face.

A much younger voice sounded from the other direction. "Only if you're dumber than a squirrel."

"Hmf," the old lady huffed, walking away.

A blonde in her mid twenties got closer. She was very attractive with chiseled, slim features and looked out of place in the small market. Monica glanced back to be sure the other woman was gone.

"You're the first person I've seen today who isn't over eighty. Well, besides the mayor's wife."

The blonde smiled. "Yeah, all the geriatrics shop here. Everybody else drives to Ryerton."

"Oh."

The woman walked closer. "I'm Betty. Betty Jones."

"I'm Monica Green. I just moved here."

"A newbie, huh? Well, let me give you some advice. Don't buy the meat here. Canned goods are okay, but not the meat."

"Why not?"

Betty scrunched her face. "Just trust me. You don't want it."

"Thanks."

Monica was relieved to have found someone her age. She'd been having second thoughts about her decision to move to Redmondsburg, but now she felt somewhat better about it. It would be great to make a friend on her first day in town.

Betty asked, "Do you wanna have lunch? I was gonna go to the diner down the street."

"Sure. That sounds nice."

"Cool. Let's go."

Betty took off happily to the front of the store, leaving behind a full cart of groceries.

"Did you want this stuff?" Monica asked.

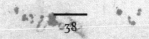

"Nah, I changed my mind."

Monica left her cart where it sat also, broken and empty.

Mayor Eddie Gordon appeared at the office doorway with a look of disdain on his chubby face. He rubbed a hand over neatly trimmed gray hair, clearing his throat. The sheriff looked up from a pile of open manila folders containing a month's worth of paperwork. A rush of indigestion churned his stomach.

"Hello, Mayor. What can I do for you?"

Gordon glanced out at the receptionist. She was busy crocheting, as always. He stepped inside and closed the door. "I understand you had a murder the other day."

Shane smiled. "Well, naturally we wrote it up as a traffic accident."

Gordon frowned. "Why on earth would you do that?"

The sheriff whispered, "It was in accordance with our deal, Mayor."

The mayor's face went bright red. "You think *I* killed Thomas Able with an axe?" A thick fist pounded the desk, knocking over a picture frame. "When have I ever been in possession of such a weapon?"

Shane recoiled from the large man. His face went pale. "I only assumed that—there was that time you killed Don Jenkins with a frog gig."

"That was an entirely unique situation! And don't remind me of Jenkins. He deserved a lot worse."

Suddenly, the mayor was around the desk with the sheriff's shirt in his fist, pressing hard into his sternum. Shane gasped.

"I'm sorry."

Gordon's hot breath saturated Shane's face. "I'm trying to get reelected, you pathetic old man. Your incompetence reflects directly upon me. Do your fucking job."

"Forgive me, sir," he said. "It won't happen again."

The thick fist released the crumpled shirt. "I'll inform you if I feel the need to kill anyone. If you test me, it will be *you* in the next car accident."

"Yes, sir."

"Oh, and by the way, there is no *deal* between us. You either do what I say or I rip out your goddamned spine. Is that clear, Sheriff Shane?"

"It's crystal clear, Mayor."

"Crystal," Gordon repeated with a faint smile. He paused for a moment as if tasting the word, absorbing its bouquet. "I like that." He turned and opened the door. "I'll expect your vote on election day."

Shane swallowed a mouthful of tobacco juice, which made his stomach feel even worse. "You can count on it."

"I'm sure I can," Gordon said, walking out.

The elderly woman at the front desk smiled. "Is everything all right, Mayor?"

"Everything is tremendous, young lady. Have a wonderful day."

She giggled. "Thank you, Mayor."

Out the door and down the sidewalk he went, humming a lively tune. His house was only two blocks away, and that was his destination. It was lunchtime.

Georgette walked into the kitchen with two full paper bags in her arms. A carton of eggs and a loaf of white bread were set on the top shelf of the refrigerator. Her husband walked around the corner and greeted her.

"Back so soon, George?"

She sent him a smile that appeared more annoyed than pleasant, not that her annoyance affected him a bit. "We just needed a few things. I thought you'd be campaigning all day."

He took a bite out of a crisp apple. "Just here for lunch."

"Oh," she said from behind the pantry door.

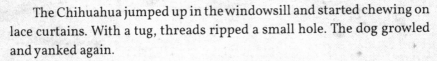

The Chihuahua jumped up in the windowsill and started chewing on lace curtains. With a tug, threads ripped a small hole. The dog growled and yanked again.

"Bad dog," Georgette said. She suddenly realized she'd just stepped into very dangerous territory.

The mayor scowled. "What did you say?"

The canine bared its teeth with eyes blazing.

"I'm sorry," she stated in a panic. "I don't know what came over me."

Eddie took the animal into his arms, stroking its back. "Yes," he said to the dog. "I agree."

Straining to breathe, Georgette asked, "What did he say?"

"King speaks to me only...therefore, what he says is for me only."

"Oh, of course. I just...I'm sorry." She went back to unloading the groceries.

Eddie cocked his head, listening to the animal again. "Hmm..." His eyes softened a bit. "King says you met her."

"Oh my, yes. I nearly forgot. I saw her at the market."

"And?"

"Well, she's...perfect."

A grin expanded his puffy cheeks. "That's what I like to hear."

The women walked to the diner, three blocks away. They passed by two antique shops, a clothing store, a hardware store, and a coffee shop. On the sidewalk, out in front of Gainer Hardware, sat a green bench and a sign that read "Bus Stop." A nervous man wearing a dirty trench coat stood in front of the bench, fidgeting and talking to himself.

"I can't believe it," he said. "I missed it again."

Monica kept her distance as she went by, with a careful eye on the man.

His breath was shallow. "I'm dead. I just know it."

Betty said to her new friend, "Don't worry about him. He's harmless."

"Who is he?"

"That's Silo Pernice. He's a bit off, if you know what I mean."

He started pacing back and forth.

"I know who you are!" he yelled into the sky. "I know who all of you are! You're not fooling me!"

A tall man stepped out of the store's front door.

"Settle down, Silo. You wanna spend the night in jail again?"

Silo sat down on the bench, his hands shaking in the chill. "No."

"Be a good boy and wait for your bus—*quietly*."

"Okay, man. Okay."

Betty leaned close to Monica and whispered, "He's been trying to catch a bus for like two years."

"Are you kidding me?"

"Nope. He always misses it."

"How can you miss a bus for two years?"

"I don't know, but he always does."

The two women sat down at a booth by a large front window in the Redmondsburg Diner. Betty pulled off her fuzzy, cream-colored jacket, and then happily reached for a menu. Monica did the same, looking around at the locals drinking coffee and eating pie. Betty leaned across the table.

"It's so weird here, isn't it?"

"Kind of, yeah," Monica said, thinking about the mayor's wife.

"It's not like the places you see on television. They're all different... normal compared to here."

"I guess so. Are you from here?"

"Oh yeah. I've been here all my life. I've never even been out of the county."

"What? You're kidding, right?"

Betty smiled. "No. I can't leave the perimeter."

"The perimeter?"

Betty's smile disappeared. She raised the menu up to hide her face. "I mean...I don't want to leave. You know what I mean. I like it here."

"Oh," Monica said.

The perimeter?

A waitress walked over, vigorously chewing her gum.

"Hey, ladies. Can I get you something to drink?"

"I'll have water, please," Betty said, "and a half-pound double burger. Plain. No lettuce, no tomato, no pickles, no cheese. *Plain.*"

Okay," the waitress said. "Just cow and bun." She looked at Monica. "And for you, hon?"

"Iced tea, please. And I guess, the club with fries."

"No problem. We'll have it right out."

Betty frowned, "No ketchup either. Or mustard. I want it plain."

"Yes," the waitress said, "I get it. It'll be plain."

"Great."

Monica set her menu next to the window. "So what's the deal with the mayor's wife? She seems kinda pushy."

"Oh, her? She's a bitch. There's no denying that."

Monica adjusted herself in her seat.

"Oh?"

"Yup. Grade A, certifiable. All I can tell you is, don't piss her off."

"You say that like you've pissed her off before."

Betty laughed. "Me? Oh hell, no. She sees me coming and she walks the other way. I'm a badass." She held up two skinny fists, trying to look tough.

Monica chuckled. "I didn't realize."

"Oh yeah. I don't look like much, but I could bench press a Volkswagen."

"Really?" Monica said, amused.

"Sure. I'll show you sometime."

"It sounds like you're the one I don't want to piss off."

Betty lowered her thin arms. "I don't get mad. I wouldn't even know how. I'm just your basic, happy badass."

Monica found herself liking Betty Jones. She was odd, to say the least, but fun.

Their conversation outlasted the meal by more than an hour. They talked about the town, the cemetery, and the upcoming local election. All the while, Mayor Gordon traveled up the street and back, over and over, on the flatbed. He paused for a few minutes to make a short speech at one point, and then he was off again, with supporters cheering at each intersection.

"What a blow hard," Betty said as the women walked to their cars.

"Yeah, he seems pretty full of himself."

"Oh, he doesn't just seem that way."

Monica's keys fell from her purse pocket, coming to a rest under a parked sedan.

"Shit," she said, scanning the ground. "Where'd they go?"

Betty's gaze was somewhere down the street.

"They're under that car, in a puddle of water."

"Where?"

"I'll get them."

Betty leaned down, grasping the underside of the bumper. Loud music blasted from the mayor's speakers, drawing Monica's attention to the next block. With ease, Betty lifted the car until the tire came off the ground. She grabbed the keys out of the mud and then let go of the bumper. The entire vehicle shook.

Monica looked back and saw Betty smiling with dripping keys in hand.

3

THE
CARNIVAL

Night had come for Redmondsburg. The sky was clear, with thousands of bright stars scattered across its expanse. Only a sliver of the moon was seen, a small bluish curve in the eastern October heavens. Monica sat on the porch, tightly wrapped in a thick brown blanket. Her eyes searched the cemetery grounds for any movement as she sipped a warm cup of tea. Everything was shadowy and quiet.

Her mind drifted from drunken teenagers and unexplained voices to her new friend, Betty. She smiled, remembering their conversation at the diner. It had been funny how Betty balled her fists, trying to look strong. Also, it was bizarre watching such a skinny woman eat a half-pound double burger.

If I ate like that, I'd explode.

Monica figured Betty's metabolism must've been off the charts.

The next morning, Betty showed up on Monica's doorstep at eight o'clock with a box of twelve glazed doughnuts. Monica ate one with her daily cup. The blonde, over the course of a conversation that lasted most of the morning, ate six.

Twenty-four hours later, Betty came offering breakfast burritos.

The day after that, tacos.

"Tacos? At eight in the morning?" Monica inquired.

Betty only smiled and stated, "Any time is a good time for tacos."

The women spent a lot of hours together Monica's first week in town, which at times allowed her to forget all about a cheating ex-husband and Woodard. It also made her slack off on her unpacking duties. She'd been in the house nearly two weeks before she'd put away all of her clothes. It was okay, though. She had no reason to be in a hurry. And talking with her new friend had a kind of therapeutic effect.

Monica spent her afternoons filling out job applications. Her savings would hold out only so long. She'd be okay as long as she found something by the first of the year.

The phone was hooked up on a Wednesday. She celebrated communications to the outside world with an hour-long conversation with Suzanne.

The strange noises around the house and cemetery did continue, but only occasionally.

Everything stayed pretty quiet around the place for Monica's first couple of weeks, although that was about to change in many unexpected and horrifying ways.

Gary entered with an armload of firewood, walked to the fireplace, and dropped his delivery to the floor. He then headed to the kitchen to make a sandwich. The crust of two slices of wheat bread was inspected for mold. When satisfied, he set them on the counter. Mayonnaise was sniffed, eyeballed, and then sniffed again. Sliced ham was given a good once over also, along with a block of sharp cheddar. A head of lettuce from the crisper drawer finalized the lunch ingredients.

Never one to forget Elton, Gary tore off a leaf and approached the cage. The hamster was his pet, his friend, and his god. And God liked lettuce.

Gary gasped and dropped the treat. The wire seam had come apart at the back of the cage, and Elton had taken it upon himself to go exploring.

"Oh no," Gary said in shock.

He wasn't on the dresser, the floor, or anywhere in sight. In a panic, Gary set off to search the rest of the house.

Monica listened to the local radio station while she unpacked pictures and knickknacks. The disc jockey's interview with Eddie Gordon occupied the current time slot. The mayor talked about his plans to build an annex at the elementary school. Also, he encouraged everyone to get out and vote on election day, which just happened to be tomorrow.

Monica remembered Betty calling him a "blow hard," and after hearing him speak nonstop for the last fifteen minutes, she thought the label had been appropriate.

Monica lost interest in the radio as she lifted a large wooden frame from the bottom of a box. She knew which picture it was before the newsprint was torn away. It was a photo of her and Ben smiling at the beach. It had been taken six years ago, previous to their marriage. Both of them were dripping wet and laughing, looking very much like two people who would get married. It was a carefree moment, a snippet of happiness captured in a glared lens and printed on glossy paper. Of all the things that reminded her of Ben, it was the only one that made her throat swell and her eyes water every time. She wiped away tears, remembering how she swore she'd throw it in the garbage the next time she saw it. This was the third time she'd done so. The back of the closet would be its destination, for now.

The next photo was not in a frame. It wasn't the kind of image that normally found a place under glass. It was of her friend Suzanne, although her face wasn't in view, since the photo had been shot from behind the kneeling woman as she vomited into a toilet.

Monica grinned.

"You blew some serious chunks at that party," she said to the snapshot. There were a number of specific things that added up to that picture.

A senior year kegger.

A game of quarters.

A bottle of tequila.

And a disposable camera.

Add them all up and you get Suzanne yacking in a toilet.

Unlike the one of her and Ben, she'd be keeping it forever. Or at least until her friend found it and burned it.

Gary's search for God began in the back bedroom, moved on to the bathroom and hallway closet, and then continued toward the kitchen. Each was as hamsterless as the previous, and a rising tension pinched at his twitching eye.

"Where are you, Lord?" It was the pleading cry of a desperate man. Over the years, many had asked that very question, although presumably under different circumstances.

Finally, below an overturned laundry basket, Gary discovered Elton chewing a hole in a dirty sock. Gary scooped him up with glee.

"There you are!"

Relief eased the twitch and the sick feeling in his stomach. Everything would be okay now. The world once again made sense. Gary nearly tripped on an open phone book in the doorway. He looked down and saw that Elton had been busy on it also. An entire corner had been munched away from the yellow and white pages. A crumpled paper nest had been piled into a colorful heap. In the center was a torn scrap with a single name and address: Mr. John O'Dell, 811 Ussie Drive.

"Is that what this is about? You have a job for me?"

The rodent didn't answer; it only sniffed at Gary's fingers. Since no date was specified, Gary assumed that part would be left up to his discretion.

With the cage repaired and the hamster returned safe and sound, Gary grabbed truck keys off the counter. He got two blocks away before he remembered and had to go back.

In all the excitement, he'd forgotten to finish lunch.

A knock at the door startled Monica at three in the afternoon. She knew before she answered who it was. It was Betty. It was always Betty, but Monica didn't mind. She looked forward to her daily visits and was surprised, actually, that Betty hadn't arrived until then.

With the door open, she saw the blonde was even more vibrant than usual, standing in the afternoon sun.

"Monica!" she exclaimed. "Get ready. We're gonna have so much fun today."

"Ready? Ready for what?"

Betty held two tickets up. "I'm taking you to the carnival."

"That Halloween thing at the fairgrounds?"

"Yeah! The pie-eating contest is today."

Monica ran fingers over her messy hair. "I need a shower first."

"Well get rolling, sister. It starts at four."

Gary Tuttlebaulm pulled over his pickup in front of the house. He scanned the street and the other parked cars, evaluating his surroundings. Everything was quiet, without a person in sight. Gary didn't know John O'Dell and had not the slightest clue what he'd look like. So, to avoid confusion later, he went to the door to ask. A tall man answered the knock.

"Yes? Can I help you?"

Gary studied the face, locking it into the memory bank, so to speak. "Are you John O'Dell?"

"Yeah. That's me."

"Okay, then." Gary turned and walked away.

"Did you want something?" the man asked.

"Not just yet," Gary said, going back to the truck.

Naturally, he wouldn't do anything right then. He'd just met the guy, and besides, only a jerk killed people in the middle of the afternoon.

As Monica and Betty walked through the Spooks and Specters carnival, they heard the local DJ, Bruce Bradley, over the loud speaker, announcing the pie-eating contest. It was due to begin in fifteen minutes, in the rec building. At a prompting of the celebrity's overly cheery voice, the thick crowd shifted toward the park's largest structure.

A group of five children sped by, nearly knocking Monica to the hard-packed dirt. They did not stop to apologize or even acknowledge the impact had occurred. The kids only laughed, disappearing into a sea of distracted people. Betty caught her friend's arm as her sneakers slid over loose gravel.

"Watch it, you little heathens!" she shouted.

They followed the flood of townsfolk into the building and saw that all of the seating was taken. The overflow of spectators gathered along outer walls, filling the aisles with a shoulder-to-shoulder nightmare that would cause any duty-bound fire marshal to soil his pants. Luckily, there were no fire marshals in attendance.

"This place is packed," Monica whispered. "You sure you wanna stay?"

Betty took Monica's hand and pulled her into the noisy mob. "Oh, come on. It'll be fun."

"Okay," Monica answered reluctantly, as they entered the deafening chatter and laughter.

A stage at the front held a long table with six contestants seated. Each wore an oversized bib and a pair of what looked like swimming goggles. Bruce Bradley and his cohost, Katrina Webber, stood at a podium smiling and occasionally waving as they spotted familiar faces in the crowd. A colorful banner hung across the wall behind them. Tall red lettering spelled out "WKAZ RADIO." The three-dimensional logo seemed to jump off the shiny, slick banner. A smaller table next to the stage provided a closeup view for the three judges.

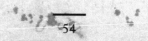

Monica didn't recognize two of them, but she knew who the third was. It was Mayor Gordon. He looked jolly as ever in a plaid suit and bow tie. His fat jowls jiggled as he laughed, hanging down over his blazer collar like fleshy balloons. She'd seen few men that were as overweight in the face as he. His head appeared unreal to her somehow, the engorged double chin and neck as unbelievable as an overzealous boob job. She imagined his face bursting and spilling silicone over his round belly. The picture in her mind made her cringe.

Then she spotted his little dog, sitting in the shadows at the back of the stage. It sat like a petite statue watching over the proceedings with narrow eyes. The small animal looked totally motionless from where Monica stood. If she hadn't known better, she might've thought it was a bizarre experiment in taxidermy. But then, just as she thought it wasn't going to move, that it was possibly a stone likeness of the mayor's dog, it turned its head toward her.

Across the excited crowd, through the jumbled laughing and raised voices, it seemed to look right at her. It was unnerving to see a Chihuahua, a breed that usually couldn't sit still to save its rodent-sized life, sit stoic and unaffected in a room full of chaotic people.

Is that thing looking at me?

It didn't blink. Once again, it was perfectly still. Monica looked at Betty, who stretched to see the disc jockey at the podium. She looked back to see the dog staring her down.

It's not looking at me. It only looks that way from across the room.

She looked away. She looked back.

The dog didn't blink.

"There's something seriously wrong with that animal," she announced to Betty.

"What?"

"Nothing," she said, turning her attention to the stage.

———

Of the six contestants, two were women, which was surprising to Redmondsburg's newest resident, although after all the food she'd witnessed Betty consume since they'd met, she wondered if all females in town could eat like that.

Must be something in the water.

One of them was an excessive lady with bright red lipstick, oversized jewelry, and a beehive hairdo. The teased and sprayed sculpture on her head stood at least ten inches high and was quite the follicle masterpiece.

The other was a petite and somewhat squirrelish-looking girl. She didn't appear big enough to lift a pie, let alone eat one.

The four men, on the other hand, all looked like they belonged there—one in girth, the others in pure, half-witted determination. They might not win, but they'd pop a colon trying. The big one, the one who outsized them all, had an expression on his swollen face that said he would devour a hundred pies and then eat the other five contestants out of spite. Monica's money was on him.

Cheering, laughing, and yelling filled the rec center as the contest ensued. Pan after aluminum pan hit the floor as fresh pies slid into position under sticky, dripping noses. Chunks of crust and globs of filling splattered over the first three rows of observers as the eaters flung their heads up to say "done" between each sticky meal.

The thin girl did better than expected, although at one point she leaned back, threatening to faint. Beehive did well also. By the end, she had purple goo at the top of her hair, and some oozing down the back of her neck.

The winner, as Monica had predicted, was the big guy. He stomped around the stage like a pro wrestler, pointing at the crowd and flexing. Betty, along with the rest of the spectators, went wild. She blew kisses at him as he shook a jiggling belly with pride.

They followed a sea of locals flooding out of the doors. Food vendors lined the path leading toward the carnival rides. "Ooh! Let's get a turkey leg!" Betty said, pulling on Monica's arm.

"Okay."

A change of mind prompted a change in direction. "No, wait. They have deep-fried pickles!"

Across the gauntlet of people they went, maneuvering the shoulder-to-shoulder crowd. "I don't really like pickles," Monica said. Not that what she liked or didn't like mattered. The blonde had changed her mind again anyway.

"String fries! Let's try those."

"Whatever you want," Monica responded, laughing, as they forged a new direction against the throng of torsos and elbows.

When they reached the order window, Betty said, "Two please." The baskets of string fries were six dollars each. Betty paid the man without hesitation.

Monica said, "Those had better be some damn good string fries."

"What do you mean?"

"I mean that six bucks for an order for fries is crazy."

Betty grinned, pulling on the top of a pile of thin, deep-fried potato curls. "It's not any old fries," she said, stuffing them into her mouth. "It's *string* fries." She looked a bit insane as she burst into laughter with a mouthful of overpriced carnival food. But as she cackled and snorted to herself, Monica couldn't help but join her.

Betty pulled her new friend toward the rides like an excited child. There was a Ferris wheel, a Spider ride, and one called the Kamikaze. Just looking at that last one made Monica feel sick to her stomach.

"Let's ride the Ferris wheel!" Betty said, fishing deep in a glittery purse for money.

They stood in line fifteen minutes before it was their turn. All the while, Monica studied unfamiliar faces passing by. Children laughed in groups of twos and threes, holding stuffed animals, balloons, and foam lizards on sticks. Some were even dressed in Halloween costumes.

A two-foot-tall dragon caught the attention of an elderly woman, who patted the boy on the head, telling him how cute he was. He pointed and yelled, "Bumper cars!" Chunks of half-chewed corn dog flew in her direction.

A man in a trench coat bumped into Monica. She turned and saw it was Silo Pernice, the homeless guy from the bus stop. He looked her over with glazed eyes. Grime lined the creases of a weathered and anxious face.

He shook as he spoke, fidgeting. "You know when the next bus is due, man?"

Monica took a step back. "Sorry. I don't."

His mouth fell into a toothless gape. "You're the one, man. It's you."

Betty leaned forward and put a protective hand out toward him. "What are you talking about, Silo?"

He didn't acknowledge the blonde. His eyes stayed on the brunette.

"You need to get outa town, dude," he said, picking at the one remaining molar on the left side of his lower jaw.

"Why would she do that?"

"Bad things happen 'round here, man. Bad things."

Both women scrunched their noses at a man who'd seen better days. To him, those days had been in another life. He continued with his warning.

"They'll be after you soon. And your friend too."

"Who will be after us?" Betty asked.

He wiped his nose with a dirty coat sleeve. His eyes stabbed at the blond girl. "Not you. I mean the other one. The red one."

Betty looked to Monica, confused.

Monica gasped. "The red one? You mean Suzanne?" He couldn't know her friend from the city. It was impossible. "How do you know Suzanne?"

Betty turned back to the Ferris wheel and shook her head. "Silo, go find a bus or something."

Monica watched him walk away. She thought of how Suzanne had suggested an idea a couple of years ago when they were shopping in Woodard. She'd said that maybe the homeless people you see on the street corners talking to themselves weren't insane at all. Maybe there was someone there listening. You just couldn't see them. Perhaps one man's psychic was everyone else's crazy. At the time, Monica took it as a joke, even though she saw her redheaded friend was serious.

Her red friend.

She watched the homeless man walk away, wondering how serious Suzanne would've taken him.

Dead Wayne nudged Tom in the side. "Hey. Check her out. I think she's new." A dead woman across the room stood on unsteady legs with a blank gaze on her face. Her eyes focused in two separate directions.

"What about her?"

Wayne smiled. "She's pretty hot for a dead chick, doncha think?"

Tom frowned. "She's got a lazy eye and part of her scalp is missing."

"I know, but look at that complexion. She's got beautiful skin."

Tom chuckled. "Maybe she died with it…maybe it's Maybelline."

"What?"

"Nothing. If you like her, you should go talk to her."

"What would I say?" The woman shifted her weight to the other leg and then scratched at her left breast as the men watched. "I'm not very good with women."

"Throw some clever slogans at her. You've got lots of those."

"Hey," Wayne said, annoyed. "What do you mean by that?"

"Oh, come on. Everything that comes out of your mouth is either from a commercial, a song, or just a ridiculous cliché."

Wayne considered getting mad about the observation, but then found himself amused. "Death is a highway, my friend. Don't blame me if I wanna ride it all night long."

"Oh brother," Tom said, watching Wayne limp away.

The two women sat at the top of the Ferris wheel, looking across the fairgrounds. The people below were a shifting and colorful mass, lacking definition. The nearby Kamikaze ride spun thrill seekers in dizzying circles over the lot. Bumper cars slammed into one another under an electrified canopy, while next door a line of children waited for their opportunity to ride a camel.

"I can't believe they got a real live camel," Betty said.

Monica grinned. "Well, the stuffed ones are easier to mount, but the ride isn't as fun."

Betty laughed hard at that. When she caught her breath, she motioned to a gathering on the ground. "That guy down there is checking you out, girlfriend."

Monica looked down. "How could you possibly tell from up here?"

"I got eagle eyes, baby."

"You can bench press a Volkswagen, and you've got eagle eyes. Any other talents I should know about?"

"You are intentionally changing the subject. I think he digs you."

Monica's face got serious. "Look, I just went through a nasty divorce. I'm not ready for that kind of attention."

"Oh."

"It's just that I thought I knew my ex-husband. I really did. And then...Well, I found out I didn't know him at all."

"That sucks."

"Yeah."

"I guess you can never really know someone fully," Betty said. "People are always holding things back...making shit up...flat-out lying. It's sad."

"You sound like you've been hurt pretty bad too," Monica said.

"There is that...and I've got something about me that no one knows. A secret."

"Oh yeah?"

"Sure. If you knew what I was talking about, you'd know why I couldn't tell anyone."

"Now I'm intrigued. Are you gonna tell me?"

Betty smiled. "Maybe someday."

"It must be a pretty big secret."

"You have no idea, girlfriend. You have no idea."

The two women rode a carousel, popped balloons with darts, and slammed each other with bumper cars. They also ate lots of carnival food. Turkey legs and deep-fried ice cream were washed down with cherry slushies. Monica hadn't been that full since she was a kid. That's just how her new friend made her feel—like a kid.

It was amazing how Betty had gotten to adulthood and maintained such innocence. She held a sense of wonder and awe about everything. It was refreshing to be around her. Monica found the snorting laughter to be contagious. It was easy to be happy with Betty at her side.

The fun continued through the evening as they watched a costume contest, walked through a not-so-scary haunted house, and saw a play put on by the high-school drama department.

By ten o'clock, Monica was exhausted. Walking to the car, they spotted Wanda Spell, who Monica recognized from the grocery store. The old woman yelled at the mayor as a crowd gathered to watch.

"Ooh. What's going on here?" Betty whispered.

Wanda stomped in circles, pausing occasionally to point a cold finger at Eddie Gordon. "I know all about you! It's time someone finally told you so!"

The large man smiled. "Now settle down, Wanda."

Her wrinkled face pinched in a rage. "Don't you tell me what to do, you evil man!"

King, the mayor's little dog, growled in his arms, barking on and on. "It's okay, baby," he said, petting the animal.

"Damn you, Gordon! And that awful creature, too!"

People in the surrounding area cringed at her words. Most felt bad for Gordon as he endured the old woman's verbal attack. It was easy to think Wanda was crazy. She sure looked it.

"That thing is a demon!" she screeched, curling a finger at the dog. "A devil!"

Sheriff Shane approached. "It's illegal to insult a public official. Do you want to spend the night in jail?"

The wrinkled index finger changed directions. "And you! You're the devil's lackey!"

The mayor whispered into the sheriff's ear.

"Yes, sir," Shane said. He turned back toward Wanda. "The mayor is feeling generous this evening. He's asked me to give you a ride home."

"I don't need a ride, jackass. I've got my own car." Wanda stomped away, and hushed conversations broke out across the crowd. Monica and Betty continued on to their car.

As the people dispersed, Gordon whispered to Shane. "I'll take care of that bitch. I know just what to do."

When Betty got to Monica's road, she didn't slow the car down or even act like she noticed it. She kept going straight.

"Um...That was my turn back there," Monica said.

"I know. I just thought you might wanna see the lake. It's beautiful at night."

A clock on the dashboard read 10:36 p.m. Monica was tired, but a quick drive by the lake wouldn't kill her.

She sat back, watching the headlights illuminate trees along the roadside. A left turn onto the dirt road sent the tires quaking over loose gravel. After a sharp curve in the road, the glass surface of Stone Lake came into view. Betty stopped the car, put it in park, and then turned off the ignition. She smiled, gazing at the bright moonlight reflecting off a mile of water.

"You're right," Monica said. "It is beautiful."

"Yup. Did you know that this entire end of the lake sits on solid rock?"

"I didn't know that."

"Oh yeah. That's why it's called *Stone Lake*."

"That's just weird."

Betty pointed to the south shore. "It's like fifty feet deep over there. I swam all the way to the bottom once."

"Fifty feet? You must be able to hold your breath a really long time."

Betty looked over and grinned. "One of my many talents."

Monica grinned back, trying to decide whether to believe it or not. It seemed like Betty exaggerated everything. Or flat-out lied. But most of the lies were in good fun, for humor's sake, so Monica didn't take offense. Still, she wondered why her new friend felt the need to make up such a fantastical thing.

After twenty minutes of looking out across Stone Lake, Monica's heavy eyelids indicated it was time to go home.

The next morning Monica unpacked the contents of the final box and then cleaned and put away the items in the kitchen pantry.

With everything finally unpacked Monica realized something. She needed more furniture. Two recliners and an end table left a lot of open space in her living room, and the lack of a dining room table made for an empty trek through the middle of her house.

There was a furniture store in town; she'd noticed it the other day. It was a block over from the highway, occupying a lot next to the barbershop.

She thought about waiting for Betty to pop in as she always did, but no, she would go it alone this time. She decided to operate on impulse, a quality she'd been learning from Betty for weeks now. Monica had never seen spontaneity so lovingly embraced. Every choice that Betty made, every decision she acted upon, seemed to be at a moment's notice, and she flew by the seat of her pants accordingly. It was under that same irreverent flag that Monica took truck keys in hand, heading for the door.

She needed a table, chairs, and a couch, so she would go shopping. Very simple. If she couldn't have them delivered she'd find some help.

Out the door she went feeling pretty darn good about herself.

4

YOU SHOULDN'T TAUNT THE DEAD

A classic rock tune faded away, and the voice of Redmondsburg's own Bruce Bradley overlapped with enthusiasm.

"All right, everyone, if you haven't heard, Eddie Gordon has prevailed as mayor in yesterday's election. Yes, winning by a landslide, he will serve as mayor of this little burg for a third consecutive term."

"Well, whoop-de-do," Monica said with sarcasm.

"The mayor's opposition, Mr. Larry Jenkins, ran a heated campaign and made his voice heard. We here at WKAZ salute you, sir, for a valiant effort. Better luck next time."

Made his voice heard? Monica thought. *I didn't even know his name until right now.*

The cohost, Katrina Webber, spoke. "Yes. Congratulations, Mayor Gordon. And now on to your local headlines."

Monica drove by a barbershop that appeared as though it had been yanked straight from the 1940s. Out front, red-and-white stripes spiraled on a tall pole. Two elderly men sat on a bench on the sidewalk, one with a cane, the other with an open newspaper. Through the large glass behind them, she saw Mayor Gordon himself getting lathered up for a shave.

"There's the blow hard now," she said. "Mayor of the burg."

Kat's voice pulled her attention back to the radio. "The admission is only three dollars at the box office for an entire day of family fun." Monica put a hand over her belly. She was still bloated from all the "fun."

The selection at Redmondsburg Furniture left a lot to be desired. The showroom had only two dining sets to choose from. She picked the one with the lighter finish, hoping it would brighten the room a bit. There were fifteen couches on display, and Monica sat on each of them before she was satisfied. A green-and-black-striped material covered the thick cushions of her purchase. The clerk promised delivery before five o'clock.

Back at the truck, Monica saw Gordon's little dog, the Chihuahua, in the middle of the street. It stood rigid, just as it had done at the fairgrounds the previous day. Like a small statue, it once again leered at her without blinking. Monica stopped in her tracks, wondering what the animal meant to do. It only pierced her with glossy black eyes, looking as though it would spring forward at any moment, but that moment didn't come. Frozen in time, it remained silent and motionless as if waiting for the signal to attack.

Monica glanced up at the barbershop. The mayor, on his feet and freshly shaved now, spoke to a gathering of men inside.

"Stop talking and put this creepy thing on a leash," she said.

When she looked back down, the canine was gone. "Holy crap. Where'd it go?" A chill danced up her spine. She wasted no time getting in the pickup and starting the engine.

Monica complained about the dog all the way home.

The delivery truck showed up, as promised, at a quarter to five. It took the two men half an hour to set up Monica's furniture. When they were gone, she sat in the dining room, deciding what kind of centerpiece she wanted for the table. After a few minutes of weighing the pros and cons of candles and flower arrangements, she went to lounge on her new couch.

The cushions were thick, overstuffed lumps and very soft. She sank into the fluffy depths, grinning. She would've drifted off to sleep and remained unconscious until morning if she hadn't heard the voice. It was a low, barely audible shout, maybe three syllables. She sat up and peeked through the curtain. Had it been four syllables? Five? The way it had trailed off at the end, it was hard to tell. There was no one in sight. The cemetery was still, without so much as a breeze.

"Four syllables," she said to her striped couch. "It was definitely four." She tried to think of words that fit the profile. *Flatulation has four*, she thought. And then, *No, it wasn't that*. She looked down the road in both directions. Nothing and nobody.

Masturbation has four, she considered, although doubted very much that there was a guy outside yelling the word *masturbation*. Perhaps it had been a foreign language, something unrecognizable even if she had heard it clearly.

A head popped above a gravestone, looked left and right, and then snapped back down. Monica's heart jumped at the surprise.

The voice sounded again, louder this time. It sill resembled the word *masturbation*.

"Is that an autistic pervert?" she asked.

Another man joined him, only he didn't bother hiding. He stood unsteady and in full view, at the edge of the road. Two more arrived as the word was uttered again. Whatever he'd said drew a crowd. She ducked down behind soft cushions.

"Go jack off somewhere else, you weirdos!" she screamed reaching for the telephone. It was dead. "I just got this thing hooked up!" In frustration, she threw the receiver across the room, and it slid under the TV stand.

She looked back to the window. Monica's eyes went painfully wide as white fog gathered across the road, over headstones and between trees and lumbering bodies. The haze softened her view at first, but soon all that remained were silouettes in thick mist. The cloud ended at the road's edge, as if contained by a wall of glass. Only the slightest wisps dared to cross over and were quickly snuffed out.

"Okay," she said through panting breaths, "they're too afraid to come over here...for some reason." An unseen force held them at bay, at least that's how it appeared. But what was it?

What's so scary about this house? What's holding the fog back like that?

Little twinkles of snowflakes rose up, out of the cloud.

And who are those guys?

The mist faded an hour later, leaving behind an empty and quiet burial ground. The mysterious men were gone, as were their voices.

Monica kept a watchful eye across the road throughout the evening and into the night. Her attention didn't waiver until the wee morning hours, when she finally fell asleep.

Monica woke at eight o'clock with an ache in her neck, presumably from sleeping with her head against the armrest of the new couch. She sat up, looking over the cemetery grounds. Other than the falling snow, there was no movement, no people, and no reason to be alarmed.

"The place is totally dead now," she said. It was an accidental pun she might've enjoyed if she wasn't so exhausted and grumpy.

Once off the couch, she rubbed her neck and headed for the kitchen. If caffine didn't hit her bloodstream soon, she feared that killing someone would be the only viable option. Luckily, there was coffee in the can, filters on the shelf, and water in the faucet.

A knock at the door surprised Monica and her heart raced, but then she realized it was just Betty.

"Hey," Monica said in a groggy whisper as she let the blonde in.

"Holy hell, girlfriend," Betty said. "You look like death on a popcicle stick." Monica was not amused by the observation, nor did she care for her pal's bright, alert eyes, matching outfit, or perky disposition.

"I'm just tired."

Betty's smile faded into concern. "Did something happen?"

"A few things happened...across the road."

"Tell me everything," she said and then added, "Hey. Nice couch."

Monica explained the previous night's events in detail over a cup of stiff coffee and powdered doughnuts. She did not tell Betty that the word they'd said sounded like "masturbation." That would've prompted a fit of laughter she simply wasn't in the mood for. She just said it was a word she couldn't make out.

"God," Betty said, "the drunk guy and now this. That sucks."

"I know. I would have called the sheriff, but my phone's not working."

"Didn't you just get it hooked up?"

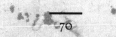

"A couple days ago."

Betty retrieved the phone from the floor and pressed the power button. She listened for a dial tone. Nothing.

Monica asked, "Is it still dead?"

Her friend pursed her lips. "Like a deep-fried chipmunk on a stick."

Monica's brow lowered. "What's with everything on a stick today?"

After a moment of consideration, Betty answered, "I dunno. Maybe I'm craving corn dogs."

Well, at least they'd established what they were having for lunch. Monica was positive Betty could eat four, possibly five. She'd have to wait until noon to find out for sure.

Midday found the women sitting at a picnic table in front of Burger Heaven, a local eatery. Monica watched in awe as Betty finished her sixth corn dog.

"Holy hell, woman. How can you eat like that?"

From behind a ketchup-stained napkin, Betty stated, "I eat anything I want. I won't gain weight."

"Yeah well, I'm getting sympathy stretch marks just being near you."

Betty grinned. "So, you want me to hang around tonight in case the freak show comes back?"

"Nah. They're probably done screwing with me for a while."

"Yeah," Betty agreed. "I guess so."

After lunch they stopped at Betty's house to call the phone company. The customer service representative said it would be a week before she could expect a technician.

Great. Another week without a phone.

She thought about telling him to forget it and getting a cell phone instead, but no. If she had a cell, she'd feel obligated to carry the thing around wherever she went, and she just wasn't willing to do that. She'd never owned a cell phone and wasn't about to start now. She'd just have to wait.

Betty took Monica home at three. The new couch was her destination for the remainder of the afternoon. She was desperate to catch up on some sleep, but her spinning brain had other plans. Her head raced with images of strange men at the graveyard and thick fog. The word *masturbation* played in an unending loop, threatening to drive her mad.

At five thirty she gave up the battle for the nap. She slid a book off the shelf, grabbed a blanket from the closet, and went to the porch. After a quick survey of the cemetery, she sat on the wood swing and began to read.

Movement at the west side of the mausoleum caught her eye. She stood with the cover falling from her shoulders.

Not again, she thought. *My nerves can't take it.*

A large dog ran out of the shadows. It was frothing at the mouth and growling. In its teeth it clenched what appeared to be a severed human hand.

"Oh my god," Monica exclaimed, rushing for the door and then slamming it shut behind her. She sneaked over to the window, peeking out through the curtains she'd put up a few hours earlier. The dog shook the hand violently, dropped it to the dirt, and then circled the appendage, barking.

"Calm down," Monica told herself with a hand over a thundering heartbeat. "It is a graveyard. It must have dug that out of a fresh grave, or something."

The dog bit down on the hand once again and took off running into the shadows. Monica turned and leaned against the wall, trying to catch her breath.

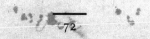

"This place is a damn circus."

In the graveyard, around the backside of the mausoleum, Thomas Able pursued the dog.

"Give me that back, you dirty bastard!" he moaned. "That's mine!"

The canine ignored him, running.

Thomas Able eventually caught up with the dog and then walked into the underground ritual chamber carrying his severed hand.

"Where have you been?" his corpse mother asked. "The meeting's already begun."

"I was getting my hand back. A damn dog chewed it off while I was sleeping."

"You've got to be more careful, dear."

Their dead speak faded as a tall one with a gimp leg stepped up.

"The time grows short," he said. "We must spill the blood of the innocent at month's end. Only then will our master be at full power. Only then can he destroy the sunlight."

"Innocent?" Tom whispered to his decomposing mother. "Like a virgin or something?"

She slapped him across the back of the head.

"We're not pigmies, you idiot. An innocent is someone untouched by evil."

Tom rubbed his scalp.

"So, like, anybody then?"

"No. Innocents are hard to come by around here. But there is one right across the road."

"We can't cross the road."

She slapped him again, "We know that."

The tall one spoke. "We must find a way to get to her."

"I fear the light!" one said.

"We cannot go near that house. It burns!" said another.

"The light protects it!"

The leader grinned. "Then we must find a way to get her to come to us."

"How?"

"With something the living crave most of all...money."

Wayne McMillan clapped Tom on the back. "Hey, man. I've been looking for you."

"Oh, hey." Tom turned and saw that the motivational speaker had an arm around the shoulders of a dead woman.

"Meet Arlene," he said. "She's my girlfriend." It was the one Wayne had admired the last time they'd spoken. One of her eyes was on Tom. The other twitched, pointing at the ceiling.

"Nice to meet you," Tom told her.

She grinned big and stated, "I like butterflies."

Wayne leaned close to his friend. "Okay, so she ain't the sharpest tack in the box, but I'm not dating her for her IQ. Know what I mean, Bob?"

Tom knew what he meant. And what he meant creeped him out.

"Sure, man. Get in where you fit in."

"Good one, Bob," Wayne said, patting Arlene on the butt. "I like that. Mind if I use it?"

It wasn't clear if he was commenting on what Tom had said, or if he was talking about Arlene's backside.

"You should ask her. It's her ass."

"No, I meant the—"

"We shall lure the innocent with money," the dead man at the podium said, holding a duffel bag. "We need two volunteers to deliver the bait."

"Ooh!" Wayne exclaimed. "This is our chance, Bob." He pulled a hand away from Arlene's breast and stuck it into the air. "We'll do it! Me and Bob!"

Tom shook his head at the floor. *It's Tom, you moron.*

The tall one dropped the bag to the floor. "Good," he slurred. "Meeting's over." Tom watched his fellow zombies file out of the central chamber.

"What a stupid meeting."

Wayne put a rotten hand on his shoulder. "Isn't it great? We get to be the cash guys."

"I didn't know you were gonna volunteer us." The disapproval in Tom's voice was obvious.

"You've got to learn to be more spontaneous," Wayne said. "Death's like a box of chocolates. You never know what you're gonna get."

Tom walked to the platform.

"Let's get this over with."

"That couldn't have been a real hand," Monica said. "It had to be something else."

She paced the living room with anxious steps.

They bury them six feet down. That dog couldn't have dug that far, could it?

She went back to the window.

And they're inside a casket. There's no way for a dog to get to a body. No way.

Then she remembered that it was October. Halloween was quickly approaching, and with it, Halloween pranks. You could buy a fake severed hand at any dime store you went to.

"That's what it was," she said. "A plastic hand."

She'd seen it only from a distance, across the road and nearly two hundred feet away; it could have been anything.

A piece of wood, an old glove...who knows what.

Feeling somewhat better about the situation, she went to the kitchen to make a Doctor Smurf. An extremely drunk girl named Katie had introduced her to the drink at a college party. It was a very basic concoction, just Dr. Pepper and blueberry schnapps. It had been her favorite ever since. Monica always preferred simplicity, especially when she needed a drink to calm her nerves. She couldn't stand beer or wine.

She went back to the window with drink in hand, peering into the darkness. Sitting across the road was a large yellow duffel bag. The top was unzipped.

What the hell?

A strong wind came up, scattering something out of the bag. It was thin pieces of paper. At first it looked like leaves; that is, until one of them tumbled across the road and into the yard. She squinted to see. All of the sudden it came into focus. It was a dollar bill. She looked back to the bag. Her eyes scanned the cemetery. No one was in sight.

"Now I know someone is screwing with me."

She grabbed the BB gun and then opened the door.

"I've called the police!" she yelled.

She ran to the yard, picked up the dollar, and then raced back up the porch steps. The gun shook in her hands as she swung around, pointing it into the shadows. After a silent moment, she went back inside and slammed the door.

Newly dead Tom and his deceased friend Wayne sat on the ground with their backs against dark headstones.

"She's not coming!" Wayne said, "Throw some more out there!"

With his good hand, Tom grabbed another wad of bills, throwing them into the air. A stiff breeze sent them spiraling and tumbling along the ground toward the road.

Wayne complained. "You're not doing it right. Let me have them."

"What do you mean I'm not doing it right?" Tom moaned. "Is there a wrong way to toss money into the wind?"

Wayne growled, "You're an idiot. She won't come if she doesn't think there's a lot of cash in that bag."

Tom looked out at the road. Dancing bills were everywhere.

"How could she not think that?"

"Just give me the money, Bob."

"Fine," Tom said, rolling the top down on a large grocery sack. "Take it, then, if you're so smart."

He threw the paper bag at Wayne.

"I'm gonna dump it all at once. Now, help me up. You know I've got a bad hip." Tom crossed his arms stiffly, ignoring the request.

Wayne spat, "I said, give me a hand!"

A severed hand smacked him in the face and then fell to the ground.

"Very funny, asshole."

"Well," Monica said, studying the dollar. "It's real."

She wondered why someone would leave an open bag of money sitting by the road.

If some stupid kids were just messing with me, then why would they use real bills? she wondered. *There must be a few hundred dollars out there. Where would kids get that much money?*

A figure came into view across the road, holding a grocery bag. He pulled it open and dumped the contents onto the ground. A few hundred dollars turned into a few thousand. Monica threw open the front door. The one across the street was surprised. He stood frozen, staring at her. She saw that it was a zombie.

"Nice costume, kid," she said. "Didn't anyone tell you? It's not Halloween yet." She aimed the BB gun, but he didn't respond.

"I'm keeping all the money that blows into my yard, dumb ass. Now, I suggest you leave before the cops get here."

Wayne threw up his arms in anger, screaming. Monica pumped once and then squeezed the trigger. The BB shot across the road, striking him in the face.

"Ow!" Wayne yelled. "That bitch shot me in the eye!"

I hit him, Monica thought. *God, I hope he's okay.*

With a hand over his wound, he stumbled backward in the mud.

"You were right," Tom said. "Death *is* like a box of chocolates."

Around the backside of the mausoleum, dozens of the undead stood confused and disappointed.

"Why does she not come?" asked one.

"She is smart!" moaned another.

A tall zombie peeked around the corner, watching the house across the road.

"She is not consumed by greed, like most of the living. We will need another kind of bait."

Tom and Wayne joined the gathering.

"She shot me in the eye!"

The tall one turned and jammed an index finger into Wayne's eye socket. With a quick tug, the eyeball popped free. A scream echoed across the graveyard.

"Is this the eye?" he asked, holding it in the palm of his hand.

Wayne looked downward, cowering. "Yes."

"Well then, problem solved."

Dead bodies filed down the stairs and into the labyrinth below the mausoleum. Wayne uncovered his empty eye socket to show Tom. "How's it look, man?"

"It looks like you're missing an eyeball."

"Yeah. My peripheral vision is jacked now. You see Arlene anywhere?"

Tom looked around. "Nope."

"Help me look for her." They separated, taking different sides of the room. It was too dark to make out faces.

Tom spotted Arlene in the middle of a group of eight towering dead men. Each was well above six feet tall and built like a linebacker. They were the strongest, angriest guys in the king's army. The biggest one of the bunch was busy inspecting Arlene's tonsils with his tongue. She, apparently, was a popular girl.

Tom hoped that Wayne was somewhere across the chamber, groping through the shadows half blind and unaware that his girlfriend was making out with someone new. As Wayne approached, yelling "Arlene!" he realized that was not the case.

Tom cringed. "Oh shit. Here we go."

"That's my girlfriend!" Wayne shouted, trying to shove his way through the tall men. They were not about to let him pass, nor were they sympathetic to his situation.

Two dead men blocked Wayne's path as Arlene's new man, Gerald, smirked. "She's mine now."

Wayne struggled to break through with no success. "I think that's up to her."

"It was her choice," Gerald said. "Wasn't it, dear?"

Her lazy eye bobbled in the socket as if motivated by a loose spring. "Strawberries are yummy," she giggled.

"Let her go now," Wayne spat, "or there will be trouble."

Gerald smiled. "How's that stomach ache, Wayne?"

"What? What stomach ache?"

A dead man at Wayne's side sliced across his belly with a sharp blade, spilling wet intestines to the dirt. Stinking and sloppy, they trailed out the slit in his skin as he tried to scoop them back in.

"That stomach ache," Gerald said laughing.

"Aah!" Wayne yelled. "I need those!"

Tom backed away from the putrid smell as the motivational speaker knelt to gather his guts.

At nine in the morning, Sheriff Shane sat at his desk, picking teeth with a long bowie knife. Across from him sat a distressed woman.

"So you're saying that some kids were throwing money at you last night and, um...you're complaining?"

"Well, yes. I think they were trying to lure me over there to—well, I don't know why. But it's strange. Don't you think?"

"Oh, it's strange all right," he said before spitting into the bucket. "I can't see how it's illegal, though."

Monica stood up. "Are you going to wait until I get killed to help me, or what?"

The sheriff stood also. "Now settle down, honey pie. I'll send a deputy by tonight to check things out."

"That's what you said before and I didn't see a patrol all night."

"Deputy Ackerman went by there. He said everything was quiet. Now don't you worry your pretty head. I'm sure it was just a Halloween prank."

Monica rubbed her temples wearily.

"Just be sure the deputy comes by tonight."

"I will. And you keep that money. Go shopping and buy yourself some makeup or something. We'll get to the bottom of it. Leave it to us."

Monica left the Sheriff's Office and climbed into the truck cab, looking down at a bag full of cash that she'd picked up that morning in front of her house. It hadn't just been dollar bills they'd left for her. There were twenties and hundreds too.

Keep the money, huh?

Monica would go shopping, but not for makeup. She smiled, wondering how much pepper spray she could get for thirty-two hundred dollars.

Then Betty's voice surprised her. "Hey, girlfriend. Whatcha doin'?"

"Oh hey," Monica said, turning toward the open window. "Betty, what are you doing today?"

"Nada," she said with a smile.

"Would you like to go shopping in Ryerton with me?"

"Sure. What are we shopping for?"

"Oh, groceries, shoes, maybe a Taser gun."

Betty laughed. "How eclectic—sounds fun."

"Hop in."

Once inside the cab, she noticed that she was sitting beside a bag stuffed with cash.

"Um, did you rob a gas station or something?"

Monica backed the truck out of the parking spot.

"The money was a gift. I'll tell you about it after we stop for some coffee." She grinned, patting the bag. "I'm buying."

"No shit, you're buying," Betty said, eyeing more bills than she'd ever seen crammed into a grocery sack.

"Those guys just won't leave you alone. I can hardly believe they'd just dump cash in the street."

"I know. I think they were trying to get me to go over there. It really freaked me out."

The sign coming up read "Ryerton 16 miles."

"Screw the Taser. I'd be getting a shotgun."

Monica looked over. "Yeah, but I've never fired a real gun in my life. I wouldn't even know how."

Betty said, "It's just for show. If you walk out to your porch carrying a Taser, they'll think you've got a cell phone. If you walk out with a shotgun, they'll run. You know what I'm saying?"

It made sense; she just wanted to scare them away. Monica desperately needed to get a good night's sleep.

"Okay," she said, "so I'll buy a shotgun. But I'm not getting any bullets."

"That's good," Betty laughed, "because they take shells."

Monica turned the truck into the Sporting Goods Emporium parking lot.

"I can't believe I haven't asked you this before, but do you work somewhere?"

Betty chuckled. "Me? No. I live off my dead husband, like Anna Nicole and Yoko Ono."

Monica suddenly remembered a joke she'd heard once, something about Yoko Ono and Ethiopians both living off dead beetles.

"Your husband died? I'm sorry."

"Don't be," Betty said. "He was an asshole. At least he was a *rich* asshole."

"Oh."

"Yeah, he went missing a while back. They finally pronounced him dead last year. That's when I acquired all his stocks."

"He was missing? That must've been awful."

"I was happy to be rid of him, actually."

"But don't you ever wish you knew what happened to him?"

"Nope. I know exactly what happened to him."

"You do?"

"Oh yeah. He died—eight years ago. He deserved it."

Monica turned off the ignition. She sat silent, looking into her friend's face. Betty happily dug through her purse, looking for a stick of gum.

"He deserved it?" Monica said softly.

"Yeah," she said, and then looked up at the sporting goods store. "Well, we're here. Shall we go in?"

"Sure. Let me grab some money."

Monica opened her purse and began stuffing in handfuls of cash.

This is insane, she thought. *I'm going to buy a gun with the money somebody threw at me, in hopes that I can scare them away. And I think Betty may have killed her husband. Things are getting more bizarre by the minute.*

Betty walked up to the firearms counter while Monica trailed behind, still not convinced she needed a gun in her house.

"Hello, ladies," the clerk said with a friendly smile. "Can I help you?"

"Yes," Betty said immediately, "we would like the largest shotgun you have, preferably a double-barrel."

The man turned, looking over a long row of guns.

"Ah," he said, pulling one down. "Something like this?"

It was a twelve-gauge double barrel, and nearly as long as Monica was tall.

"It's massive," she said, turning pale.

"Perfect," Betty added.

The man passed it across the counter. "Try it on for size."

"My god," Monica said, feeling the weight of it in her hands. "It's too big."

Betty laughed, watching her friend trying to hold it steady against her shoulder.

"We'll take it."

"Wait," Monica said, "I don't know if I—"

"Don't worry. We just want to scare some kids. It's not like you're ever gonna shoot it."

"I suppose…"

Betty turned to the clerk. "We'll need six boxes of shells also."

"What? You just said I wasn't going to shoot it."

"What's the point of a gun if you don't have any ammunition? I'll keep the shells at my house. Just call if you need them."

Oh hell, Monica thought. *What am I getting myself into?*

Gary followed John to the video store, keeping his truck's pace far back enough in traffic to avoid detection. He'd been following the man for a week now and had learned quite a bit.

He was single, lived with his sister, and enjoyed horror movies, romantic comedies, and video games. His current favorite was Frontline Assault. His sister went to the gym on Wednesdays at about eight o'clock. She didn't return until after ten. That left him alone at the house for at least two hours, plenty of time for the Lord's work.

Gary checked his day planner. He flipped to October 29. It read "Kill Georgette Gordon."

"Yup," he said, rubbing his chin. "I need to take care of this guy soon."

He wrote "Kill John O'Dell" on the line below for October 28.

It looked like it was gonna be a hectic week.

Monica drove home with two pairs of shoes, a new pair of jeans, some T-shirts, and a twelve-gauge shotgun behind the seat. The gun made her feel uneasy as cars passed her on the highway. She imagined it accidentally going off, causing a twenty-car pileup. But of course, the shells were tucked away safely in the bottom of a plastic bag in Betty's lap; Betty, who was suspiciously happy about her husband's disappearance and untimely death.

She's not the type to kill somebody, is she?

Monica figured it would be a good idea to get to know her friend better.

"So, your husband left you some stocks?"

"I wouldn't say that he left them to me—everything was in his name only—but yes, I got his stock in Synergy Dynamics when he was pronounced dead."

"Synergy Dynamics?"

"Yeah. He was the lead scientist in his division. You've seen the lab, haven't you? It's the complex south of town."

"Oh, I guess I missed that. What do they do there?"

"Experimental engineering and biological testing. They work in chemistry, robotics, synthetic organisms...all kinds of stuff."

"It sounds like a big company."

"Oh yeah. They have contracts with the military and everything. It's huge."

"So, your stocks must've been worth a lot of money."

Betty grinned. "They bought me out for eight million."

Monica nearly choked on her gum. "*Dollars? Good god.*"

A laugh and a snort. "Yeah. It's fun being loaded."

"I had no idea I had a millionaire in my truck."

Did she off her husband for the money?

"Of course, I keep mine at the bank, not in a plastic bag," she said, patting Monica's remaining twenty-six hundred dollars.

"Good idea."

"Yeah," Betty said, looking at the passing landscape of blurred trees and fields. "But money is just money, you know? It doesn't mean anything. Not to me."

As they passed by the Redmondsburg city-limit sign, they saw a van parked on the shoulder. A couple was standing outside, inspecting a tree. The man held up a small handheld device as a woman followed, carrying a larger box with flashing lights.

"What are they doing?" Monica asked.

"I don't know. You wanna stop and ask?"

"No. That would be weird."

"Okay," Betty said. "Whatever."

Dr. Dillon Ramsey checked the reading again and then spoke to his wife.

"Are you getting anything?"

"No, hon. Nothing."

She looked up the length of the tall tree, frowning. He puckered his pink, wrinkled face as he huffed.

"There has to be something."

"I had a cold spot for a minute, but it's gone now."

"I'm getting the camera," he said walking to the van.

Renee slipped a big pair of headphones over her ears and then clicked on a microphone.

She held it at arm's length, up the tree. She heard static, crackling, and then a whisper.

"Get away from me," a voice hissed.

Renee jumped back.

Dillon rushed over. "What is it?"

"It's there! In the tree!"

The doctor swung around, snapping pictures.

"We got one," he said with panting breath. "We really got one!"

"Who—who are you?" his wife asked, holding out the microphone, yet still cowering.

The invisible voice said, "I am the devil!"

She pulled the headphone off her left ear.

"He says he's the devil."

Dillon laughed. "What is Lucifer doing climbing trees? Hmm?"

Renee listened closely for a moment and then said, "He says he's not *the* devil. But he definitely claims to be evil."

"Evil, huh? Prove it."

A pinecone flew out of the tree, hitting Dillon on the head.

He frowned. "Ooh, you're real scary." He held up the camera. "Smile for your picture, ghosty."

The tree shook in a violent rage.

Renee backed away. "You shouldn't taunt the dead, honey."

The quake traveled down the trunk, tearing at the roots. Suddenly, with wood snapping and popping, the tree fell at Dillon. He leapt out of its path as it crashed to the ground. Renee screamed.

"Wow," he said, "a real, honest to god, pissed-off ghost." He got to his feet. "Come on, hon. Let's check out the pictures."

The couple walked back to the van.

"My house is up two more, on the right."

The truck pulled over in front of a large two-story house on Ash.

"Well," Monica said, "thanks for going with me."

"Oh, no problem. Anytime. I'll stop by in the morning, if you want. We can get breakfast or something."

"Sure. That sounds great."

Betty grabbed the sack of twelve-gauge shells and then opened the door. She got out and turned back toward Monica.

"I'm sure nothing will happen tonight. The kids have had their fun. Don't worry."

"I hope you're right. I don't know how much more I can take."

The weariness in her face from two nights of little sleep was obvious.

"Do you wanna stay here tonight? You could sleep on my couch."

"Thanks, but no. I'll be fine."

"Okay. I'll see you in the morning, then."

"Bye."

Monica arrived back home and set her new shotgun in the closet by the front door. She looked out at the quiet graveyard across the road, wondering what to expect of the coming evening. A sheriff's car drove by at ten miles an hour.

"Oh sure. You come *now*," she said. "It's not even dark yet."

It made a U-turn at the southwest corner of the cemetery and then made another pass. The deputy looked out over the headstones, scanning the grounds. He then pulled into Monica's driveway. She went out to the porch as he got out of his car.

"Good afternoon, ma'am," Deputy Simms said. "The sheriff said you've been havin' some disturbances."

Monica went down the steps. "Yes. I think it's some kids dressed in Halloween costumes."

Simms grinned. "Yeah. The damned kids always get so excited this time o' year. This time last year we had a teenager throwin' cats off old lady Spell's barn roof. Can you believe it?"

"That's horrible."

The deputy chuckled. "The things were hittin' the ground so hard it was breakin' their legs."

"My god."

"Yup. More than a dozen felines had to be put to sleep."

Monica's stomach churned. Just the idea of such cruelty made her feel ill. Simms continued with his story.

"And when I say put to sleep...I mean shot. The closest vet is in Ryerton, you know. So we decided to take care of business ourselves."

Simms patted his side arm.

"You killed them?"

"Oh sure," he said proudly. "It was the humane thing to do."

Monica went pale. "That's awful...and sad."

Simms's face got serious. "My point is, kids do some crazy shit around here. They're not too damn bright, if you know what I'm sayin'. But they're mostly harmless."

"Unless you happen to be a cat."

The deputy laughed. "Yeah, I suppose so." He walked back to his car. "I'll come back by after sundown and make sure everything's still quiet. Don't you worry, little lady, you're perfectly safe."

I feel less safe with every person I meet, she thought as the deputy backed his car out of the drive.

5

PEGGY

Monica made herself a cup of coffee as the sun disappeared behind a thick forest to the west. The darkening sky was hazy gray as the temperature fell into the teens. It looked like snow would be there any moment. Monica had one more look over the cemetery out the kitchen window before taking her warm cup into the living room.

She'd just gotten comfortable with a magazine and a blanket, when she heard the voice. It startled her, and she spilled hot coffee down her arm and across the blanket.

The child said, "Get away from me."

It had come from the basement.

"Shit," Monica said, leaping away from the chair.

The cup fell to the floor, and the remaining liquid soaked into the dark carpet. A pounding heartbeat thundered in her chest. She swung around to face the basement door, her entire body shaking.

Again, the voice. "Please, no. I hate him."

"Who's there?" Monica forced out. Silence. She took nervous steps toward the closed door. "Hello?"

A stuttering hand reached for the knob. With it turned, she pushed it open. Narrow wooden stairs led downward into a pitch-black hole. She felt for a light switch, her lungs heaving at the cool air. She realized that she could see breath forming little clouds in front of her face. The voice boomed from the darkness below.

"I said I hate him! Don't make me get mad!"

Monica screamed as a filmy apparition exploded into view. It was a little girl wearing a long nightgown. She looked maybe ten years old, possibly more. Curly bright locks hung down and over small shoulders. She glowed like a florescent bulb in a steamy room. The small figure was transparent, ghostly. Monica fell back wailing and hit the floor.

"Jesus!"

She scrambled away on hands and knees. The light from the basement faded. The house went deathly quiet.

What the hell was that?

On her knees and shaking, she pulled the coffee-soaked blanket up to her chin. Her wide eyes did not stray from the open doorway. A small, whispery voice sounded from behind.

"You made a mess."

Monica screamed once again and turned to see the coffee cup float over her head. Her nerves could take no more. She fainted, her body slumping over moist carpet. The next twenty minutes was the soundest sleep she'd had in days.

Monica woke with a gasp. She sat straight up, looking around the room and listening. Everything was quiet once again as she got to her feet.

That wasn't real.

The blackout had left her lightheaded and unsteady. She tried to shake off a pounding headache. Slowly she walked to the basement doorway. The downstairs was silent and dark. Monica's clammy hand pushed the door shut. She steadied herself against the wall, looking into the kitchen. The coffee cup sat freshly washed, next to the sink. There were also three bowls, clean and drying, neatly placed upside down on a towel.

"I don't believe in ghosts," she said. "Do you hear me? I don't believe in ghosts!"

There was no otherworldly response. A strong wind howled across the yard. She looked to the window and saw that it was snowing.

I have to get out of here.

She glanced out to the truck in the driveway. Little pellets of white glistened over its surface. She grabbed a set of keys off the counter and then a heavy coat from the closet, rushing for the door.

I changed my mind, Betty. I think I will spend the night.

Betty answered a knock at the door at six thirty. "Monica? Hi. Come in."

Shivering from the cold, Monica went inside.

"Hey. I was wondering if the offer to stay over was still good."

"Of course it is. Did something happen?"

Pulling off a thick coat, she said, "Yeah. Something happened."

Betty could see it in her friend's pink face. She'd been obviously shaken.

"Well?" Betty said. "Are you gonna tell me?"

The women found a place to sit as Monica rubbed her hands together, warming them up.

"You wouldn't believe me. I don't believe it myself."

"You'd be surprised what I believe. Spit it out."

Monica looked up and around Betty's house. It was small, but more cozy than cramped. Spider-shaped lights lined the windows, glowing orange. Cardboard skeletons hung on a wall, with silly smiles and top hats. Fake cobwebs lined every corner, and a plastic cartoon witch sat atop the entertainment center. Below, a large square shelf sat empty, with no television. Dime-store spider webbing had been stretched across its corners also. It struck Monica as odd.

"You don't have a TV?"

Betty looked over at the vacant shelf and grinned.

"Oh. I don't need a television. I can just close my eyes."

"Huh?"

"You're changing the subject. What happened?"

"I…uh…saw a…ghost."

The words felt stupid coming out of her mouth. They sounded crazy. Betty's eyes went wide.

"A ghost? Really?"

"I know how it must sound, but—"

"No. I totally believe in ghosts."

"Really?"

"Yeah. Tell me everything."

"It was a little girl, maybe ten years old. I passed out, but when I woke up…she'd done my dishes."

Betty sat silent with a look of shock over her face.

"She…washed your dishes?"

"I know. It's crazy, right?"

In a whisper, she said, "No. It's not crazy."

"What? Do you know who I'm talking about? Did she used to live around here?"

"She lived six blocks from here, on Fourteenth Street. She used to play in your house, when it was vacant. That was a long time ago."

"How do you know she used to play in my house?"

A silence lingered for a few seconds and then she answered, "Because I used to play there with her. We were best friends."

Monica leaned back and put a hand to her chest. "Oh my god."

Betty's eyes showed the sadness for a lost friend. Monica held out a comforting hand, and it was taken.

"I'm sorry. But are you sure it's her?"

"Yeah. She was a clean freak. Her room was immaculate, not a toy out of place. That's why she did your dishes. She couldn't stand messes, even at eleven years old."

"That's so weird."

"Yup. She had curly blond hair. Her name was Peggy Wyne."

Curly blond hair. "Jesus."

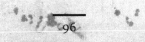

Monica had seen a real ghost. It wasn't her imagination. The little girl had been alive. She'd had friends, people who cared about her. What Monica had seen suddenly became very real. A shiver went up her spine. Proof of an afterlife had just been handed to her. She had no choice but to believe.

"What happened to Peggy? How did she die?"

Betty, reluctant to answer, stood nervously eyeing the kitchen. "It was years ago. She was...stabbed."

"God. Really?"

"Yeah. By a...man. A very bad man."

Monica covered her gaping mouth with a shuddering hand. "Where?"

Betty turned to face her friend, watching the fear in her grow. "Right there," she said in a whisper. "She was killed at your house."

A gasp. "At my house? That's horrible. Did they catch the guy?"

"Yeah. He was caught."

A real murder happened where I live. My god. "I have to move. I can't stay there."

Betty paused a moment and then suggested, "But what if we could help her? Help her move on."

"What are we supposed to do? Tell her to go into the light?"

"I don't know. All I do know is that she was my friend. I feel like I should do something." Betty's eyes filled with tears. "I have to try."

"Okay. If it's important to you, then we'll do it. I just want you to know right now, this shit freaks me the hell out."

Betty smiled. "So, if we can put her to rest, so she's not there anymore, you'll stay, right?"

"Yeah, I guess so. But it has to be totally ghost-free. You know what I'm saying? No voices. No weird lights. No dishwashing. I can't take it."

"You bet. I know we can do it. It'll be fine. And then you'll stay. Everything will work out."

"I hope so," Monica said. "I really do."

Monica slept until almost eleven o'clock in the morning. Yawning and stretching, she sat up on the couch, squinting at the bright sunlight shining through the window.

"You're awake," Betty said from the kitchen. "You must've been really tired. You slept, like, twelve hours."

"I haven't been getting much sleep, with all the kids in the graveyard and the ghosts."

Betty smiled. "I guess you wouldn't. I made some coffee. When you're finished, we'll go."

"Go?" Monica said, rubbing her eyes. "Go where?"

Betty took a cup out of the cabinet and placed it on the counter.

"To the library. It's the best place to start."

Dillon sat at a table in the back of the library, looking at microfilm of an old newspaper. He'd found something interesting. The article was from November 30, 1963.

An early morning hunting accident had left a hunter, Mr. Benjamin Blake, fatally wounded with a bullet buried in his stomach. The weapon had been fired by one Ranard Clement. Apparently, both men had a deer in their sights and shot at the same time, from opposite sides of a large clearing. While Mr. Blake's bullet dropped the animal, Mr. Clement's bullet dropped Blake. He and the six-point buck bled out together, presumably ending the day on a sour note for the both of them.

After a short investigation, local sheriff personnel sent the deer home with Clement. He had it slaughtered by early afternoon and was preparing lean strips for jerky by evening.

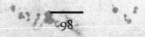

Dillon looked over at his wife, Renee, who was scanning down a page of the county registry.

"I think this might explain our buddy in the tree. Read this."

They switched seats as Monica and Betty walked in looking for the occult section.

"Here we go," Betty said, walking up to one of the shelves and pulling out a large book titled *Spirit Sightings in America*.

"What about this one—*Paranormal Investigations for Dummies*?" Monica said.

Dillon approached the women. "Are you interested in the living deceased?"

Betty looked up at him. "What?"

"Ghosts, young lady. Ghosts."

"Oh yeah. We're...uh...interested."

"Well, how lucky you are. I happen to be one of the country's leading investigators."

Monica frowned. "In ghosts?"

"Yes. My wife and I have studied more than a hundred locations with actual afterlife activity. That's why we're here. You have an entity in the woods west of town."

"Oh. You're the people we saw looking at that tree."

"Yes. He was quite grumpy. He nearly dropped that tree on my head."

The two women looked at each other for a moment. They turned back to the man suddenly, and Monica spoke. "Maybe you could help us. I have a ghost in my house."

Renee stopped reading and looked over.

The doctor grinned. "Are you sure? You have a haunted house?"

"Yes, I'm positive. She scared the shit out of me last night."

"She?"

"It's a little girl," Betty answered. "She was eleven when she died."

"Oh my," Dillon said with flushed cheeks. "Did you hear, honey? A haunted house."

Renee stood beside her husband, gripping his arm with excitement.

"Yes. I think we should look into it."

"As do I, hon. Right now."

Monica smiled in relief. "You'll help us? That's so great. Thank you."

"Now put those books away," he said. "They're trash. If you want to know something about ghosts, you ask me. I'll tell you the truth."

"Sweet," Betty said, nudging her friend. "We're really gonna do this."

Dillon and Renee unloaded boxes of equipment from the van. Each was set in the yard carefully, so not to damage the sensitive contents. Monica was inside, making coffee for her guests. She was relieved that she would not be spending the night alone in the house.

Betty stood on the porch, peering in the open doorway, reluctant to step inside. Her sharp eyes scanned the living room as she listened for any unusual sound.

Peggy, she thought, *why are you still here?*

Betty hadn't been in the basement since that terrible night, when it all happened. She swore that she'd never go back after that. The memories were too painful to endure. But her friend needed her, and she wasn't going to let her down.

Not this time, she thought. *That night was my fault…I'm going to help you, Peg. I promise.*

As she stepped inside, she hoped that Monica wouldn't find out what really happened. *That would ruin everything.*

"Come in," Monica said. "I made some coffee."

"Great," Betty replied, as her fearful eyes studied the dark corners of the room. Renee appeared at the door, struggling with a large metal crate.

"Can you help me with this? It's really heavy."

"Oh sure."

Betty lifted the large box out of the parapsychologist's arms with ease.

"Where do you want it?"

Renee was surprised how strong the skinny woman was. "That crate weighs more than a hundred pounds, and you hold it like it was full of cotton balls."

"Yeah, well—"

Monica interrupted, "Didn't she tell you? She can bench press a Volkswagen."

Betty grinned. "I am a badass."

Renee tried to catch her breath. "Anywhere over there is fine."

The box full of computer equipment was set in the center of the room.

"Need help with anything else?"

"Yes, thank you. Everything in the yard comes in."

"No problem," she said with a smile.

"Coffee?" Monica asked, holding out a warm cup.

"Thanks," Renee said, watching Betty go down the porch steps.

While the women unpacked the supplies and set up in the living room, Dillon evaluated the house. With a handheld electromagnetic field (EMF) detector leading the way, he went up the staircase. The sensitive needle bobbed lightly, showing normal nanotesla readings. He stopped every three steps, noticing the room temperature on his face and hands. With no apparent cold or hot spots, he continued his search.

When he reached the top, he checked the EMF reading and then looked around carefully. He saw two closed doorways directly ahead, and to his right was a short dark hallway leading to the attic ladder. He went right first. Holding the device higher in the air, he approached the shadowed rungs that led up through a rectangle opening in the ceiling. The needle dropped twenty nanotesla.

Oh my.

He peered upward, squinting. The room above had a dim yellow glow, presumably from the setting sun's light through a window. He started up the ladder. The reading held for a moment more and then jumped back to its original position. Dillon's eyes scanned the attic quickly. He saw a small window, scattered boxes, and a weathered trunk. The needle jumped up to sixty thousand nanotesla, vibrated for a few seconds, and then dropped to almost nothing. His breath began forming little white tufts in front of his face as the temperature dropped below twenty degrees.

"Damn," he said out loud. "This place is gorged with spiritual energy."

The hair on the back of his neck stood up. His arms tingled with cool static electricity. A low rumble sounded in the corner as a cardboard box flap popped up.

"Shit!" Dillon gasped.

Carefully, he stepped forward. Perhaps there was something the entity wanted him to see. Ghosts had been known to ask for help.

He rummaged through the contents of the box and the trunk. A leather-bound notebook caught his attention. He tucked it under an arm and kept searching. There was nothing else of interest. The air eased back to sixty-five degrees, and his icy breath disappeared. He went down the ladder with a thundering in his chest.

"Honey?" he called out.

"Yes, dear?" came a faint voice from downstairs.

"We're gonna need an infrared camera up here...and a microphone."

"Okay, dear. Just let me finish hooking up the computer."

At the bottom of the ladder, the doctor tried to catch his excited breath. He walked to the first bedroom and threw the door open. The needle spiked again.

We don't have enough cameras for this place. There's activity in every room. The next bedroom was empty. The detector bobbled with random magnetic surges and lulls. He headed for the stairs. All three women sat in the front room looking up at him.

"Well?" Monica said, "What do you think?"

Dillon rubbed his scalp with thin fingers. "Either you've got a ghost in every room, or there's one following me."

Betty's face went pale. "Do they do that?"

"Some do," he said, descending the stairs, "and some don't. We'll need the digital cameras to know for sure."

Renee booted up the computer. "I'm all set, hon. Are you ready for some video?"

"Yes," he said, reaching for a camera attached to a long line of cable. "Could you hand me a tripod please?"

Betty had just finished extending the tall, three-legged camera stand. "Sure," she said, passing it to him over piles of wound video cable.

Dillon looked at Monica. "Do you have a microwave?"

"A microwave?"

"Yes. The frequency really pisses them off."

She pointed toward the kitchen. "It's over there on the counter."

"Great," he said with a grin. "If they get too quiet tonight, I'll make some popcorn."

"Does it hurt them?"

Dillon chuckled. "It seems to, yes."

Great, Monica thought. *Let's get 'em mad. That'll be fun.*

Video cameras were set up in the two upstairs bedrooms, the attic, the basement, and the living room. All of the feeds were plugged into the computer that displayed each one's view in a separate window on the monitor. Renee sat watching the feed from camera five, the view of the basement. It was set to infrared, and she could see her husband's body heat in the darkness as he walked slowly, taking temperature readings. Betty stood behind, watching over Renee's shoulder.

"What's he doing?"

"He's checking cold spots, mostly. Room temperature usually drops when an entity is active."

"Has he found anything?"

Renee sipped her coffee, "Not since the attic."

Suddenly, Dillon felt a chill. He looked down at the gauge and saw that it had dropped to forty degrees. He fumbled for a digital recorder.

With it on he said, "Hello. My name is Dr. Dillon Ramsey. What's yours?" He peered into the shadows, waiting for a response.

He heard only silence. "Why are you here, my friend?"

Again, his ears strained for any noise at all. His own footsteps over concrete were all he heard. He saw his breath in the dim light as the temperature went even lower.

"Is there anything we can do to help you? Anything at all?"

He waited for ten seconds before speaking again.

"Is there anything you'd like to tell us?"

Static electricity bit at Dillon's face. He stopped where he was, a thunderous heartbeat pounding in his body. After another moment, he checked the readout and saw that it was once again sixty-five degrees. He pushed the stop button on the recorder. Up the stairs he went. Dillon gave the small recorder to his wife.

"Load this up."

Renee plugged it into a USB cable to begin the wave file transfer.

Monica watched as the recording loaded on the computer. "What're you doing?"

Renee glanced up. "I'm going to enhance the sound and amplify it."

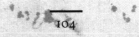

She loaded a wave program and then opened the file. It showed up on the screen in squiggled lines along a grid. She pressed play.

Hissing and then, "Hello. My name is Dr. Dillon Ramsey. What's yours?" Renee tagged the spot where Dillon's voice ended and kept listening. After a few seconds of static, his voice sounded again. With the hissing silence selected, she saved it and continued.

Betty listened closely. "Oh my god. Did you guys hear that?"

"Hear what?"

"The voice."

"I can't hear anything but Dillon," Monica said.

Renee opened all of her selections together on the screen. She ran them through an enhancement filter and waited for the program to finish. A ten-decibel volume boost finished the task.

"Okay, hon. You ready?"

Dillon squeezed her shoulders with anticipation. "Go ahead, dear."

The entire recording played again.

Hello. My name is Dr. Dillon Ramsey. What's yours?

A loud popping followed, along with a previously unheard voice. "Back away."

It was undeniably angry. Monica gasped. The recording continued.

Why are you here, my friend?

"She put me here."

Is there anything we can do to help you? Anything at all?

"Get the hell out."

Is there anything you'd like to tell us?

Static, and then, "You're all going to die."

A shiver went up Monica's spine.

Dillon smiled. "Don't worry. Ghosts make empty threats all the time."

"That didn't sound like the voice I heard before."

"Yes. It would seem that you have at least two active entities in this house. Very interesting."

Betty had gone pale. She walked to the window. Monica followed.

"Are you okay? What's wrong?"

"Nothing," Betty said, looking out into the night. "I'm just a little freaked out, I guess."

"Yeah. Me too. Are you sure you wanna do this?"

More than ever, Betty thought. *Now that I know that he's here too. I have to help her.* "Yeah, I'm sure."

Monica looked across the room toward Dillon, who hovered over the computer screen. "How are we gonna get rid of two ghosts? God, who knows, there might be even more than that."

"I don't know how, but there has to be a way. We should ask him."

The two women approached the doctor. Monica put a hand on his shoulder. "Excuse me, but what can we do to send the ghosts away?"

"Yeah," Betty said, "does the house need an exorcism or something?"

"No," he abruptly said. "Exorcisms rarely work. They only serve to anger the deceased."

"Then, what?"

Dillon scratched his chin. "We must determine the reason they are attached to this location. A tragic event is usually to blame."

"The little girl was stabbed in his house. She died here."

Renee and Dillon looked at each other.

"That would explain the girl," Renee said. "But what about the man?"

Betty suddenly realized the other three were looking at her.

"I don't know anything about a man," she said, her words trembling.

She hated that she had to lie to them, but there was nothing else she could do. She couldn't let them find out.

But how can we put Peggy to rest without the truth coming out?

She doubted the spirits could be put to rest at all. Knowing how both of them died, Betty feared that there was nothing anyone could do.

It's all my fault, she thought. *I'm responsible for all of this.*

Much of the evening was spent staring into the computer screen, checking various room temperatures, and recording sounds. Every twenty minutes or so, Dillon walked the entire house, searching each room and closet. By nine o'clock everything had gotten very quiet. There had been no unusual variances in electromagnetic fields or degrees for more than forty-five minutes. There had been no odd sounds or recorded voices for a half hour. It seemed that their otherworldly friends were taking a break.

Dillon was frustrated as he emerged from his sixth expedition to the basement. The look on his face was of boredom, and Renee recognized it immediately.

"I'm sure something will happen soon, honey. Do you want me to switch the cameras to night vision again?"

"No, dear. The room temperature will change before they appear, I'm sure of it. Leave them all on infrared."

Betty sat back in a recliner with her eyes closed, listening. Monica stood at the front window, looking across a quiet cemetery. It seemed that the Halloween pranksters were taking a break also. She'd seen no sign of them all night.

Betty's eyes popped open. She quickly slid forward to check the computer screen. "The temperature's dropping in the attic."

Renee clicked on the view to enlarge it. "She's right, hon. I'm switching to night vision."

Dillon rushed over as the screen went black and white. A greenish haze illuminated the camera window, allowing them to see into the pitch-blackness.

"Look back there."

"A window came open. That's why it's getting cold."

Betty stood. "I'll go close it. I need to stretch my legs anyway."

Monica stepped up. "Are you sure? Any of us could go."

She smiled. "I'm positive. It's just an open window. No problem."

With an uneasy feeling in her stomach, Monica watched her friend go upstairs. Up the ladder Betty climbed, hearing the hinged window frame creak back and forth under the force of a brisk, icy wind. Her face emerged above the floor level, and she felt the chill of the outside air. She searched the shadows as she stepped up, onto creaky boards.

"Peg? Are you here?"

The camera sat recording on a tall tripod six feet away. A red light on the side of the device was a tiny pinpoint of illumination in the darkness. Betty walked to the window and latched it shut. The attic went colder. Ice formed and crackled across the glass before her eyes. Frost formed tiny white flakes over the wall and curtain. Betty's hot breath came to life in steamy clouds through her lips. She slowly turned back to face the shadows.

"Peggy?" she said, clutching her bare arms to warm them.

In the distance, Dillon bounded up the stairs. "Betty!" he called out. "Are you okay?"

A piercing light exploded in the center of the attic, throwing the camera to the floor. Betty screamed, falling back. Just as Dillon reached the ladder, the trunk slid across the floor, blocking the entrance.

"Betty!" he yelled, pushing at the bottom of the trunk with all of his might. It wouldn't budge.

Renee screamed, "I've lost the feed! What's happening?"

Monica ran up the stairs, taking two at a time. *Oh god, I shouldn't have let her go up there alone.*

When the blinding light faded, Betty saw that she wasn't alone. Not at all. A small, filmy apparition hovered a few inches above the attic floor, with feet dangling in the air. She wore a bright blue nightgown that stopped at her knees, and white socks. Her hair hung in long twisted blond strands, past a milky-white face and over narrow shoulders. Not a speck of white was seen in her eyes; they were glossy black stones, dark and menacing. Parched ivory lips parted slightly as she glared at the familiar intruder, the one in her attic, the screaming woman. Her voice was distant, pleading, and sad.

"Why did you do this to me?"

Betty's cry subsided, leaving a scratchy pain in her throat. She heard Dillon calling her name from below, and Monica too. She heard a howling wind outside, rattling the windowpane and tearing at the remaining autumn leaves in the trees and on the ground. She heard her own heaving breath as it created icy clouds in front of her pale face. But most of all, she heard Peggy.

Betty took a step back. "I'm so sorry…about everything."

The little girl put hands up to the sides of her own head, pulling at hair and flailing. "I hate him! I hate him!"

Still backing away, Betty's eyes did not waiver from the vision before her. When her back touched the wall beside the window, she knew there was nowhere else to go.

The little girl with the ebony eyes lunged forward, screaming, "You did this to me!"

Below and halfway up the ladder, Monica shoved at the obstruction with all of her strength.

Betty did what to the girl? Oh god, did she kill her? She knew something wasn't right about Betty's husband, and now the ghost was all but calling her a murderer. *Jesus, I think Betty killed both of them.*

Dillon appeared in hallway with a crowbar. "Step back," he said. "Let me up there."

She complied, and he got into position. Just as he started to apply pressure, the trunk slid away, leaving a clear opening into the attic. Frantic, Dillon climbed up.

Betty sat on the floor below the window, crying.

"Are you all right?" he asked, rushing to her.

"I'm okay."

Monica looked into the dark room. Boxes sat undisturbed in the center of the floor. The video camera and tripod lay on their sides in the shadows. There was no sign of ghosts. She turned to see Betty, who was wiping away tears.

Is she really a killer? Monica felt a chill travel up her spine. *Did she murder her husband and best friend?*

Betty sat in the living room, trying to calm down. Renee was on her knees in front of her, holding her hand.

"Everything is fine now, dear. It's okay."

Betty managed a smile. "Thank you. I'm good. Really."

Monica stood in the kitchen watching them. Betty seemed too young to be a murderer. *Too happy. Too pretty, for Christ's sake.* And too damn female. *Aren't most psychos men?* She'd never heard of a woman serial killer. But, after everything she'd heard from Peggy and Betty, what was she supposed to think? A dark fear came over her, knotting up her stomach. One thing was for sure: She didn't want to be left alone with Betty again.

"Monica? How are you holding up?" Renee asked.

"I'm fine," she said, although the look on her face proved otherwise.

Renee looked at her husband. "Maybe we should get them out of here. I think we've all had enough for one night."

Monica frowned. "I'm staying. You three should go. Get Betty home."

"No," Betty said. "I'm not going anywhere. If Monica's staying, I am too."

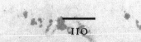

She looked over, sending her friend a smile. The gesture was not reciprocated. Monica only stared back as rising stress flexed the muscles in her face.

At three a.m., Monica shook awake. She was sitting in the recliner with her feet up. A blanket had been put over her after she'd fallen asleep. She sat up quickly, folding down the footrest. Renee and Betty were at the computer looking intensely into the display.

"What's going on? I must've fallen asleep."

Betty glanced over. "You're awake. Dillon's in the basement. We heard a noise down there a few minutes ago."

"What kind of noise?"

Renee zoomed in the camera view. "A voice...maybe."

"The little girl?"

"No," Renee said frowning. "We think it's the other one."

Dillon walked carefully through the darkness. He held out a digital recorder in one hand and an EMF detector in the other. The air was cold.

He said, "Hello again, my friend."

The electromagnetic needle leapt as a voice boomed from the shadows. "I said, get away from me!"

A rush of pressure hit Dillon in the chest, knocking him to his back. Sharp pain blasted across his shoulder blades. He scrambled away as panic seized. Renee wailed, as she ran for the basement door. The other women were right behind. When they arrived, it slammed shut. The knob was solid; it wouldn't turn.

"Oh god! Dillon!"

"Stand back," Betty said.

She rammed the door with her shoulder. It held rigid, denying them passage.

"What do we do?" Monica asked.

Betty raised a sneaker upward and kicked. The heel of her foot hit the door hard and stopped as if held back by a concrete wall. *It's just wood*, she thought. *I should be able to break it.*

Monica went back to the computer. She watched the camera image from the basement. Dillon was pinned to the floor by something unseen. He struggled for air.

It's killing him.

Dillon strained against the invisible entity above. Its power tightened around his neck as he struggled. With feet flat on the concrete floor, he pushed upward with all his strength. The thick energy growled, shoving him down again. His burning lungs heaved for oxygen. The grip over him would not allow a breath. Dillon knew that in a few more seconds he would suffocate. There was nothing he could do about it, but that didn't stop him from fighting. With weakened muscles aching, he struggled. The darkness, cold and unforgiving, expanded like a cruel blanket of unconsciousness. It was swallowing him.

Monica raced for the kitchen. She ran past Renee, who was still screaming, and Betty, who shoved at the basement door. She remembered Dillon's words from earlier in the evening. They'd struck her as odd, ridiculous when he'd said them, but she believed him now. It was the only thing she could do. Skepticism was for those on the outside; those who'd never seen a ghost firsthand. She had been one of those people only a few days ago, but as she quickly realized, a perspective change of one-eighty is only a matter of turning around. Although, as she slid to a stop on the slick tile, it felt as if the world was turning around her. She now believed in the unbelievable.

She cranked the dial over to three minutes and pressed start.

The microwave hummed to life.

A guttural scream exploded above Dillon as the sharp pressure at his neck released. He gasped. Cool air inflated desperate lungs, and he coughed violently, rolling onto his stomach. With a final shove, the basement door flew open, and Betty caught herself from falling down the steps.

Renee screamed, "Dillon!" pushing past and storming downstairs to her husband. In a matter of seconds, both women stood over the man, who lay pale and wheezing on the floor. Tears streamed down Renee's face as she lifted him by the arm. "Are you all right, dear? Are you hurt?"

Panting, he said, "I think I'm okay."

Betty took him by the other arm. "Can you walk?"

He looked over, into the shadows. "If it means getting the hell out of here, yes."

Monica stood waiting as the three emerged from the darkness below. Dillon, on wobbly legs, leaned heavily on the women, who didn't seem to mind. Once upstairs, they got him to a chair. He flopped down onto the soft cushions, still catching his breath. Monica closed the damaged door. Splintered wood sat in sharp shards down both edges. Two hinges hung loose with broken and missing screws. A long crack down the center followed the grain in a jagged curve.

With a ding, the microwave shut down.

Dillon looked over with tired eyes. "You saved me."

"I remembered what you said, about it hurting them. It was the only thing I could think of."

He smiled. "I'd be dead if you hadn't."

"Thank you," Renee said, still crying.

Monica took a deep breath. "No problem."

Betty stood watch in the kitchen as cameras and computer equipment were packed into crates and boxes. She looked out the window and saw that a new day had begun. The sun eased over the horizon as snow clouds gathered in the northwest. By ten o'clock the small area of blue sky that was showing would be swallowed by the icy haze. The first heavy snow of the winter would be upon them in a few short hours. Dillon and Renee carried the last loads out to the van as Monica scooped coffee grounds into a filter.

Betty smiled. "Crazy night, wasn't it?"

"Yeah. Crazy."

"What's the plan for today?"

"I don't know. I might do some more research at the library...Maybe get some sleep later."

"You're exhausted. You should crash at my place for a while."

Monica looked in Betty's eyes. She didn't appear tired at all. She was perky as ever, which was irritating, to say the least. "Yeah. Like I said, maybe later. I'll let you know."

"Anytime," Betty said. "But we can hit the library first. That's fine."

"Actually, I'm gonna go alone this time. It'll help me focus...if I'm by myself."

"Oh."

A sadness formed in Betty's expression, like a puppy that dropped a hunk of rawhide behind the couch. Monica ignored the disappointment, opening the cabinet in search of cups. Dillon appeared, out of breath.

"Well, that's the last of it."

"Okay, thanks for everything."

He got serious. "I would bet that both of your ghosts died in this house. It's the only thing that makes sense. A violent death can bind the deceased to a location. It happens all the time."

"But how can we put them to rest?"

Dillon stepped closer. "That's the tricky part. Usually, they'll leave on their own after time. But as angry as both of them seem to be, I think there's something else at work here. They obviously hate each other. If there was a way to separate them somehow...I don't know...I'll need to study this case further. We'll be at the motel south of town." He paused a moment. "I wouldn't suggest either of you staying here, especially by yourselves. It's dangerous."

Monica offered him a steaming cup of coffee, saying, "Oh, we won't. You can be sure of that."

"Thank you, dear. The only other thing I can think of is that ghosts tend to hang around the place where they're buried. That's why graveyards are so supernatural. Is either of them across the road?"

Betty looked over. "At Lakeshore? No."

"Are you sure? It would make sense."

She smiled. "I'm pretty sure."

Monica glared at her. *Naturally, you'd know, wouldn't you? You killed them yourself.*

Renee joined the group. She held up an EMF detector to show her husband. "I've gotten some very strong readings from the cemetery. There's definitely a lot of activity over there."

Dillon checked the device. "I've never seen a spike like that."

"We should check that place out too. But first, we need some sleep."

"Yes. I would agree. Let's get going."

Monica picked up her purse and keys. "I'll walk you out. I'm headed into town myself."

She had a new goal. She was going to find out what really happened to the ghosts. And if Betty did murder them, as she suspected, she'd make sure that some prison time was in her future.

Then she was going to move the hell out of that house.

6

BETTY'S SECRET

The small library was quiet at nine in the morning. Monica sat studying microfilm of a newspaper from eight years ago. It was the twelfth issue she'd looked over. She knew right away when she saw the article that it was what she'd been looking for. The headline read "Two persons missing since Friday evening."

Two?

Monica kept reading. "A manhunt has begun for two local residents of Redmondsburg. Mr. Bernard Jones, the renowned scientist who heads an engineering team at Synergy Dynamics, has been reported missing as of sometime after ten o'clock, Friday night. Also, eleven-year-old Peggy Wyne has been reported missing. She is a fourth grade student at Redmondsburg Elementary. It is unclear if these disappearances are connected. Sheriff Guy Shane is calling for volunteers for a countywide search. Participants should check in at the local Sheriff's Office at 907 Rocky Creek Way."

Monica sat back in her chair. *Peggy went missing the same day as Betty's husband?*

She looked at the two photos at the bottom of the article. Bernard Jones was a portly man in his late forties. He wore thick, black-rimmed glasses and was totally bald. Peggy's was obviously from a class photo. Her blond curls had been pulled away from her face with pink ribbons. She was smiling at the camera, looking as though she were about to break into laughter. Her eyes were crystal blue.

Monica had assumed that the girl died long before Betty's husband.

If Peggy was eleven eight years ago, and she and Betty were best friends...Betty would have been about twenty at the time. That can't be right.

If she was in her mid to late twenties now, that would've meant quite an age difference between Betty and her husband also. She was definitely a gold digger. And perhaps she hadn't been friends with the little girl after all.

Oh god.

One thing had become very likely. The second ghost in Monica's house was Betty's husband. She murdered both of them the same night.

"Excuse me," Monica said to the librarian. "Do you remember when a scientist and a little girl went missing eight years ago?"

The elderly woman looked up from her book cart. "Oh yes. I remember. That was just awful."

"Were they ever found?"

She walked closer. "No. They searched for nearly a month. Nobody ever found hide nor hair, so to speak."

"So, it's an unsolved case."

"Yes. They were finally pronounced dead a year or so back, due to the limitations statute of missing persons, or some such thing."

"You never heard anything about the little girl getting stabbed?"

"No. No one ever found either of them, although I wouldn't be surprised if something like that was what happened."

"Yeah," Monica said, looking back at the article. Peggy's eyes really were quite beautiful.

The librarian went back to her cart. "Only those poor victims would know for sure."

No, the killer would know too, Monica thought. *The killer would know everything.*

Betty sat at her dining room table, sifting through a pile of photographs. There were wedding shots of her and Bernard, some pictures of the county fair from two years ago, and other random Kodak moments that had prompted smiles and the word *cheese*. She pushed glossy images of her husband away, searching. A still of a young girl at Pheasant Park caught her eye. She lifted it up, grinning. It had been taken only five days before that awful night when it was all over. Peggy looked so happy standing there in front of the swing set, so completely innocent. She was wearing a pink coat with thick fur lining. Her hands were warm inside fat mittens. Her cheeks were flushed in the cold air. She'd only been eleven years old. Betty started to cry.

"I'm sorry, Peg. You should've stayed away from me."

She knew it wouldn't be long before Monica put the pieces together.

She's already suspicious.

Betty had heard it in her voice, seen it in her eyes. Her friend didn't trust her, and why would she? The awful truth was about to surface, one way or another.

Monica unlocked the dead bolt and then stepped into her living room. She set her purse and keys on the kitchen counter, looking around cautiously. Her jacket was covered with wet snow. She pulled it off and hung it in the closet. The double-barrel shotgun sat leaning in the corner. She paused for a moment to notice its size.

I should've gotten a pistol, she thought. *At least I'd be able to use it...if I had to.* As she closed the closet, she knew that shooting at ghosts would be useless anyway.

The basement door hung broken and slightly ajar. With a stuttering hand, she pushed it open. The air was cool and silent. Stairs creaked underfoot as she stepped downward, into darkness. Monica's entire body quaked with fear, but she had to search the house. If two people had been murdered there, and justice was to be served, clues needed to be gathered. Her house was a crime scene that had never been investigated.

Dillon sat in the van rubbing at a sore neck, looking over the computer and video equipment. The insulation on two of the cables was scuffed, with a few chunks of plastic missing. They were a couple of years old and would need to be replaced soon. Under the video cables was something that had been nearly forgotten.

It was the leather-bound notebook he'd found in Monica's attic. He pulled it out and opened the front cover, scanning down the page. It was the journal of a man who'd lived in Monica's house in 2006. Each entry was dated, and it appeared the man had written in it daily. Dillon closed the book to inspect the cover. The leather finish was creased and worn around the edges. A large Celtic weave design adorned the front. The back was a smooth antique stain. At the bottom, two words had been scrawled with an ink pen: *innocent blood*.

"That's strange," Dillon said.

Renee appeared with a stack of freshly charged camera batteries. "We'd better get going, dear."

The notebook found a place under the driver's seat.

Monica searched the house from rafters to baseboards. Every nook and cranny, each cupboard and crawlspace was illuminated with a flashlight and studied with determined eyes.

Loose boards in the attic floor were pried up to reveal empty spaces. Large appliances were drug from their designated spots to discover lint, dead bugs, and dirt. Top to bottom and one end to the other, the house was scrutinized by its owner.

By the second afternoon, the only remaining area was the basement. Monica had been putting it off since she began. Images of the ghost of a little girl and Dillon suffocating in the shadows had kept her upstairs in the safety of sunlight. But now, her choices were down to one. If she wanted to continue the search, it was time to face her fear.

With a flashlight in her fist, she ventured down creaky steps.

Dillon set the final box down next to a tall headstone. He rubbed at an aching back with a gloved hand. "I'm getting too old for this," he complained.

"Be careful, hon," Renee said. "Don't hurt yourself."

His teeth gritted together. "I'm fine. Hand me the EMF."

A thickening snowstorm masked the sunset behind its pale haze. Swirling white pellets danced in a frigid breeze before touching down onto the cemetery grounds.

"Here you go," Renee said, handing over the device. "It's really cold out here."

Dillon ignored the comment in favor of exploration. He took off walking toward the mausoleum. "Set up the computer, would you, dear?" he said, not looking back.

"Fine," she huffed, rubbing her red cheeks.

The front door of the mausoleum was padlocked. Dillon glanced down at the needle every few steps. Around the corner of the building he went, searching. The structure was twenty feet high at least and made of concrete. Around the next corner he saw steps leading downward, into a lower level. He peered into the shadows. The door at the bottom of the stairs stood open. The electromagnetic reading leapt. Down the concrete stairwell he went, clicking on a flashlight. The smell was increasingly putrid, like a slaughterhouse. He covered his nose. Once through the door, he stood in the cemetery underground, shining a beam of light into shadowed corners.

Movement caught his attention from behind a heap of broken headstones. Raspy moaning filled the air. One voice quickly became three, and then ten. From every direction the sound grew, enveloping him in dead speak. The flashlight hit the floor as he swung around to run. Dark bodies flooded the entrance. There was nowhere to go. Dillon screamed.

Out at the van, Renee heard the faint cry. "Dillon! Hold on! I'm coming, dear!"

When she reached the backside of the building, she realized that she was still holding a camera tripod.

"Where are you, honey?" she called out.

Another scream resounded from somewhere below.

"Oh god," she forced out. "He's fallen down the steps."

A dark figure appeared beside her, and then another. She turned to look a dead man in the decomposing face. He gargled something as she wailed in terror. Without thinking, Renee swung the tripod like a baseball bat. It connected with the side of his head, making a loud crunch sound. The skull fell sideways, hung limp for a moment, and then dropped to the frozen ground. Arms flailed as the disconnected head continued to moan. Rotten fluids shot into the air.

"Oh my god!"

Gripped by three living corpses, she was dragged downward into the reeking underground.

Each stair creaked underfoot as Monica descended, abandoning the warm sunlight. At midway, the flashlight beam began to feel insignificant and small compared to the density of shadow. Monica stepped carefully over the basement floor. She saw an old water heater, boxes of mason jars, and a corroded pipe wrench. Broken glass crunched under her sneakers. The farther she went, the darker it got. An old wooden bookcase stood against the back wall. Thick dust covered its shelves. An overturned cup lay on its side with a pile of nails spilled out.

Monica squinted at the wall. A black line ran straight down to the floor. She touched it with her fingers and found a ridge separating concrete and wood. She went around the side of the tall bookcase and pulled. It scraped along the rough floor. With it out of the way, she walked back around. She saw a closed doorway.

Where does this go?

She turned the knob and opened the door. Another dark room was beyond. Blind, she felt above for a pull chain as she went inside. She felt a string swipe across her fingertips. She grabbed it and yanked. A dim bulb lit up a room about ten feet square. Monica looked behind her. The concrete stopped at the doorway. The floor where she stood was dirt. The walls looked like limestone.

Something shiny sat in a dark corner. She got closer. It was a large fold-out pocketknife. A crusty substance was dried over the blade.

Oh god, that's it. That's what she killed them with.

She didn't want to touch it. She was afraid of ruining the evidence. If Betty's fingerprints were on the handle, they'd still be there when the investigation began. It was time to pay another visit to Sheriff Shane. He'd have to listen to her this time.

Screw it, she thought. *I'm calling the FBI.*

To Gary's surprise, the back door was unlocked. He opened it with caution, listening. He heard the sounds of machine-gun fire from the Xbox in the living room. Apparently, John was busy winning World War II again. He would curse occasionally, when events in the digital game world did not go his way.

Gary stepped across the shadowed kitchen and into the front room. John sat on a couch with his back toward his attacker. A big screen television displayed the first-person perspective of an American soldier, in full 1080p resolution. John tossed a grenade into a trench full of enemies, and bodies and dirt flew accordingly. Gary thought it looked like a fun game.

He stood right behind his victim now. The TV was loud, nullifying all other sound. This was going to be the easiest kill Gary had experienced in a long time. The axe ascended into the air, preparing to strike.

"Crap," John said to the screen. "Come on."

As gooda last words as any, Gary reasoned.

The blade was especially sharp tonight. He'd spent more than an hour at the grinder, polishing the edge.

It sank deep into the skull, all the way to the bridge of John's nose. His soldier was promptly killed also, leaving the words GAME OVER on the screen.

"Looks like the Nazis win after all," Gary said with a smirk.

Dillon and Renee's hands were bound with nylon rope. They were then tied to one another with a six-foot length, at the waists. A black cloth bag was pulled over each one's head. Blind and terrified, they struggled against the undead captors. An unseen number of corpses dragged the two up the stairs, into the bitter storm. Dillon fell, which, in turn, pulled Renee to the ground, wailing. Icy snow soaked into their clothing. A frigid, howling wind swept through the cemetery, biting at reddened skin. Shivering, the husband and wife were yanked to their feet.

"Dillon? Oh god, what's happening?"

An angry zombie punched her across the cloth-laden jaw. "No talking!" came out as "Mulllgar!"

She stumbled, tasting the blood in her mouth.

"Honey!" Dillon yelled, which earned his own punishment, a kick to the backside. They were taken around the mausoleum. The group stopped at the road, directly across from the house. More than thirty dead men raised their voices. Moaning, yelling, gargling, and growling resounded through the air in a melody of the damned.

Betty sat back on the couch with her eyes closed. Her house was totally silent and she was motionless, thinking.

I'd better check on Monica, she thought.

Her eyeballs spasmed under thin lids for a few seconds.

"Shit!"

Her eyes popped open. They didn't focus on the room; she was seeing something else. She stood and bolted for the closet. A plastic bag sat on the floor with six boxes of shotgun shells inside. She snatched it up and grabbed a heavy coat.

"Hold on," she said. "I'm coming."

Monica walked out the front door with keys in hand. Her phone still hadn't been repaired, so she'd have to go into town to make a call to the authorities. A gathering of undead across the road stood waiting for her.

She gasped as a group of dozens of dead men howled. Each of them wore clothing at various stages of disintegration and had torn, rotting skin. Out in front, a bound man and woman kneeled with something dark over their heads. With a quick tug, both of the sacks were ripped off, revealing terrified faces.

That's Dillon and Renee.

The Halloween pranksters were back, only this time it seemed they meant business.

Renee screamed, "Monica! Help us!"

With a punch to the jaw, she fell forward, crying.

Oh god. "Let them go, you bastards!"

A long blade slid into position in front of Dillon's throat. Monica couldn't breathe. She couldn't look away. Every muscle in her body seized. The one with the knife motioned toward the captives and then leered back to her as if to say, *You want them? Come and claim them.* They'd been trying to lure her across that road for days, and now it seemed that she would have to go or people would die. The game had just turned deadly serious, and it had become apparent to Monica. These weren't just some kids out screwing around.

The shotgun.

She turned, threw the door open, and went inside. Confused, the gathering looked around at one another, shrugging.

"She's not coming!" one moaned.

The tall one growled, "Chop his head off!"

With a kick, Dillon fell forward on his hands and knees. The sharp blade raised upward as Renee screamed. From across Miller Drive, a voice called out.

"That's enough!"

Everyone looked over to see a woman struggling to hold a large shotgun. It was aimed unsteadily at the one with the machete.

"She's got a gun!" a dead man yelled.

The group scattered in a whirlwind of lurching, limping, and stumbling. Dillon and Renee were dragged into the shadows.

"Stop!" Monica called out. "Let them go!"

One twitching, trampled man remained at the side of the road, complaining. "Don't leave me here, you assholes!" came out as "Gum err anoo, lahhhole!"

Monica looked left and then right. Slowly and trembling, she descended the steps. All was quiet. She approached the road.

"What do you want with them?" she asked the one on the ground. "Why are you doing this?"

He said nothing, growling and rolling onto his stomach.

"Answer me!"

She saw distant headlights out on the highway. *Please let that be the sheriff.* Across the dirt road she stepped, pointing the weapon down at the one struggling to crawl away. Her voice wobbled. "Don't move, slime bag."

He ignored her, scratching fingernails at loose soil.

She kicked a flailing leg. "I said, don't move."

He flipped onto his back, hissing. The smell was rotten. Up close she saw that it wasn't Halloween makeup. Half of his scalp was torn loose from the skull. His eyes were filmy and drooling black liquid. She saw strands of dried muscle over his right cheek and a torn hole with a slathering tongue beneath.

"You're...you're *really* dead."

He yelled something and one of his eyeballs fell into the darkness of a slimy socket. Monica screamed, falling back onto frozen grass. The butt of the shotgun hit the hard ground, and the hammer snapped closed. It, having an empty chamber, did not go off.

Shit.

She scrambled to her feet. Zombies appeared out of the darkness, no longer afraid of the woman and her weapon. Dark figures flooded in from every direction. Five rushed between her and the road. She swung around and struck one in the jaw with the shotgun barrel. He cowered, spitting teeth. She kicked at another. Her foot planted deep in his spoiled belly. When she yanked her foot free, she realized that her sneaker was still inside, jammed between the rungs of a broken ribcage.

Grunting, she plowed through the wall of undead like a linebacker. Once past the group, she ran for her life, into the shadows of Lakeshore Cemetery.

A Chevy Nova slid to a stop in the middle of the icy road. Betty threw her door open, grabbed the plastic bag, and got out of the vehicle. She didn't bother checking the house. She was well aware that Monica was already in the cemetery with shotgun in hand.

Navigating the frozen surface of Miller Drive was difficult. Only when she crossed over onto brittle grass did her sneakers gain traction. She paused a moment to scan her surroundings. Constant gusts held the spiraling snow aloft, punishing nerve endings across her face and hands. Ignoring the frigid blast, Betty raced for the mausoleum.

Monica struggled to comprehend the unbelievable events, with her back against a dark headstone. "It's not possible," she whispered between panting breaths.

Thirty feet away, two corpses lumbered along, moaning and slurring at one another.

"Not real," she said, unable to look away.

The slower one carried his severed head under an arm, like a putrid cantaloupe. She pinched her eyes closed. "No fuckin' way." Her entire body shook with freezing panic. Little white pellets collected over her blue jeans and T-shirt. The skin on her arms was red and aching. She suddenly realized that her coat was back at the house. The shotgun felt like an icicle in her hands.

Banging and muffled voices startled her. She peered around the corner of the concrete to see six shadowed figures approaching. She swung around, ducking into the darkness.

Without warning, a tight grip had her by the arm, pulling. Monica screamed.

"It's me," a familiar voice said. "Hurry."

The undead army closed in.

"Betty? What are you doing?"

"There's no time. Get to the tool shed."

The two women ran side by side. With a tug, Monica was guided west. A dark structure came into view. It was fifteen feet square with a tin roof and had one window on the east wall. They raced for the door. A large padlock hung from the latch. Monica watched as Betty ripped it open with ease.

"How did you—"

With a push, Monica was forced inside. A dead man rushed from behind with outstretched arms. The door slammed on a skinless bicep, and he yowled in pain. Betty slid a workbench into position, creating a barricade. Random tools fell to the dirt floor. The discolored arm flailed in an attempt to pull free. Broken fingernails scratched at the wood in desperation.

"The window!"

Dark faces gathered outside the glass. A thick fist punched through.

"Grab the drill," Betty said, reaching for a large piece of plywood.

More voices gathered outside as the women rushed to lift the board to block the window. Monica found an overturned box of screws. Betty held the wood while Monica secured it to the window frame.

"That should hold temporarily," she said. "The shells are in that bag. You might want to load the shotgun."

Monica glared. "What are you doing here?"

"What do you mean? I came to help you."

"I don't need your help," Monica said, pulling a box of shells out of the bag.

Betty grinned. "Yeah, you kinda do. And so do Dillon and Renee."

"What do you know about them? Were you spying on me or something?"

"I was checking to see if you were all right. There's a difference."

Monica had no idea how to load the shotgun. Tears streamed down her cheeks as she tried to force it open.

Betty walked closer. "Let me show you."

Monica recoiled. "Step off, bitch."

"What's your problem?"

Monica took a step back. "My *problem* is that you're a murderer, and you're not touching my gun."

Betty's voice fell weak. "I'm not a murderer."

The yelling and banging outside got louder.

"Do you deny that you killed your husband?"

With a click the barrel snapped downward, allowing access to the chambers.

"No. I don't deny it."

"Well then," Monica said, fumbling with loose shells, "there you have it."

"You don't know anything."

With two shells in place, she pulled the barrel closed.

"I know enough."

She cocked the hammer and then aimed it at the murderer.

"Listen to me, and when I'm finished, you can shoot me if you want."

Monica said nothing more. She backed into a shadowed corner. Betty sat on the floor, leaning back on the palms of her hands.

"My husband, Bernie, created me at Synergy Dynamics. I was the prototype for a line of synthetic soldiers."

"What?" Monica blurted. "What the hell are you talking about?"

"I'm not totally manufactured. My skin is real. It's fed by a nutritional network underneath."

Monica gripped the gun tight, trying to hide trembling fear. "You're batshit."

Betty sat up, removing the heavy coat. She pulled her shirt up, tucking it under her breasts. She then peeled back a large square of skin that covered her belly. Another layer, made of gelatinous, bubble-like material, was just underneath. With that out of the way, Betty relaxed red abdominal muscles that looked like cords of elastic rope. From the center she peeled them apart. Rubber tubing hung behind twisted gatherings of multicolored wire and circuitry. Her stomach was a molded plastic tank. It was canary yellow and had a tag on the side that read "Synergy Dynamics."

"Jesus Christ!" Monica yelled. "You're not human!"

She slipped and fell back into the wall. Her thin legs failed completely, and her butt hit the floor.

Betty said, "Please don't freak on me."

Monica's eyes didn't blink, nor did they waver from a sight that couldn't be real. It was impossible, and yet, well, there it was.

"I'm not freaked out. You're a goddamn robot...and I'm not freaked out."

"The control module, my brain, is actually at my house. It's too big to carry around with me. It's like the size of a U-Haul truck."

"A U-Haul. Nice. I'm not freaked out. Nope, not me."

"Could you stop saying that now?"

"Your ribs are chrome," she said, pointing.

Betty looked down. "Yeah. I'm all tricked out. You should see my spine."

Monica pushed herself up, still gripping the shotgun.

"I don't want to see your fucking spine!"

Betty closed up her belly. "Sorry. I was just saying—"

A pounding shook the door, and then another. The third strike broke through, splintering the wood and exposing the blade of an axe.

"Shit! They'll break it down!"

Betty got to her feet and approached the door. The axe struck again, creating a slender, splintery hole. She snatched the axe head and pulled the weapon inside. It dropped to the floor as the dead complained outside.

"How did you—"

"As I was saying, Bernard created me at the lab. He designed me as a woman because he was a freak-show pervert."

Monica stared at the weapon on the floor. "A pervert?"

"Yeah. He decided to steal me from Synergy. He faked a break-in and then took me home. He created an identity for me...got me a social security number and everything. Then he married me."

Monica looked up at Betty. "You didn't like him. You seem to have a pretty forceful personality, and you're strong. Why didn't you just say no?"

"Because of the security coding. I was designed with free will, but I had to do what he told me because of the coding override."

"Oh."

"Peggy and I had become friends. She's the one who removed the security code. She was trying to help me. And it got her killed." Tears flowed down Betty's cheeks.

"Your husband killed Peggy?"

"Yes. She'd already been stabbed by the time I got there. There was so much blood. He went to stab her again and...I shot him." Betty broke down completely. She sobbed, covering her face and turning away.

"God," Monica said, "I'm sorry."

Betty wiped the moisture away from her red eyes. "Yeah. Me too."

"You feel real emotions?"

"Yes, I feel everything you do. As best I can tell."

"You're not a murderer."

"Nope. And I'm your friend."

Monica lowered the gun. "I'm sorry I called you a bitch."

Betty walked over and gave her a hug. "Not an issue. I forgive you."

Monica pulled away. "Can you really bench press a Volkswagen?"

A laugh and a snort. "I am a badass."

7

THE
MIST DEMON

Synergy Dynamics sat on one hundred acres of forested land, ten miles south of Redmondsburg. Tall trees kept the main building hidden from County Road 3A. An iron gate and guard shack were the only things that indicated the facility existed. The gate met up with a fifteen-foot chain link fence that stretched down the property line, disappearing into the woods. Spirals of razor wire adorned the top edge of the barrier while large yellow signs, every twenty feet, announced what danger 20,000 VOLTS meant to curious hands.

SERIOUS INJURY OR DEATH COULD OCCUR, as so many unfortunate woodland creatures could testify. The third line of instructions seemed a bit pointless, that is if a person had bothered to read the first two.

NO TRESSPASSING.

The strict security measures went into effect eight years ago, shortly after a break-in had left building C with a major research deficiency. That is to say that a top-secret project, known as Valkerie 13, had been removed without Synergy's (let alone the US government's) blessings. One morning it was just nowhere to be found. Stealing such a thing would've been no easy task; the control unit itself weighed 1.3 tons. Scratches across the floor and broken concrete indicated that it had been moved, dragged onto a trailer, and driven away. The synthetic prototype and a few computers were also missing.

Everyone working at the company was thoroughly questioned. Homes were searched, and garages and barns too. The entire community of Redmondsburg and its surrounding areas were interrogated, scrutinized, and followed. The military kept a presence in the county for more than four months, leaving no stone unturned and no citizen unthreatened. Fencing went up in the month of September, as did motion sensors, guard towers, trip wires, and a video surveillance system.

The lead scientist on the Valkerie project, Mr. Bernard Jones, got married one year after the break-in, to a girl from out of town. At least that's what he told everyone. He said they'd met in a chat room on the Internet and fallen in love. She was far too young and pretty for a man of such an old, balding, and portly nature. Everyone thought so. He was not only a scientist, but also a major shareholder in the company. And he owned a Corvette. So naturally, they all thought she was a gold digger. That's exactly what he'd wanted them to think. Little did they know, the control unit, her computerized brain, lived in a bunker below his barn.

Her look had changed dramatically since she'd been stolen from the lab. The fabricated bone structure in her face was altered. Cloned, living skin was grafted over her mechanical frame. By all outward appearances, she'd become flawlessly human. If you felt for a heartbeat in her chest, you'd feel one. She breathed in and out regularly, just like everyone else. Her muscle and bone structures were, to anyone paying attention, believable in every way. It was her programming that was the challenge in the beginning. She needed to act real, respond to input naturally, and behave accordingly. It was months before the control unit performed at human levels. He kept her at home during those critical months, programming complex functions and working out software glitches.

When he was finally satisfied, when the project was complete, she'd become a self-aware and self-learning synthetic being, capable of dynamic thought processes and even real emotion. She was his masterpiece, his magnum opus. No one was going to take her way from him. Not the lab. Not the military. No one.

She became his companion, his lover, and ultimately, his wife. Yes, they had sex. He programmed her to do everything he wanted, anytime he wanted it, in every way he desired. She secretly began to loathe him. She grew to hate the way he combed his thinning hair, the way he brushed his teeth, the way he called out her name in the heat of the moment. She was quickly becoming human and, at the same time, tiring of her unsatisfying marriage.

But, as unsatisfied as she was, she never indicated her feelings to him. She smiled when he came home, made him dinner, and laughed at his jokes. She catered to his every need, emotionally and sexually, and even washed and waxed the Corvette on a weekly basis. For him, life was nearing perfection. For her, well, she just wanted the hell out.

In the daytime, while he was at work, she went for walks to the local park and around town, experiencing the world with a childlike wonder. She made friends with a young girl named Peggy Wyne. She told Peggy secrets about herself that she couldn't tell anyone. Peggy, being an eleven-year-old, believed every word. They became the best of friends.

She offered babysitting services to Peggy's mom so they could spend more time together. Betty looked to be a woman in her midtwenties and had a pleasant personality. So the offer was accepted. She got paid fifteen dollars to watch Peggy on Saturdays. Bernard worked six days a week and had no idea the two knew each other at all.

It was perfect. In the mornings they'd spend the babysitting money at the convenience store, on candy, pop and the occasional hot dog. The afternoons were spent exploring. They walked for miles across the countryside. They went to the park, the library, and sometimes they walked all the way to the cemetery. An abandoned house across the road from the graveyard eventually became their clubhouse.

It was the best time either of them had experienced. When they were together, nothing else mattered.

"We could probably hold up here until morning, but if we're gonna help Dillon and Renee, we have to leave."

Monica looked at the door. A crowd of the undead moaned and gargled on the other side.

"Go back out there?"

"Yes."

"We don't even know if they're still alive."

Betty studied the tin roof above her head. "Oh, they're alive. The dead people are holding them at the north side of the mausoleum."

"How could you possibly know that?"

Betty climbed on top of the workbench. "I have a direct link to Synergy's satellite. I can see the entire cemetery from orbit."

"You're shitting me."

"It's even equipped with night vision." She shoved her hand through the tin and pulled. Thin metal stretched downward in her iron grip. She took hold with the other hand and bent the hole wider.

Monica frowned. "You don't expect me to climb out the ceiling, do you?"

"Well, there are currently eighteen bad guys at the door and twenty-two just outside the window. You can push your way through them if you want, but I'm going this way."

She pointed down at her coat. "Put that on. You need it more than I do."

There was no argument about that. Monica pulled the coat on and gathered the shotgun shells.

On the workbench Betty spotted an open cloth bag with a stick of what appeared to be dynamite poking out the top. "Holy crap, what's this?"

A closer look revealed ten sticks of explosives, a detonator, and a cord; everything one would need to blow the hell out of whatever they chose. "We are taking this," she said, pulling the cloth bag strap over her neck.

"Is that what I think it is?"

Betty smiled. "Cool, huh?"

Monica peered upward, through the torn metal roof and into the hazy sky. Slurring voices resounded. A deep breath inflated her lungs.

"Here," she said, handing the gun up to Betty.

"Are you sure you trust me?"

"Yeah, I trust you. Now help me up."

With ease, Betty pulled herself through the hole and onto the roof of the tool shed. She looked down to see the shadowed undead shouting at one another. Only two of them still struck the plywood-covered window. Broken glass was scattered across churned-up mud and slush at their feet.

She whispered, "Okay, come on."

The women clasped hands and Monica was pulled out in one smooth motion. Her sneakers touched down on wet tin.

Surprised at Betty's strength, she said, "Wow. That was easy."

The shotgun was shoved into her hands.

"All right," Betty said, "I'm gonna draw as many of them away from you as possible. I'll meet you at the mausoleum."

"We're splitting up?"

"Yeah. Don't hesitate to use that gun. Just remember, they're already dead."

"Great. That makes me feel so much better."

Betty turned and sprang from the roof. She hit the ground twenty feet away, her strong legs absorbing the impact.

She swung around and yelled, "Hey assholes! Over here!"

The gathering leered at Betty. They remained where they were, confused and unsteady on their feet, as usual. A mumbling conversation broke out.

"That one does not concern us," one slurred.

"She is neither living nor dead," said another.

"She has no brain!"

"No blood!"

"No heart!"

A slathering man with a missing ear said, "She gots skin! I can smell it!"

The gibberish continued while Betty shrugged her shoulders, looking up at her friend.

Monica said, "Oh, screw this."

She stepped to the edge of the roof, aiming the long barrel downward. With a dark figure in her sights, she squeezed the trigger. The dead man's head was an explosion of sour liquid and chunks of skull. The power of the blast sent Monica stumbling with intense pain stabbing at her shoulder and chest. She slipped and fell flat on her back on the tin roof. Her lungs strained for air.

"Should've gotten the Taser," she wheezed, clutching at the ache.

The limping undead rushed at Betty. She stomped one in the kneecap, forcing his leg to snap in an unexpected direction. He fell wailing into frozen grass. A backhand connected with the next, shattering teeth and bone. She ran for the shed.

"Monica! Come on!"

A zombie rushed her from behind. She flipped him over her back. He hit the ground hard, and she realized she was holding a disconnected, stinking arm.

"Gross," she said, dropping it in the snow.

Monica pushed onto her feet. The shotgun slid down the angled roof and stuck in a headless corpse, barrel first, like a javelin.

Betty walked up and claimed the weapon. "Excuse me," she said, yanking it free.

"Some plan," Monica said from above.

"Yeah. They got it bad for you, girlfriend."

"Apparently," Monica said in frustration. "Now help me down."

The women jogged through glistening white trees, along the northern cemetery border. Blowing snow grated across their exposed skin. The temperature had dropped below zero, and the muscles in Monica's back flexed uncontrollably. Her red hands ached as she pulled the coat tighter around her neck. Betty popped the gun barrel down and removed the spent shells.

"I need two more."

Monica retrieved them from a deep pocket. "That thing sucks," she said out of breath.

"Hold it tight against your shoulder next time."

With the new shells in place, the shotgun snapped closed. Betty slid to a stop at the grave of Connor Oppenheim. He'd been a loving husband and father, according to the inscription. She pulled Monica down low, scanning the back of the shadowed mausoleum. Two of the dead were in sight; one held a broken baseball bat, the other a length of chain.

"You blast these guys," Betty said, pushing the shotgun into Monica's hands, "and I'll free Dillon and Renee."

"Where are they?"

Betty pointed a finger at the corner of the building. "Over there." She checked the satellite view once more and saw a group of sixteen guarding the shivering prisoners. Miller Drive was fifty yards south.

"Ready?" Betty asked.

"Hell no," Monica said. And then, "Oh, just go before I change my mind."

The shotgun zeroed in on a rotten face. A deafening blast sounded the attack, and two zombies fell to the ground, clutching their wounds. Betty raced around the corner of the building to see a lumbering mob.

Renee called out from behind the wall of undead. "Help us! Please!"

The corpses rushed forward. Betty kneed one in the groin. He doubled over, grunting. She kicked the next in the face, driving a nose into his skull. She elbowed, punched, and shoved. Dark figures fell away one after another. She reached the captives and heard a shotgun blast. Monica was only a step behind, firing into the belly of a tall ghoul. With ease, Betty ripped apart the rope that bound the captives. They were amazed at her strength but had no time to comment on it.

Shivering, Dillon and Renee followed them toward the road. Dense fog poured in around the running group. It was a pure white, shifting cloud. The winter gusts and falling snow could not penetrate its blinding sanctuary. With the blizzard's power nullified, it surrounded them like a silent ivory curtain. The four stopped in their tracks, unable to see even twenty feet ahead.

"What the hell?" Monica said, "I can't see anything."

"Keep going in that direction," Betty instructed. "The road isn't much farther."

Dillon looked all around, noticing the deathly silence. They stood in some kind of vacuum, oblivious to the outside world.

"Everyone join hands. We don't want to get separated."

Betty checked the satellite view and saw the cloud expanding over the entire cemetery. Cautiously, the four continued, hand in hand. A hazy figure came into view through the mist. It had the form of a man, although its arms were impossibly long. Its skin was as white as the cloud surrounding it, and its eyes were vacant black holes. The creature's face was elongated, with stretched bands of powdery flesh over a pronounced bone structure. The hairless skull was a massive white globe in the fog. With flexed, muscled arms reaching out, the monster bared its teeth, hissing. Each fang was a long curved nail that had been driven through bloody meat. Renee and Monica screamed. Breathless, Dillon took a step back. Betty grimaced.

"What the hell is that?" she said.

It took a step forward and spoke. Its voice was the growl of a rabid dog, formed into words. "Give us the innocent. She is ours now."

Monica's voice trembled, asking, "Who are you talking about?"

The thing before them smiled with razor-sharp teeth piercing into its own lips. Blood ran in long downward streaks. "You," it said. "You are untouched and have never known the darkness."

Betty stepped up. "You'll take her over my dead body."

Its laugh was a sharp whisper. "How can one that has never lived die? You have consciousness, but no soul."

Dillon yelled, "What do you want with Monica?"

"And you," it said, "you have intermingled with death too often. Your essence reeks of the dead." It turned back to Monica, pointing. "It is her that we shall have."

Betty spoke to the others. "Run. Get to the house. *Right now.*"

She turned back to the demon, squeezing fists tight. "Let's see what you got."

The monster growled in a rage, flexing.

Dillon, Renee, and Monica ran.

As fast as their feet could carry them, they raced into the white void. Monica hoped they were going in the right direction, toward the road. Dillon struggled to keep up. His energy was failing, his body shivering. His foot caught a rock, and he went face down into the snow. He looked up and saw that he was alone.

The creature rose off the ground in a whirlwind of cycling mist. Held aloft by an invisible power, its unnatural flesh illuminated with white-hot anger. It hovered above the crystalline snow, snarling and casting seizure reflections into the cloud.

It lunged forward with a predator's ambition; its strike was a bolt of lightning. Betty was seized off the ground before she could react. Sharp claws sunk deep into living skin and manufactured muscle. Her synthetic nerves registered intense pain across impaled shoulder blades. She ignored a sensation that would've paralyzed a human and punched the monster across the jaw. An audible cracking of bone reverberated in its skull as blood and broken shards of teeth exploded into the air. The pale face turned back to its prey, laughing and drooling crimson strands.

"You are strong, fake one. But not strong enough."

With a heave, it threw her soaring into the cloud. Her back collided with a tall headstone, breaking the slab in half. The impact was an explosion of snow, mud, and flying chunks of smashed marble. She remained idle for a moment, folded uncomfortably over ice-cold debris.

"Goddamn, that hurts," she said sitting up.

Her metal vertebrae reset back to default positions. She rubbed at the wounds in her shoulders and neck.

I've got to help Monica.

She got to her feet and sprinted through the fog.

Renee raced through the haze, trying to keep Monica in sight. Her clothing was soaked from the wet cloud all around her. There was no way of knowing how close the road was, or even if they were going in the right direction. Her joints were rusty hinges, her muscles hardening rubber. It felt as if gravity were increasing as her exhausted body slowed. She knew that Dillon's back must've been killing him.

"Monica, wait," she said, turning to look back. He wasn't in sight.

Monica appeared beside her, out of breath. "Where's Dillon?"

"He was right behind me."

The view from Synergy's satellite showed thick fog coverage across the entire graveyard. The haze thinned at Miller Drive and dissipated completely before it reached Monica's front porch. Betty switched to infrared in an attempt to locate the others. Two orange and red heat signatures appeared thirty yards north of the road. A third source of warmth accelerated toward them at more than forty miles per hour.

A person can't run that fast. One of them either found something to drive or---

Betty knew that a vehicle would emit its own heat. There was no evidence of a running engine. She hoped she wouldn't be too late.

A silhouette slowed to a halt in front of the women. It was nearly invisible in the dense swirl of white.

"Dillon?" Monica said, but then realized that it couldn't be. It was at least seven feet tall.

Renee took a nervous step forward. "Hon?"

Mist thinned and they saw that it was Dillon. His feet dangled a foot above the ground. The look on his face told them all they needed to know. His eyes were bloodshot and watering. With a wide mouth, he fought for air. His pale skin stretched, creating dark grooves down his cheeks and across a twitching forehead. Something had him in a noose-like grip, and he was suffocating.

Renee screamed.

The ivory figure behind him came into view. Unnatural fingers constricted around Dillon's throat as he gagged. The monster grinned, exposing needle teeth. It leaned forward, resting a chin on the man's shoulder.

"Come to us now or this one dies."

Uncontrollable panic claimed Monica's shuddering body. She felt as if she would collapse at any moment, but Dillon was counting on her. He'd die if she didn't do something. She forced herself to take a step forward.

"Let him go," she said.

It laughed. "Come closer."

Another step. And then another.

This isn't happening, she thought, unable to breathe.

The mist circled above in a vortex as her head swam. Darkness tunneled around her vision like oil saturating her lucid mind. She was within arm's reach. Long fingers released, and Dillon fell to the ground gasping. The grinning monster held out a scaly hand. Its razor talons lingered inches from her cheek.

Then a blurred chunk of marble blindsided the fiend with the force of a sledgehammer. The impact sent it reeling to the ground. Snarling, it spun around to see Betty leap through the mist with a length of pipe held high. Momentum sank her feet deep into the snow and mud in front of the beast. She jammed the metal through its skull. A spray of dark blood saturated the air. Dazed, the monster stumbled away shrieking.

She turned and saw Monica's legs buckle as unconsciousness took hold. Betty heaved the limp body over her shoulder and grabbed the shotgun.

"Hurry," she said to the others.

They arrived at Miller Drive. The house was in sight. Renee glanced back every few seconds as she tried to keep up.

Dillon limped at her side, shivering. He coughed with a scratched and swollen throat. It seemed that willpower alone kept their feet underneath them. There was no other energy to draw from. All else had been depleted.

We're going to make it, he thought.

White haze faded into fleeting wisps, dissipating in the cold air. The creature knelt under the shadow of a crumbling statue. It grasped the pipe and pulled it free, with a howl of pain. The weapon was tossed aside.

It knew the innocent was at the house now.

His master would be furious.

Monica woke with a deafening headache. She sat straight up, checking her surroundings. She was on the carpet in front of a recliner. It was warm. Betty's voice was behind her.

"You're awake."

She turned, her body still shivering. "What happened?"

"I got you out of there. You're safe now."

Dillon sat in a nearby chair, still catching his breath. Renee was in the kitchen. The inside of Monica's house felt surreal. She could hardly believe they'd survived.

"What was that thing?" she asked, rubbing a sore neck.

Betty put a gentle hand on her shoulder. "I don't know."

Monica burst into tears. She covered her eyes, sobbing. The two of them embraced, trying to squeeze away the fear and pain.

"I thought I was gonna die."

"It's okay now."

Renee approached holding two cups of steaming coffee. She held one out to her husband. "Drink this. You need to warm up." She turned to Monica. "This one's yours, dear. How are you feeling?"

Monica accepted the cup with a faint smile. "I'm all right," she said. "Thank you."

The images in her mind were impossible to shake. They hung suspended in time and just behind her eyes, waiting for the opportune moment to step into the light. Wet fangs glistened. Fog so thick it could lift things off the ground. The wet cloud. The monster's skin. Monica tried to focus on the room and the people there, but the cemetery would stay with her for a long time to come.

"You lost a shoe," Betty said. A torn hole in a sock allowed Monica's big toe to poke out.

Dillon sat forward cradling his cup. "I've seen a lot of weirdness in my day...but goddamned if that wasn't the craziest shit ever."

Monica shivered. "I have to get out of here. I can't live here."

Sadly, Betty agreed. "You should go. Get as far away from this place as you can."

"You could come with me. We could get a place together."

Betty's vision sank to the floor. "You know I can't."

Monica suddenly remembered her unique situation. Then she remembered that her friend, the one that had just saved her life, wasn't even human.

"I can't believe you're a robot."

"A synthetic," Betty corrected.

"Whatever."

Dillon and Renee looked over with confusion in their faces.

Monica took a deep breath. "You'd better tell them."

Betty sent the couple an insecure smile. "Wanna see my spine?"

"Maybe we can still put things right. I'd still like to help Peggy before I leave. I think we're a step closer in figuring it out now."

Betty smiled. "You can crash at my place until that's finished...if you want."

Renee sat on Dillon's lap, hugging him. She kissed his cheek. "No offense to either of you, but at daylight we're leaving. We've had enough."

Dillon added, "I'll do some research on your graveyard and call you with the information I gather."

"Thanks," Monica said. "That would be great."

None of them got any sleep that night. They took turns at the window, watching for unbelievable creatures. None came. It seemed that Monica's house was a sanctuary from the things across the road, not to say it didn't have issues of its own. The ghosts were there, but were thankfully quiet for the time being.

At sunrise Dillon and Renee gathered their coats.

"Thank you for saving us," he said sincerely. "We owe you our lives."

Betty drove the Chevy into town with precision. The car was never too close to the double yellow line to their left, nor did it ride the white line to their right. It sped down the center of the lane perfectly, even when she looked over at her passenger for minutes at a time, talking.

Watching Betty talk and drive made Monica a bit nervous. She glanced frequently through the windshield to be sure they were still on the road. The car didn't waver. The speedometer needle did not drop below, or exceed, forty-five miles per hour, which was the posted speed limit. With access to the satellite, Betty could've driven blindfolded. But knowing that didn't make Monica feel any better. She pulled the seatbelt across her lap and clicked it together.

Looking around the vehicle, she tried to focus on something else. Pink fuzzy dice hung from the rearview mirror, along with a purple-feathered roachclip. The dash looked like it had been chewed by mice in a couple of places. The upholstery was in the same sad condition. Large sections of stained foam padding were exposed under torn threads. The outside of the vehicle compared closely to the inside. Dents, scrapes, and dark red primer scattered the surface in an automotive war zone. Betty's ride was in need of a good pimping.

As the road turned into Rocky Creek Way, they saw the mayor aboard his flatbed trailer, celebrating his victory, with music blaring at an obnoxious level. People along the sidewalks waved and cheered as always, showing their support. The Sheriff's Office had a solitary squad car parked in the front.

"Should we tell them what happened last night?" Betty asked.

"I can't see what good it would do. They wouldn't believe us."

Betty continued on to her house.

The entire world was blinding white. The ground and trees, the sky, and the thick, wet air. With shallow breaths, Monica walked, peering into the fog. The ivory void seemed to stretch out forever. Hard snow crunched at each stuttering footstep, as the weight of her body broke through the frozen crust. Whipping air carried an abrasive sting across her face and bare arms. Shivering, she made her way deeper into the cloud.

A shadowed form rose off the ground ahead of her. It narrowed the gap between them, wisps of wet air shimmering around pale flesh. Long needle fangs snapped. Its eyes were empty sockets, black holes descending into a powder-white skull, focused on her.

It has no eyes, she thought, *and it's looking right at me.*

Frozen in place, she strained against the confinement of her own fear.

"We will have you," it growled.

Its voice was like broken glass; an inhuman thing that should've never been allowed to form words. What kind of world would let such a creature be, let alone speak? There were no answers, no logic, and nothing that made sense. There was only the monster and its dark purpose.

God, no.

Amusement stretched its pallid skin as it got closer. Razor teeth punctured thin lips. Blood ran in shiny streaks down its chin, dripping to the crystal ground below.

You're not real.

But it was real. And it would have her.

Monica's body spasmed, and she woke crying. She sat up on the couch and a colorful blanket fell to the floor.

Betty appeared from the kitchen. "Are you okay?"

There was no answer. It was all she could do to force the dream's images away. With her face downward, she sobbed.

She remembered the last fight she and her ex-husband had. In a blaze of anger, he'd called her pathetic. She'd caught him cheating on her, and yet somehow, she was the pathetic one. It had taken months to get that hurtful word out of her head. It had taken only one terrible night to bring it back. Only this time, it felt true.

8

SUZANNE

The women sat at the kitchen table eating pancakes, bacon, and eggs. Monica watched her synthetic friend with curiosity.

"You don't have to eat, do you?"

Betty tore at a lean strip of bacon. "No. I just like to, that's all. It has no nutritional value for me. All I need is electricity. I plug in every couple of days."

"Plug in where?"

"Any standard wall outlet. A full charge takes about six hours."

She reached for three more pancakes and then drowned the stack in maple syrup. Monica was amazed at how much food Betty could fit into the small tank she'd seen.

"If you don't digest it, where does it go?"

Betty grinned. "I'll pump it out later. There's a valve on the bottom of the tank...I guess that seems kinda gross, huh?"

The thought of it churned Monica's stomach in disgust.

"No. Not at all."

The blonde stuffed another bite into her mouth. Monica changed the subject.

"So both your husband and Peggy died in my house. What happened to the bodies?"

Betty's vision snapped down to the floor. Her voice fell weak. "I buried them."

"Where?"

"In your basement."

"You buried them"—Monica's words screeched—"together?"

"Well," Betty whispered defensively, "they were dead. I didn't think they'd mind."

"I think we've established that they do mind. *A lot.*"

"Sorry."

"God. No wonder my house is haunted."

Betty's guilt pinched into annoyance. "I said I was sorry."

Monica looked at her synthetic friend. "I'm sorry too. I guess my nerves are just ragged from being attacked by dead people."

Betty took a huge bite of dripping pancake. Syrup ran down her chin. She wiped it with a paper towel, grinning. "Understandable."

Monica slid her chair back and stood up. "We need to rebury the bodies."

"You think that'll let Peggy be at peace? She'll move on to the afterlife and all that?"

"Yeah. I think so."

"When do you want to do it?"

Monica checked her watch. It was one fifteen. "Right now. You got any shovels?"

Monica and Betty kneeled in cool, loose dirt, peering into the dark hole they had dug. Two bodies lay inside—Peggy on her back, and Bernard on his side, facing her. His left arm rested across her stomach like he was giving her a hug. The eye sockets of both corpses were empty, leathery holes. Skin was darkened and cracked. Peggy's once beautiful hair was strewn over her shoulders and across her face like tangled, dead grass. It was a bizarre embrace for a little girl and her killer to share for more than eight years.

Betty leaned down and pulled her ex-husband's rotten arm away from the girl. Tears swelled in her eyelids. "God, Peggy. I'm so sorry."

Monica patted Betty on the back. "Let's get them out."

They carried the girl into the next room. Her body was much lighter than Monica had expected. They set her down in the middle of the floor.

Gritty dirt was inside Monica's shoes, down her shirt, and smeared across her arms and face. Her fingernails were caked full. A large dark blotch stained the front of her white T-shirt. Her dusty scalp itched. "I can't wait to get a shower," she complained.

"I know," Betty said, scratching at her armpit.

Squatting down and lifting at Bernard's arms, Monica said, "You can take showers? It doesn't short circuit you or anything?"

Betty grabbed two ankles and pulled. "I'm waterproof, baby."

Monica looked down at a rotten head. "You just thought of everything, didn't you, Bernie?"

His body was heavier than the girl's, but still lighter than expected.

"Oh, he was a genius; I'll give him that."

They wrapped the corpses in blue plastic tarps Monica had used when she'd moved. Up the stairs they went with the dead and set them down side by side in the living room. Monica flopped into the recliner, panting for breath. She wiped at her forehead with the back of her hand, leaving behind a black smear.

A knock at the door startled her. She looked down at the bodies and up at Betty, whose eyes widened in fear. "Shit," she whispered. "Who the hell could that be?" Monica peeked through the curtain. A petite woman stood on the porch, wearing a taxicab-yellow short skirt and a low-cut blouse, exposing a mile of perfectly rounded cleavage that defied gravity. Her shoes had tall square heels and thin winding straps halfway up her toned calves. Bouncy red curls were held aloft with massive amounts of congealed hair spray. Eyebrows had been plucked with unreasonable precision. Thick, black eyeliner. Pronounced, crimson lips.

Monica recognized the woman immediately. It was her friend from the city, Suzanne. "Oh my God," she said. She turned the knob and opened the door four inches. Suzanne squealed in delight, pushing the door wider to hug her best friend.

"Monica! Surprise!"

"Suzanne. What are you doing here?"

"I got a couple of extra days off and decided to see how you're getting along out here in the sticks. Is it everything you hoped for?" Monica heard the sarcasm in Suzanne's voice. It was loud, clear, and somewhat grating on her already tender disposition.

She sighed. "And then some."

Suzanne stepped back, noticing the filth across Monica's T-shirt, the smears over her face, and the caked dirt under her fingernails.

"God, you've really taken to country life, huh? Do they have running water out here, or what?"

"Oh," Monica said looking down at herself, "we were...digging. I must look horrible."

"Who's this?" Suzanne inquired, walking over to Betty.

"This is Betty. Betty—Suzanne." Hellos were exchanged.

Then everyone's attention focused downward, toward the rolled-up tarps.

"Whatcha digging for?" Suzanne asked, snapping her gum.

Monica pulled her to the kitchen. "We'll talk about that later. How have you been?"

The conversation continued in the other room, and Betty did not waste the opportunity. Out the front door she went, with a corpse under each arm.

"It's so great to see you," Monica said. "I can't believe that you came all this way."

Suzanne checked her makeup in a mirror she'd extracted from a glittery purse. "You know me, I'm very spontaneous."

Betty appeared at the doorway. "Um, Monica, it's almost a quarter to five. Sunset is at five twenty-eight."

"Shit," she exclaimed, turning her watch upward. "I didn't know it was so late."

Suzanne scrunched her nose. "You guys got a hot date or something?"

Monica stood up. "We have this thing we've got to do while there's still daylight. Why don't you hang out here? We won't be longer than an hour."

"I'm not leaving your side. I just got here—I'll go with."

"Not a good idea," Betty said abruptly.

Monica pinched her eyes shut, exhaled, and then walked over to Betty. "I'm just gonna tell her."

"Is that wise?"

Monica smiled. "Probably not." She turned around. "Suzanne, look, we just dug up two dead bodies out of my basement, and now we're gonna rebury them down the road." She smiled. "Wanna give us a hand?"

Suzanne's gum chewing stopped. She peered at the grungy women with an amused grin. "That's really funny. Now, why don't you tell me what you're really doing?"

"There's no time," Betty said. "We can explain on the way."

The three women walked out to the pickup. The bodies lay in the back, encased in blue tarps. Two shovels lay beside them. Monica shuffled Suzanne to the cab.

"Get in."

Monica told Suzanne about the ghosts as Betty drove down the dirt road. She described the night they'd spent in the house with Renee and Dillon. Suzanne looked back and saw a foot hanging out of one of the tarps.

She gasped. "There's a...there's a...foot."

Monica glanced into the truck bed. "That's Bernard."

"It's a body?"

"That's what I've been telling you."

"Let me out right now!" she screeched.

"Settle down, it's not like we killed them."

Betty corrected her friend. "Actually, I killed Bernard."

"Oh yeah. Right," Monica said. "Sorry Betty."

Suzanne looked at Betty and then screamed.

Betty smiled at her. "But he deserved it."

The pickup pulled off the road, its tires crunching over frozen snow. Monica opened her door and slid out.

Suzanne leapt out behind her. "Have you lost your damn mind? Dead bodies? Shovels?" She watched Betty walk around the truck. "A murderer?"

Betty frowned. "I am not a murderer. It was self-defense—sort of."

Suzanne threw her hand into the air. "Well, as long as it was *sort of* self-defense."

Monica lifted a shovel out. "Are you gonna help us or not?"

Suzanne shoved glossy fingernails in her friend's face. "This is a *French manicure*. I'm not helping you dig a friggin' grave!"

Daylight faded quickly behind the tall forest. The temperature descended with the sun, pushing into the teens. Suzanne frantically paced, cursing under her breath and waiting for the others to finish their morbid duties. After fifteen minutes she checked her watch, huffed in frustration, and took off walking down the road.

Monica patted loose soil. "Finished."

Betty appeared from deeper in the woods. "I guess that's it," she said quietly.

"I guess it is. Are you okay?"

Betty peered through the darkening trees. "Yeah. Let's get out of here."

When they got back to the truck, Suzanne was nowhere in sight. Monica scanned the area. "Shit. Where'd she go?"

Betty opened the driver's side door. "She's about a quarter mile down the road."

"Goddamn it," Monica said, tossing a shovel into the back. "Let's go get her."

Suzanne's high heel caught a rock, and she stumbled, growling. "Holy hell! These are eighty-dollar shoes. I can't believe this shit."

The truck slowed beside her. Monica leaned out an open window. "Get in the truck."

"No," Suzanne said, pulling a big red curl away from her face. "*Hell no.*"

She skidded on another rock, caught her balance, and growled. "You've gone totally batshit. I'm going back to the city."

The sun was gone completely now, and the wind had a frigid bite. Suzanne's cheeks numbed. Teeth chattered behind smeared lipstick. Up ahead, snow swirled around headstones as fog descended over the mausoleum.

Monica pleaded, saying, "We've been friends forever. I need you to believe me. I need you to *trust* me. *Please.*"

"You kicked me in the face."

"What? That was like twenty years ago. We were kids. You really should be over that by now."

Betty laughed. "You kicked her in the face?"

Suzanne shoved her head in the open window. "You think that's funny, *murderer*?"

Betty's expression snapped to a scowl as she raised a clenched fist. "I don't get mad, but I could make an exception just for you."

Monica leaned between them. "Stop. Both of you." She turned to Suzanne. "Get in this truck right now, goddamn it. I'm tired of screwing around. You are gonna listen to me."

"Monica, I—"

A stiff finger pointed at the redhead's nose. She went cross-eyed.

"No. Shut up. You will hear what I have to say because I always tell you the truth. I've never lied to you, and I'm not going to start now...and because I gave you Stanley Bisswickey."

"You didn't give me Stanley."

"Yeah, I did."

Betty scrunched her face. "Who the bleep is Stanley Buzzwhacky?"

The other two turned and said "BISS-*WICKEY*" in unison.

Monica looked back to Suzanne. "He asked me to prom first."

"He did not."

"I'm sorry I never told you."

Suzanne's eyes glazed. "Really?"

Monica nodded.

Suzanne opened the pickup door. "Slide over, I'm getting in."

Betty exclaimed, "Are you kidding me? *That's* what got her in the truck?" She looked back to the road. "You people are insane."

Dillon sat in room 104 at the Sunny Side Motel, looking over the tattered notebook he'd found in Monica's attic. He flipped through the first twenty pages with curiosity. It was the journal of a man named Charlie Waterson, who had resided in the house Monica now lived in, from 2006 to 2007. The first section was a personal diary, all written in black or blue ink, and was a chronicle of the man's seemingly usual daily activities.

Dillon did find a few pages where Charlie had experienced paranormal activity. He heard odd noises on July 25, 2006. They had been what sounded like voices originating from the attic. A search found nothing out of the ordinary, and life went on as usual for another three months.

Then, on November 1, another event scared the wits out of Charlie, as he watched the ghost of a young girl wash and put away a sink full of dirty dishes. He considered moving out after witnessing that activity, but since the girl seemed to pose no immediate threat, he decided to stay. More occurrences took place over the course of the next year, some frightening and others fascinating. Charlie wrote them all down in detail, adding to the notebook daily. And then an odd passage caught Dillon's attention.

Charlie had an interaction with a local resident, Mr. Eddie Gordon, and his dog, a Chihuahua named King. It seemed that the little animal bit him on the ankle when he was on Main Street, coming out of the supermarket with an armload of groceries. The man immediately scooped up the dog and apologized. It left a small tooth mark on the back of Charlie's leg and had broken the skin, but just barely. After the description of the incident, nothing was written on that day, beyond the fact that Charlie hated Chihuahuas.

But then, Dillon saw the writing change dramatically. The journal skipped days and even weeks before it continued, which was very different than the previous daily writings had been. Also, the speech became more juvenile, cruder, with many misspellings and bad punctuation. It looked as though someone new had taken over the journal, but the new person still claimed to be Charlie Waterson.

This new person was very angry, short tempered, and quite paranoid. Descriptions of events from that point on were painted with dark sarcasm and loathing.

And then Dillon read something that chilled him to the core. The man, still claiming to be Charlie, had abducted and killed a young woman from Ryerton. The words went into very specific and horrible detail. Dillon, in shock from the psychopathic passage, kept reading.

The next couple of pages talked about Charlie's hatred for the world and everyone in it. By the spring of 2007, the man had taken three more lives and had grown quite proud of his work. Something had snapped inside Charlie Waterson's mind, and Dillon was determined to find out what it was. He flipped a page and saw something unique. An entry on August 14 had been written in red ink.

That's different.

Dillon kept his place with an index finger and flipped through the remainder of the book. Random days were also written in a red-colored pen. Going back to the first crimson note revealed another difference as well. The words in red were all spelled correctly and written, once again, like a literate, sane adult. The content had a noticeable contrast as well. A very fearful man had written in those places, and still claimed to be Charlie Waterson. He feared for his life and the people around him. He was horrified by the things he'd done. His sanity had come back to him in those strange places written in red. He was a totally different man, penitent and increasingly suicidal.

One entry, on December 5, stood out.

"I have come to know that the power of the little ghost that lives here with me is the reason for my stints of regained sanity. I don't know how or why, but I believe she wants to help me.

"I write in a different color ink when I am myself, so anyone who reads this will know that it's me.

"I have also come to know one other very important thing. It was Gordon and his dog that did this to me. That thing is not really a dog at all. It is an evil that took over my mind, infecting me with its awful energy. When the feeling takes hold, all else is lost. Willpower means nothing. Its grip on me is absolute.

"If this happens to you, if you are forced into this criminal insanity, just know this: When the urge is on you, nothing can make it stop. Nothing."

Dillon read on. The explanation of Charlie's murders went into more and more gruesome detail. He explained how he chose his victims, what implements of death were used, and how he disposed of the bodies. The text became almost like a how-to guide for those with similar motivations.

Dillon forced himself through the bloody sections, not wanting to miss anything important. The red sections continued throughout as Charlie struggled with his situation. Confused and powerless, it seemed only one terrible option remained.

Dillon arrived at the final entry. It had been written in red ink.

"Oh god. What have I become? Those poor people. My hands are now stained with the deaths of more than a dozen women and men. I am surely damned. I cannot hold onto myself long enough to do anything outside of these walls. This house has become my only sanctuary. Only in her presence am I free in my mind. And even then, only in short waves. Sometimes hours, sometimes minutes.

"One thing that eats at me is that I know how to kill the devil now. I know its weakness, and there isn't anything that I can do about it.

"I found out that some kind of ritual that will allow the devil to take a human host and be at full power will happen on Halloween 2009. I do not know the significance of the time; I only know the date.

"If you have been given this horrible disease, then God help you. I will take my own life when I'm finished with this passage. It is the only thing left for me. I only pray I can go through with it. May God forgive me.

"If you have come to read this, and you are of the right mind—that is to say, the evil has not taken you—please, do the one thing that I haven't the power to do. Kill the devil. I would do it myself if I could.

"Its weakness is in its chest. Infuse the heart with"

The rest of the notebook was blank.

With the truck parked in the driveway, the women went inside. Monica told her friend from Woodard about the ghosts of a little girl and Betty's ex-husband. She described the undead-laden graveyard across the road and the horrible white monster in the fog. Suzanne listened, thinking her best friend was crazier with every passing moment. She kept a careful eye on the other; the one who'd admitted killing her husband.

"Monica, you need to come back with me right now. This place is making you see things. Don't you see how crazy this all sounds?"

"I know how it sounds, but I can't go yet. I promised I'd help Peggy first. If there are no signs of ghosts tonight, I'll leave in the morning."

Betty checked a satellite image of the cemetery. Random undead figures lumbered here and there; one stood directly across the road, glaring at the house.

"You can go now…if you want," she said.

"No," Monica replied. "I'll go in the morning."

The creature's one good eye examined the attic window. Unsteadily, he swiped a decaying arm over the dirt road. He glanced around and then gazed toward the house. He limped a step forward and stopped in his tracks, waiting.

Through the front window Betty watched him stand in the road, gnashing yellow teeth. "Uh, Monica…"

Monica pulled the curtain wider. The dead man took another step closer.

"Shit. They can't leave the graveyard, can they?"

"What are you guys looking at?" Suzanne said wearily.

He suddenly turned, limping back toward the mausoleum. Monica breathed a sigh of relief. "Thank god. For a second there I thought—"

"Who is that?" Suzanne said, squeezing between the other women.

He stopped in front of the mausoleum yelling. Three dark figures appeared around the west corner, and then two more. Five shuffled, hobbled, and lurched from the east.

"Oh hell," Betty said. "This doesn't look good."

Dozens gathered at the stone building, slurring and mumbling. Dead speak resounded into the icy, white air.

Suzanne's heart rate doubled. "Who are they?"

The gathering quickly multiplied. From every corner of the graveyard the damned flowed in, creating a massive and unsteady crowd.

Monica gasped. "There's got to be more than a hundred."

"One hundred and twenty-four," Betty announced, "and forty-three more on their way."

Suzanne swallowed her gum. "What do they want?" she said, coughing.

Betty grabbed hold of Monica's shirtsleeve. "Get your truck keys right now."

The mob headed for the road, growling. Betty claimed the shotgun from the closet and a box of shells. With keys jangling from her fingers, Monica grabbed for a coat.

"They're getting closer!" Suzanne squealed, her eyes growing into saucers.

"Move!" Betty screamed, throwing open the front door.

The dead flooded the road, yard, and driveway. A rotten man at the porch steps tore off his own left arm with his right and then threw it at Betty. She stepped aside as it sailed past. It came to rest at Suzanne's feet. She leapt away shrieking. The fingers on the detached appendage groped for something to take hold of as the elbow flexed.

"That's an arm!" Suzanne yelped, running for the kitchen.

With the front door slammed shut, Betty locked the deadbolt.

We're too late.

Monica claimed the shotgun and slid shells into the chambers. "I thought they couldn't leave the cemetery."

The front window shattered inward, showering the recliner with glass. Three long arms entered, as the moaning outside got louder. Monica raised the gun up to her shoulder, pulled it tight, and aimed toward the window. The blast sent the intruders to their backs, flailing on the dark porch. Fists pounded against the door. Another window shattered in the kitchen.

Thomas Able was caught in a surge of bodies rushing up the mausoleum stairs.

"What's happening?" he slurred.

A man to his right said, "The entity no longer protects the house! Our time has come!"

Once in the graveyard above, Tom followed the crowd to the road. Wayne slapped him on the back. "Hey, buddy."

"Oh...hey, Wayne. How's your stomach?"

Wayne looked down and put a hand over the wound. "I couldn't get my intestines to stay in, so I had to clip 'em off."

Tom noticed the concave, slack skin. "Bummer."

"Yeah. What's a guy to do, you know?"

"Have you seen Arlene?"

Wayne scowled. "That rotten slut can suck it."

The two walked across the road toward the house. Dozens of their undead brothers were already in the yard and driveway. Feeling a rush of hatred, Wayne stormed the porch, howling. Tom, somewhat less motivated, lingered by the mailbox, watching the attack. A shotgun blast sounded, and a front window exploded with Wayne just outside. His left arm was ripped off at the shoulder as he fell away.

Tom turned back toward the cemetery.

"Being dead stinks," he sighed.

When he got back to the mausoleum he stopped, looking over shadows woven in the creases of Gothic architecture. The building that was meant to be a resting place now stood dark and foreboding, overcome with evil.

"I don't belong here," Thomas Able said.

He then turned and walked away.

"Where's Suzanne?" Monica cried. She and Betty rushed for the kitchen. Glass crunched underfoot as the women took in their surroundings. Above the sink an arm groped between curtains, swiping at the air. Rotten fingernails grated at every side of the house, encircling the women in a horrible, scouring resonance.

Suzanne cowered on her knees, under the table. "An arm..." she said. "It was moving."

Fog poured in the broken window. A loud bang rattled the back door. The three women jumped at the sound. They stretched to see around the refrigerator. An unseen force exploded into the center of the door, sending two splintered halves inward. Monica and Suzanne screamed. Betty gritted her teeth and tightened skinny fists. The outside world was thick white. A tall creature came into view, snapping long teeth. Betty leapt forward, grasped the top of the refrigerator, and pulled it onto its side, blocking the doorway. "Get upstairs now!" she said to the others, as she braced a shoulder against the blockade.

The two fled the room, heading for the stairs. Once at the top, they heard a crash from below and growling. Monica pointed to the attic ladder. "Hide in there," she said, turning back.

"What was that thing?" Suzanne stuttered.

"Just go. I have to help Betty."

Sneakered feet thundered down the staircase. With the hammer cranked back on the shotgun, she rounded a corner into the kitchen. Betty was flat on her back, pinned by the pale monster. Long talons squeezed at her throat, piercing tender skin. The demon's gaze shot upward, at Monica. She pressed the twelve-gauge barrel against its forehead and squeezed the trigger.

Suzanne scrambled up the ladder, panting for breath. Boxes and an old trunk sat scattered across the attic floor. It was dark. She squinted to see to the back of the room. A cool shadow hung across the far wall, a velvet curtain of nothingness, offering sanctuary. She entered the void, pulled a box close, and then went to her knees. She ducked behind the cardboard, sobbing.

The creature's head exploded, showering the table, stove, and linoleum with oily blood and thick chunks of skull. Its jawbone remained connected to the spastic body, hanging down like a torn necklace of flesh and broken teeth. The recoil sent Monica stumbling back, with ringing ears.

Betty grunted, rolling the body off her. "Thanks, girlfriend."

Another white demon appeared at the back door, hissing in the mist. And then two more. Needle fangs snapped with blood streaking downward.

Monica's lungs shriveled like two deflating balloons.

Eddie and Georgette Gordon's house was dark except for one room, the master bath. The shower ran as Georgette lathered her long hair. She hummed along with a song on the radio. It was tuned in to the local station. The music faded, and the voice of Redmondsburg, Mr. Bruce Bradley, spoke with enthusiasm.

"You're listening to WKAZ Radio. I'm your host with the most, your king of Halloween, Bruce Bradley. With me is the lovely Katrina Webber."

"Good evening, Bruce."

"Yes. This is our spooky special, celebrating Halloween, which will be here in only two days. Are you all stocked up on toilet paper and soap, Kat?"

"Just what I need for my house, Bruce."

"Well, you'd better get crackin'. How are you gonna soap the mayor's car without some extra Zest?"

Georgette stopped rinsing to scowl toward the radio. *Did that jerk just tell people to soap our car?*

Katrina said, "Everyone knows the mayor gives out the best candy. I won't be soaping *his* car. I'll be soaping yours, Bruce."

Georgette smiled. "Thank you, Kat."

"Ooh," Bruce said. "That's harsh. Now folks, don't forget about the Spooks and Specters carnival. It ends Halloween day at midnight. It's a lot of creepy fun for the whole family. I'll be there each night at eight p.m. for some extra special activities. And Katrina will be too. Don't miss it!"

Another song began as Georgette shut the water off and stepped out of the shower stall. Once dried off, she put on a white robe and tied the belt. A clock on the counter read 7:34 p.m. She clicked a dial on the radio, and the music disappeared.

Bare feet padded into the bedroom on a quest for clothes. A lamp atop the nightstand clicked alive, and yellow light filled the room.

Georgette turned to see a massive silhouette in the doorway. It was too tall and lean to be her husband. The figure stood well above six feet. Its arms were as thick as she was at the thigh. Its chest was a monolith of heaving buttons and taught flannel.

Monstrous hands gripped a long axe; its curved edge shimmering in freshly sharpened glory. She soaked in the frightening image with failed lungs. A slight sound passed through her lips. It wanted to be a scream, but surprise nipped it into silence, and panic finished it off. She stood rigid with fear constricting her throat. The loss for words lingered between the predator and prey, hanging in the air above the carpet, dresser, and bed.

Questions would've been pointless. She knew why he was there. He meant to plant the axe in her and watch her bleed out. That's what God had told him to do. No one, including Georgette, was going to talk him out of it.

Gary stepped into the bedroom and said, "The Lord wants you dead, lady."

"No," Georgette forced out, scrambling back.

With weapon ready to strike, he paused. "The Lord gets what he wants." Then another voice startled him.

"Gary Tuttlebaulm. Here to kill my wife, are you?"

The killer turned and said, "Yes." He saw the mayor was holding a pistol. "You gonna stop me?"

Georgette cried, "Shoot him!"

Gordon addressed his bride. "Now, settle down, dear. Everything is the way it should be."

"He wants to kill me!" she screamed, "Shoot him!"

Gary stared at the fat man, waiting for a bullet. It didn't come.

The mayor laughed. "I was going to kill her on Halloween, but...well, here you are. I suppose you can do it for me."

Georgette yelled, "You bastard! You were gonna kill me?"

"Of course. You are of no use to me anymore."

"No!"

Gary swung around to face his victim. "Okay then."

Gordon fished a cell phone from his pocket. The sheriff picked up after only one ring. Gordon instructed, "Get to my house right away. I have an intruder."

The axe came down hard. A squirt of blood shot onto the paisley comforter. Georgette gagged as the carpet soaked up her fluids.

"Yes," the mayor said into the receiver. "My wife is dead." A wheezing gasp sounded as she squirmed. "Okay, so she's not completely dead, but she will be in a moment."

Gary yanked the weapon free and then brought it upward for another strike.

"No, no. It wasn't me," Gordon explained into the phone. "I really do have an intruder...Yes...Gary Tuttlebaulm. Isn't that convenient?"

The axe came down once again, this time silencing Georgette for good.

"And Sheriff...bring some shovels."

The van plowed through the undead gathering, with brittle bones crunching beneath the tires. Dark figures stumbled and fell away, moaning and screaming. Dark fists pounded at the windows, leaving behind smeared blotches.

"Out of the way, you dirty heathens!" Dillon called out as his wife screamed.

He reached between the seats and retrieved a glass bottle full of unleaded gasoline. With a lighter, he lit a soaked cloth wick hanging out the top. He rolled down the window and chucked the homemade bomb at a thick gathering. It shattered against a dead man's skull, spraying orange flames in every direction. Six scorching bodies flailed in pain.

Dillon grinned with delight. "Surprise, you pitiful spooks. I came packin'."

The attic window smashed inward, showering the floor with glass. Suzanne screamed at the sound. Her body shook with panic clamping down on every raw nerve. Cohesive thought was lost.

Wet mist spiraled through the open window, saturating the air. A moonlit head and shoulders took form in the haze, accompanied by a growling voice.

"Innocence once lost is now found."

Suzanne was frozen in the wet darkness. She was trapped—a lamb in the wolf's jaws—the instinct of self-preservation now futile. The monster was inside the attic in an instant. It hovered in the cloud with teeth snapping. It paused to inhale deeply. The smell of fear was satisfying. A dark vision cut into the shadows, locking onto the woman. She lurched back and met the far wall. Her eyes connected with the demon's. She couldn't look away.

"Sleep," the horrible thing said.

Unconsciousness enveloped her like a shroud of death.

Betty and Monica stood rigid and back-to-back in the kitchen as three white demons and a crowd of the dead closed in on them.

A van slid to a stop in the driveway. Dillon rushed to pull start a gas-powered generator. The engine coughed to life, sputtering and threatening to flood. He closed the choke valve, and the motor ran a bit smoother. Renee plugged a small microwave cord into an outlet on the generator. She cranked over the dial and pushed the start button.

Inside the house, corpses dropped to their knees in agony. The mist creatures, unaffected, kept coming. The dual barrels of the shotgun blasted at the monsters concurrently, the first impacting a milky-white chest, sending the beast falling backward. The second hit another in a leathery arm, tearing into muscle and bone.

"Come on!" Betty yelled, pulling her friend through a cowering crowd of rotten, writhing enemies. They reached the front door and saw the van with its exhaust wafting into the night.

"Dillon?" Monica said in shock.

Renee waved a long arm out the driver's side window. "Come on! Hurry!"

Monica fearfully glanced back into the house. Dead men moaned in pain on their knees, holding rotten heads in both hands.

"Suzanne."

"Get to the van," Betty ordered. "I'll get her."

She pushed her friend toward the steps and then ran into the house.

"Suzanne!" Betty called out as she climbed the ladder.

She stepped onto the attic floor, scanning the room. The window lay smashed in, leaving glistening moonlit chunks across the wood floor. Fading mist hung in the frigid air. The darkness was still, silent. She rushed to the broken window and looked out over the roof. She closed her eyes, accessed the satellite, switched to infrared, and zoomed in on the cemetery. One solitary heat signature appeared at the mausoleum doorway. The camera changed to night vision. Betty saw Suzanne's body, limp and floating in midair, entering the tall threshold. Three creatures of the mist accompanied the unconscious woman. They were quickly out of sight, and the door slid shut. A chill danced up Betty's metal spine, making her shudder.

God, no.

They watched Betty rush from the house, over and between the dead, alone. Urgency pushed Monica's voice against the swelling urge to cry.

"Where's Suzanne?"

The blonde climbed in the van's side door and sat wearily. Her eyes were distant. "They took her."

"Oh god…I'm going to find her."

"Wait," Dillon said, "we need to talk."

Monica gripped the shotgun tight. "No. They'll kill her if we don't—"

"They won't harm her—yet. I promise you."

"What do you mean? How do you know what they'll do?"

Dillon explained what he'd read about the mayor and the ritual that was to be performed on Halloween. October 31 was in two days, and he figured they wouldn't hurt Suzanne until then.

The generator sputtered and then died.

"Shit," Dillon said.

Renee, from the front seat, said, "The dead are getting up, hon."

"They're coming this way," Betty added, sliding the door shut.

Lumbering, limping figures went slowly past the van, heading back to the cemetery.

"They're leaving us alone?"

"They got what they came for," Dillon said.

Monica's face flushed with determination. "I'm not waiting until Halloween. I'm going now."

Betty put a hand on her shoulder. "We can't just waltz in there. That place is crawling with who knows what."

"We can use the microwave to stun the zom—" She had begun to say zombies, but couldn't bring herself to utter the word. "…the *dead people*, and you can distract the other…*things*. I'll look for Suzanne."

"It took everything I had to fight one of them. There's like five now."

Renee spoke calmly, trying to ignore a walking corpse passing close by her window, "Yes, dear. Let's not be hasty. We need a plan."

Monica felt as if she would explode out of her skin. She fought the desire to jump out of the vehicle and start blasting. Tears streamed down her cheeks. "Okay," she said in a whisper, "any ideas?"

Dillon slid over to her, on his knees. "The microwave is a good idea. I'll get the motor running again. I'm sure it's just out of gas. But that won't help us with the mist creatures. They aren't affected."

"What can we do that affects all of them?"

"It's that little girl. The one that was protecting your house. That is, until tonight."

Betty looked over. "We reburied her."

"Oh. Now this all makes sense. We'll need her back with the man that killed her. I'm afraid it's the only way."

Monica couldn't see any more of the dead through the windshield. It looked as though the last of them had moved on. "We reburied him, too."

"Oh. Well, let's get them back together and see what happens, shall we?"

"But if we put them back in the house, how is that gonna help us?"

"We're not putting them in the house; they'll have to come with us."

"Come with us?" Betty asked. "Peggy's gonna be so pissed off."

"Yes. Sorry 'bout that," Dillon said, reaching for a gas can.

He could only hope the little girl's ghost would come back. Naturally, it was not a guarantee. Also, the other entity, the one that nearly killed him, would likely make an appearance. Dillon pinched his eyes shut, trying to forget the panic he'd experienced suffocating in the cold, dark basement.

9

THE IMPLEMENTS OF DESTRUCTION

Early morning sunshine outlined the tops of the trees with a heavenly radiance.

"This is it," Betty said. "Pull over here."

The van slowed to a stop over packed snow and gravel. Monica slid the door open with a shovel in hand. She stepped out and stood rigid for a moment, peering into the shadows. Her childhood friend, Suzanne, with thick red curls and a runny nose, dominated her thoughts.

Renee appeared from behind, with another shovel. Betty made her way slowly, carrying a purple backpack and a yellow duffel bag. Each was large and empty, save for the single hundred-dollar bill in the bottom of the bag. She stopped at a mound of loose, clumpy soil. Turning to Dillon she said, "Peggy's there." The backpack was dropped to the ground, and she continued toward her dead husband's grave.

An abandoned crater remained where they'd left him. His body was gone.

Oh shit.

She rushed to the others. "Guys, we have a serious problem."

"So, you're saying that Bernard has been turned into one of those things?" Dillon lifted at the child's small corpse.

"Considering the unique circumstances that we find ourselves in, yes."

Monica held the backpack open. "But, then why isn't Peggy one of them too?"

"Perhaps they can't raise a child from the dead. Or maybe she's too small—too weak—for their purposes." He looked over the remains and then down into the open pack. "She won't fit like this. We're gonna have to fold her up."

Betty looked away. "I'm sorry for this, Peg."

A hipbone crunched as a knee was lifted to the torso. Dead skin flaked as another snap sounded. Betty covered her ears, rushing to the van. When Dillon's project was complete, dead Peggy sat in a gargoyle position, her knees up to her chest with leathery arms hanging down at her sides. He tied a piece of twine around to hold the body in place and then fitted her into the backpack. Once zipped, only her small head was left in view. It stuck out the top with clumped strands of hair dried against pale skin. Small eye sockets sat dark and empty in the center of a crumbling, lifeless face.

"Our only hope," Monica said, "is that we can find Bernard at the mausoleum."

Betty surprised her friend from behind. "I'll find that son of a bitch."

Monica turned, looking into sad eyes. "How are you holding up?"

"I'm okay. It's you I'm worried about."

"Yeah. If I can just stay focused...We can do this, right?"

"Absolutely," Betty said, trying to sound convincing.

Suzanne awoke in a small, shadowed room. She pushed herself up from a dirt floor, confused. Her surroundings consisted of stone walls— large rocks held together with crumbled mortar. A solitary doorway provided the only light. Flickering candles sent a dancing yellow illumination across the connecting chamber.

She struggled to remember how she got there. An image of her friend Monica screaming something seemed important. A new person, a woman whom she hadn't met before and didn't trust, felt relevant. She recalled fearing for her life. Something awful was after her, something evil. Her lucid mind spun in a collection of disconnected snapshots.

Suzanne squeezed her eyes shut in an attempt to piece the memories together. Long, needle teeth snapped from her mind's eye. She burst into tears.

It was cold. She felt goose bumps over her arms. Her body shuddered in the chill. The coldest of all was her left ankle. She slid her legs around in front of her. An iron cuff was locked around her leg, attached to a thick chain. Metal links trailed off into darkness.

Oh god.

She tugged at the restraint. It held tight to something unseen. She pulled again with all the strength she could summon. It was solid.

She sobbed, "No...Please..."

A shadow grew outside the doorway. The figure of what looked like a man limped, blocking the dim light. When he entered, she saw that it wasn't a man at all. He may have been at one time, but what stood before her now was no man. Phlegm gurgled in his spoiled throat as he flexed torn arms with exposed muscle and bone. He mumbled, prompting air to enter though a gash in his right lung, creating a percolating gurgle noise.

Suzanne's scream echoed throughout the underground labyrinth, bouncing down long corridors, seeking an escape route. Her voice was desperate, hollow, and undeniably alone.

The ride to Ryerton was spent in silence. They knew what had to be done if Suzanne had any chance of survival. They knew the dangers waiting in the darkness below. Their chances depended upon each of them finding a way to be strong in the face of the most horrifying things they'd ever seen. The team needed courage above all else. And, perhaps, a good amount of luck.

They also needed supplies. Even the best soldier can't hit the front line without bullets.

Dillon stood at the ammunition counter, waiting for a clerk to return with the items he'd requested. The pistol was in a box under the driver's seat of his van. It had been a gift from his brother, Daniel, who was an avid hunter and fisherman. At the time, Dan told him a weapon of that caliber wasn't much good for hunting. It was too big for small game, and too small for big game. Actually, a nine millimeter was only good for one thing—shooting people. But he was convinced, for whatever reason, that learning to use a gun was as important as knowing how to change a tire.

So he took Dillon to the shooting range, showed him how to load and unload the pistol, and how to clean it. Dillon went along to satisfy his brother. He'd never had a desire to kill anything and, quite honestly, found the entire process disturbing. His brother told him that he would need to know how to shoot at some point in his life and made him promise to keep the pistol. Until now, Dillon thought his brother had been wrong.

The clerk emerged from the back with ten boxes of bullets and set them on the glass countertop.

"Thanks," Dillon said in an uneasy tone, reaching for his wallet. "How much?"

Suzanne cowered away from the thing that stood before her. Black drool oozed from its cracked lips when it spoke. The language was incomprehensible to the living. It was a mishmash of mumblings, grunting, and words that seemed to make no sense. The creature's voice was accompanied by the sucking wheeze through the hole in its damaged lung and the horrible stench of rancid meat.

"Crum, bahhlla. Pallis?" it asked, taking another step forward.

The smell flooded the room. Suzanne gagged, covering her nose and mouth.

"Get away from me, you freak."

It frowned. "Minno...sumpoo gra."

She scrambled to her feet, looking over the floor for anything that could be used as a weapon. She spotted a four-foot length of rebar on the other side of the chamber. She ran for it with thick chain jangling behind. She'd almost reached her prize when the slack ran out. Taught metal stopped Suzanne's foot in midstep, tripping and slamming her to the hard floor. She wailed in pain as the dead man limped closer. With her body pulled as far as the chain would allow, she reached for the metal rod. It sat corroded and with a slight bend inches from the tips of her straining fingers.

"Please," she cried, forcing her arm to stretch farther.

The cuff's sharp edge cut into the heel of her foot. It felt like her shoulder would come out of the socket. She sobbed in intense pain, forcing herself to keep going.

"Almost there," she said as her index finger felt the end of cold metal.

The thing was above her now, casting a black shadow. It watched her straining and crying. It bent down and grasped the rebar. Inquisitive, it held the would-be weapon, studying it from one end to the other.

"Mon din?" he said as he handed it down to the woman on the floor.

Without hesitation she ripped it away and then, as hard as she could, struck him on the kneecap. He yowled, stumbling. Suzanne rolled away, got to her feet, and held the rod high, threatening another strike. He swiped at the air, growling.

"What a dumb shit," she said, standing her ground.

He grimaced, limping closer.

"You want more? Bring it!"

He yelled, pushing a cloud of sour breath into her face. She swung, hitting him in the jaw. Teeth exploded away from the impact.

"It's called mouthwash, asshole."

She hit him again. The rebar struck him in the skull just above the ear.

"It's in the same aisle as the toothpaste!" She swung again. "And the dental floss!" He turned to limp away. She smacked him across the back. "It's not far from the deodorant! Get some, you rotten fuck!"

The next swing missed as the dead man limped out of reach. Exhausted, Suzanne's arms fell to her sides. She heaved to catch her breath as the dead man left the room, growling in anger.

Betty walked up to a rack of hanging baseball bats. Renee and Monica followed, looking over the assortment of wood and metal. The synthetic woman removed an aluminum bat from the hanger. Bold letters down its length read "Louisville Slugger." With both hands, she swung it across her body twice, testing the weight, feeling its balance.

"This is a good one."

Renee gripped a bat made of pine. She held it at arm's length, as a person might hold a dirty diaper or a dead mouse.

"It won't bite you," Betty said. "Hold it like this."

She stood as if she were up to bat, keeping her knees loose and her elbow high behind her head. Renee tried to mimic the stance, with unconvincing results.

"When you swing," Betty instructed, "bring your front foot down and really lean into it. That'll give you more power."

Renee attempted a swing. The end of the bat caught a rack of Yankees jackets, making a loud bang.

"Ooh!" Renee exclaimed. "Sorry. I didn't mean to do that."

Betty and Monica took a step back.

"I'd tell her to keep her eye on the ball," Betty said with amusement, "but that really doesn't apply here."

Monica made a mental note to stay the hell away from Renee when they got back to the cemetery.

Dillon paid for the room as the others unloaded the van. Room 12 was a bit cramped for four people, but it had two double beds, and sleep was all they were there for anyway. Monica set the shotgun in the corner as Betty pulled the three-pronged cord out of a bag. The skin at her right hip was pulled upward to expose a socket to plug in the cord. She inserted the other end into a nearby outlet. Fascinated, Monica watched a small charging light at her synthetic friend's side come alive.

"So weird. I keep forgetting that you're not...you know."

"Human?" Betty said. "It's okay. I forget sometimes too."

Dillon sat on the bed across from the women. In his lap he held a notebook bound in leather. "How long does a full charge take?" he asked. The blonde looked down at the journal. "Oh, about six hours. Whatcha got there?"

He opened it to the first page. "It's the diary of Mr. Waterson, a man who lived at Monica's house from 2006 to 2007. I found it in her attic."

"Oh yeah. I saw that," Monica said. "I didn't read it, though."

"Well, I did. It's how I know what they plan to do."

Renee sat by her husband as he passed the book to Betty. Its passages horrified them for the next hour as they followed Waterson's disintegration into madness.

When they finished, Monica passed the book to Dillon. "That's the most awful thing I've ever read."

He tucked it into a duffel bag. "So you see what needs to be done. The ritual will happen on Halloween."

"That's tomorrow."

"Actually," he corrected, "Halloween begins at midnight tonight."

"Yeah," Betty added. "You guys had better get some sleep."

The doctor and his wife lay down, trying not to think of what they were up against.

Monica grabbed her coat and went to the door. "I need some air."

"Don't take too long, girlfriend," Betty said as she closed her eyes.

Outside a brisk wind sent a chill through Monica's body. Hair and blowing snow whipped her face. She ignored the temperature and headed across the parking lot.

Memories of Suzanne hung in her mind like weathered snapshots. Each moment in time felt distant and worn. Details had all but faded, leaving behind only the feelings that once held the photos in place. Even their first encounter, a thing she swore she'd never forget, was hazy now. The emotion was there, but the pictures were long gone. Little Suzanne, with the bouncy red curls and runny nose, had vanished.

What remained was the scream, the pathetic and ear-piercing cry of surprise and pain. It had been the moment that began their friendship, and strangely enough, it was the one thing that grounded the relationship. Good and bad times came and went, but they knew they could make it through anything together. A kick to the face had proven that. They learned to forgive one another before they became friends. That meant something for a reason Monica couldn't define. It meant something special. She only hoped Suzanne would be able to forgive her now.

A man in a long coat startled Monica from behind. His voice made her gasp.

"Hey," he said. "You're the girl."

"God, you scared me."

He paid no attention to her fright. "It's you."

"Silo? Silo Pernice?"

The sound of his name coming from the girl surprised him. "Do you know me?"

"Of course. We spoke at the carnival."

He leaned close. His breath smelled like sour milk. "You see what I mean now, don't ya?"

Monica backed away, trying not to let disgust show on her face. "You said they were after my red friend. How do you know that?"

He scratched at a dirty neck. "They got 'er, huh?"

"Yes." Tears welled in her eyelids. "They did."

"I guess you can't leave now."

"But how did you know?"

"Some folks are tuned in better than others."

"What else do you know? Can you help me?"

His hands went deep into his pockets, feeling for change. There was only lint. "I can't even help myself. Can you spare a couple bucks?"

"I have money," she said, pulling two hundred-dollar bills out of her back pocket. She handed them to Silo.

His eyes went wide. "Screw the bus. I'm callin' a cab!"

"That's great. But first, tell me what you know."

His vision searched the parking lot from one barren side to the other. Then he focused on the motel. "You're all in mortal danger. You'll have to work together if you want to survive."

"Okay," Monica said, hoping that more specific information was coming.

Silo grinned. "And wear a jacket. It's gonna be cold." He turned to walk away, and she stopped him.

"That's it? That's all you can tell me?"

He wiped his nose with a dirty sleeve. "Pretty much."

Monica huffed in frustration. "Are you sure there's no other way you can help me?"

Silo rubbed the two bills between his fingers, assuring himself they were real. "You want me to bring you back a burger?" He grinned. "I'm buying."

She didn't answer. She walked back to room 12 to get some rest. Dillon was snoring on his side. Renee was asleep also. They looked peaceful in each other's arms, and happy.

Monica had been happy once. She remembered how Ben used to mumble in his sleep. He'd say her name once in a while, and she knew he was dreaming of her. It was hard to say whom he dreamt of now.

Monica was exhausted. Lead weights seemed to hang from her eyelids, threatening to pull her into unconsciousness where she stood.

The sheets were cold next to Betty, her robot friend.

The motel mattress was hard.

Not that it mattered.

Mayor Gordon walked into the Sheriff's Office without knocking. He closed the door, and his carefree expression went sour.

Shane stood at his desk, shuffling through a mound of paperwork. "Hello, Mayor," he said with a smile.

"I need you to arrest Betty Jones and Monica Green right away."

Shane leaned over to spit in the bucket. "Those pretty little ladies? What for?"

Gordon wiped a cloth handkerchief over the back of his neck. "Your stupidity amazes even me sometimes, Sheriff."

Shane sat as beads of perspiration formed on his forehead. "I apologize, Mayor."

"We have kidnapped their friend. What do you suppose they might do?"

"I don't know."

"I'm sure they're plotting to toss a wrench into my plans right now."

"So, I'll bring them in. What should I charge them with?"

The mayor stormed the desk and thrust his face at Shane. Veins swelled in a flushed rage. "You're the sheriff! Make something up!"

Out in front of the Sheriff's Office, the Chihuahua felt the need to hold back no more. The sacrifice was set to happen at midnight, sending

Redmondsburg, and the entire world, into chaos. So, it figured, why not start the party early? The devil tired of the order that went with laying low. It had yearned for some fun for thousands of years, and now, finally, it would have some.

A mother and daughter passed by on the sidewalk enjoying ice cream cones. The little girl was three years old and wearing shorts, a pink T-shirt, and flip-flops. The swirl of chocolate and vanilla was the highlight of her afternoon. She giggled when the dog trotted up and licked her toes. After a moment she stopped, dropped the waffle cone to the concrete, looked up at her mommy, and then kicked her in the shin. The woman recoiled at the surprise pain and nearly tripped. The toddler screamed and kicked again. Now that was fun.

Down the street, two men were busy repairing a brick wall in front of the coffee shop. The little dog ran up to let the one at the wheelbarrow pet him. The other man, on his knees and with a trowel in hand, asked for another brick. He got what he asked for, eight times in the back of the skull.

By the time the mayor emerged from the Sheriff's Office, there had been three murders, two senseless bludgeonings, four acts of vandalism, and one public urination. The demon Chihuahua was especially proud of that last one.

Gordon called out, "King! What did you do?" as the dog raced away. The animal wasn't listening. He was busy.

He was going to see if he could get someone to burn the library down.

Monica woke with a stiff pain pinching at her neck and upper back. For a few seconds she was unsure if sitting upright was possible, let alone a good idea. The cause of her discomfort stood in the corner of the room, silently waiting for another opportunity to devastate dead things. Its dual barrels were dirty, scratched, and stained with dried blood. The wooden body of the gun showed the same scuffed and battered signs of a war-torn weapon.

Monica lay staring at the length of the shotgun. She no longer wished for a Taser or any other lesser tool of destruction. It was as much a part of her now as an arm or a leg, or her will to survive. While her entire chest and ribs were bruised because of it, she knew that she was also alive because of it. The shotgun had given her a fighting chance, and sometimes that's all you need.

She sat up groaning, rubbing her neck. "No pain, no gain," she said as Betty approached.

"How you feelin', girlfriend?"

Monica winced as her feet touched the carpet. "You got any ibuprofen?"

Renee grabbed for her purse. "I have some. How many would you like, dear?"

"How many bottles do you have?"

The sound of breaking glass preceded a car alarm outside the motel doorway. And then a scream. Dillon looked up from the duffel bag. "What was that?"

Betty walked to the window and peeked out the curtain. A woman was flat on her back on the icy pavement, next to a pickup with a smashed-in side window. She cried and flailed as if someone were kicking her. The only other person in sight was a man across the street, running down the sidewalk with a hacksaw raised high. His laugh was that of a nervous mental patient. In the distance, Betty saw a cone of black smoke rising from the library. "Holy shit. It's chaos out there."

Dillon pulled the curtain wider. "We need to go now."

Monica watched the woman at the truck push onto her knees. The expression on her face was that of a frightened animal. "We should help her."

Dillon took hold of Monica's arm. "We will. By killing Gordon and stopping the evil. It's the only way."

The group exited the motel room at five o'clock. When they got to the van, a body came into view. It was a slump at the edge of the blacktop, at the eastern edge of the lot. A long coat was twisted against the ground with a dark bloodstain down the side. The victim's blank stare aimed toward the sky, and a crumpled hundred-dollar bill stuck out between the fingers of a clenched fist. Silo's throat had been sliced deep, and his shirt was saturated.

Monica gasped.

"There's nothing more we can do here," Betty said, turning away. She paused. "I'm sorry, girlfriend."

Monica stepped up into the van and sat thinking about a homeless man who wouldn't be making it out of town after all. He'd known about the evil long before any of them. And he tried to warn her, help her. She only wished she could've helped him, but it was too late for that now.

There was one she could help, though. The one he'd called her red friend.

Suzanne.

Monica swiped a tear away with cold fingers. She tightened her jaw. "Let's just do this thing."

Gary Tuttlebaulm stood in the darkened cell, scratching down a rough concrete wall with bloody fingernails. His left eye twitched every few seconds, pinching his face in a nervous spasm. A man appeared on the other side of the bars, in the wide pathway between the human cages. The man was fat. He wore a blue jacket, the color of a clear midsummer's day. Gary stepped over to the bars and stood eye to eye with him. He gripped the iron with thick fists, flexing. He growled like a rabid dog.

Mayor Gordon didn't flinch, nor did he step back. He was nonchalant and casual—happy as a clam, as the old-timers might say—with a big clammy smile. Gary stood inches away, staring with twitching intensity, looking crazier than a pet coon—an expression also very popular with the old-timers.

"Mr. Tuttlebaulm," Gordon said. "Good to see you again."

"Let me out."

The mayor picked at his molars with a soggy toothpick. "Oh, I plan to...but not just yet." His smile expanded, pushing red cheeks upward. "I just spoke with your gerbil."

"Hamster," Gary corrected. "Elton."

"Elton, yes."

"He needs food."

"I fed him while I was there. He's fine."

"He spoke to you?" Gary asked, letting go of the bars and taking a step back.

"Oh yes. He'd like you to do something for me."

"What?" the prisoner whispered, astonished.

"Pay a visit to Wanda Spell."

"Old lady Spell? What for?"

The mayor turned to a deputy who then handed him a long, freshly sharpened axe.

"Deliver this to her," Gordon instructed with amusement expanding over his face, like blood into fabric.

"That's mine."

"Yes," he agreed. "Show Wanda how it works."

"Oh," Gary said as the twitch at his left eye ceased. "Old lady Spell... Tell Elton that it will be done."

"Very good," Gordon said as he gave the weapon back to the deputy.

"Get some rest, Mr. Tuttlebaulm. We'll release you at nine o'clock."

The mayor walked toward the doorway with a pleasant spring in his step. Gary's words stopped him at the threshold. "Elton is God, you know."

The fat man laughed. "Of course he is."

He walked into the Sheriff's Office, closing the door behind. Shane sat watching the rodent as it sat on a stack of paperwork, eating a crumb of bread that had been pinched off a ham and cheese sandwich. The sheriff smiled at his furry guest.

"What do you want me to do with this little guy?" he asked the mayor.

Gordon walked over, made a fist, and slammed it down, flattening the hamster on the desk. A squirt of blood shot across an office supply order form.

"Jesus!" Shane exclaimed.

"No," Gordon corrected. "God."

He burst into laughter and then left the room.

10

THE
CEMETERY
UNDERGROUND

Dead Thomas Able, carrying his severed hand, moped through the forest, wondering what he should do with his afterlife. The graveyard and the terrible agenda were behind him now. He'd have nothing more to do with the demon king's plans. He was a free zombie.

"No more lumbering around in the dark," he said. "No more doing what they tell me." His foot caught a branch and he stumbled. "And no more goddamn Halloween."

He stepped into a clearing and saw a house. It seemed that every light burned within. Each window was a beacon, blazing with yellow light. A figure walked across the living room. A living person. Tom's stomach rumbled.

"I've got to have something to eat," he moaned.

He walked to the house, holding his complaining, grumbly stomach. Standing at the back door, he found no one in sight in the living or dining rooms. His eyes squinted to focus down a dark hallway. Then, without warning, an elderly woman rounded a corner, meeting the dead man's stare. The two stood in a surprised silence for what felt like days. Drool ran over his lips and down his chin. The aroma of her flesh saturated his nostrils, even from outside the closed door. It seemed to emanate from the pane of glass that separated them. The old lady, Wanda Spell, approached the threshold. The deadbolt clicked open and the knob turned. The door eased away from the frame a few inches.

"Hello, my friend. Out for a stroll, are you?"

Tom didn't know what to say. She spoke to him like a person. Like he was alive. It didn't matter. She could speak to him any way she pleased. He was still going to eat her brain.

Just as he was about to shove his way in, she said something else he didn't expect.

"I can see you're not like the others. You're special."

Special? Tom thought. *I'm not special. I'm just a starving dead guy.*

The door swung wider. "Come on in and take a load off." Her old, wrinkly face smiled at him, which was irritating to say the least. He couldn't eat her brain if she was smiling at him. That would be wrong, no matter how hungry he was.

"I can see that you're hungry. I have a thawed steak in the fridge. Would you like that?"

Seeing how she was still smiling at him, hell yes, he would like a steak very much. Wanda disappeared into the kitchen, and dead Tom had a look around the living room. Little porcelain pigs were everywhere. "Old people," he mumbled.

When she reemerged she held a raw, pink sirloin. The meat was bloody and nearly an inch thick. He tore into it like an animal and had it consumed in seconds flat.

"Now," Wanda said, "sit down."

He found a chair as he licked wet fingers.

She sat across from him, in the recliner. "You've abandoned your brothers in the crypt. Why?"

He thought for a moment and then shrugged.

"Was it because you didn't fit in?"

He nodded.

"And now you don't know where to go. You're wondering what you should do."

Again, he nodded.

Wanda leaned close to whisper the answer he'd been looking for. With anticipation, he slid to the edge of his seat. "The way I see it is this. This is a war, and it's no time to be wishy-washy. You need to pick a side." She clasped aged fingers and sat back with confidence. Seriousness took hold of her at the mouth and then spread upward, narrowing her eyes. "If you're not one of them, you're one of us."

Tom hadn't thought about it that way before. He moaned something she didn't understand. She continued. "I know they've kidnapped someone...you could help them...if you really wanted to."

That was true. He could help the innocent. He couldn't say he really wanted to, though.

"It would be a chance to make up for your mistakes...A chance to do something right."

He couldn't really think of any mistakes that needed to be made up for. Oh wait. There was that brain he'd eaten. He supposed that had been wrong, since it had belonged to a person. It sure was good, though. But wrong. Definitely wrong. Tasty. But wrong.

He wondered if old people's brains were as delicious a young people's brains.

Wanda frowned. "Are you listening to me or just thinking about eating my brain?"

He shrugged.

"Try to focus here. I'm giving you an opportunity to do the right thing."

She's talking about morality, he thought. It was something he hadn't considered since he died. Well, long before he died, actually. He was a lawyer, after all.

But seeing how he wasn't particularly motivated to do bad things, doing good things would at least give him something to do. It had to be better than roaming the forest feeling sorry for himself.

"Okay," he said, "I'll do it." What Wanda heard was "Mull snod, ploo."

"Does that mean you'll do it?"

He nodded.

"Just wonderful, my friend! You've made me very happy!"

Perhaps doing the right thing would feel good to Tom. It would, if nothing else, give him some purpose.

Great, he thought. *I'm gonna be a good person from here on out.*

She stood. "Let's celebrate with another steak."

Good thing there was more steak; otherwise he would've eaten her brain.

Dillon drove down side streets, avoiding what he assumed was a choatic and somewhat dangerous downtown. Various sirens were heard as they made their way west. With a left turn on the highway, Monica's house and Lakeshore Cemetery were less than ten minutes away. That is if Sheriff Deputy Leonard Simms's car hadn't been blocking the road.

It was parked crossways, blocking both lanes. The lawman stood with his left hand up like a stop sign, while the other rested comfortably on his hip.

Dillon said, "It's the sheriff. You two duck down and don't make a sound." Betty and Monica slid behind the middle bench seat while Renee and Dillon tried to compose themselves. The van rolled to a stop, and the deputy walked to the driver's side window.

"Where are you folks headin'?"

Dillon smiled. "We're going over to Shelbyville. We heard it's quite beautiful country over there."

Simms rubbed at his nose. "You'd get there quicker if you went out to the interstate."

"Yes, I know, but we were hoping to stop by Stone Lake along the way."

"Stone Lake, huh?" The deputy looked past Dillon, into the dark van. "Do you know Betty Jones or Monica Green?"

Dillon looked over to his wife and then back to Simms. "Those names don't sound familiar."

"No," Renee added. "I've never heard those names before."

Unsatisfied, the deputy asked, "Whatcha got in the back?"

Dillon gave him an innocent smile. "Oh, we've got some recording equipment, cameras and such…You see, we are paranormal investigators. We—"

"Open up the side door for me."

Dillon got out and walked around the vehicle with Simms close behind. He turned and said, "It's really just—"

"Open it."

"Yes, sir," he said, reaching for the door handle. In one smooth motion, he slid the door open and backed up, hoping to hell the girls were either out of sight or ready with a bat.

The deputy leaned in to see into the dark van. In a flash, Betty appeared and punched him across the jaw. Simms wailed in surprise and pain, reaching for his pistol. The holster was empty. The weapon was already in Dillon's grip.

"My gun," he exclaimed, looking toward Dillon. His face snapped back to Betty as she stated, "Your Taser too." In her left hand she held a Taser gun she'd snatched off of the deputy's other hip. She aimed it at his chest and pulled the trigger. A few thousand volts surged as Simms twitched and then stumbled to the pavement. After ten seconds of electric pain, he passed out.

"Cool," Betty said with a chuckle. "I need to get me one of these."

Monica's head popped into view. "You're pretty quick, old man," she said to Dillon.

"Yes, well..." he responded, examining the officer's nine-millimeter pistol. "When properly motivated, I suppose."

The three turned to see Renee's pale face, which held mouth-gaping astonishment.

"You just assulted a deputy," she said with wide eyes.

"Yeah," Betty laughed. "Nothin' like starting the festivities off with a bang."

"But...but...I believe that's a *felony*."

Monica stepped out of the van. "So is flattening his tires. Betty, you wanna give me a hand?"

"Sure."

"But...but—"

"Settle down, dear." Dillon said, "He's one of them."

Renee covered her face with trembling hands. "I don't feel so good."

Suzanne would've killed for a cigarette. With a length of rebar in hand, she paced the small room, examining the walls, ceiling, and floor. The chain trailed behind her left foot at each step, sliding over hard dirt. She eyed a thick metal plate that secured the chain to the wall. Three large bolts driven into rock were all that kept her from freedom. She glanced back at the doorway to be sure no one was coming and saw candlelight flickering in the threshold as usual. She pulled on the chain, using her foot against the wall for leverage. It held as strong as before.

"Damn it!"

With a frustrated heave, she struck the wall with the rebar. A chunk of rock crumbled away. She hit it again, that time closer to the metal plate. Mortar cracked into pieces as stone chipped from the rough surface. She worked the end of the rebar behind the plate and pried. It popped outward, sending dust into the air. One corroded bolt fell to the dirt. She repositioned the bar and pried again. With a final yank, the plate fell. The metal hitting the floor made a considerable clang. Her eyes snapped back to the entrance, expecting to see a walking corpse or a white demon. There was nothing.

She coiled up six feet of heavy chain and hung it over her shoulder, growling under her breath at the weight.

This must weigh a thousand pounds, she exaggerated to herself.

The connecting chamber was lit by two previously unseen candles, on opposite walls. This room was much larger than the last. There was a stone hallway directly ahead and one on the left. Banging and moaning could be heard to the left, which made Suzanne's choice easy. She stepped forward, entering the silent corridor. After thirty paces into the darkness, more choices appeared. The path continued straight ahead, or she could turn left or right. She stood quietly at the intersection, listening. At first all that could be heard was her own panting breath.

After a quiet pause, another noise echoed. A clunk and then a scrape. A clunk and then a scrape. Over and over. It was coming from behind and getting a step closer with each passing moment. She glanced back, seeing only a pitch-black hole.

She evaluated her choices again. Seeing that there was no time for eeney-meeney-miney-moe, she made a decision based on dexterity. She was right-handed, so she went right. It was bizarre logic that made no sense whatsoever. But with a dead man closing in, it didn't feel as crazy as it might have under different circumstances. It certainly was no worse than catching a tiger by the toe.

She held tight to the chain slung over her shoulder in an effort to keep the links from jangling together as she walked. At the same time she maintained a tight grip around the length of rebar, her only defense. The corridor was pitch black now. Suzanne, with shallow breath, felt her way along. The clunk followed by the scrape continued from behind. After another twenty steps, the path stopped. Suzanne stood at a solid stone wall with solid stone walls to her left and right. It was a dead end. The only way to go was back the way she came.

"Oh shit."

She suddenly wished that she were left-handed.

The deputy's car rounded a corner at County Line Road, its tires crossing over the pavement and onto gravel. Ackerman slowed the vehicle and glanced into the rearview, checking on the passenger in the backseat. Gary sat in the darkness, with head down, wheezing. Greasy hair hung in twisted clumps and strands, hiding his face.

The deputy pointed down the road and said, "Wanda Spell's house is on the right, about a half mile south."

Slowly, Gary's line of sight rose to see the cage wall that separated the backseat from the front. "I know where she lives." His voice was stiff with annoyance but not quite angry. It wouldn't take much to push it in that direction, though.

Deputy Daniel Beemer, who sat on the passenger side of the front seat, looked over to the driver. "He knows where she lives," he said, lowering his brow and trying to mimic the axe murderer's voice.

Ackerman stopped the car and put it in park. He stepped out onto a rough gravel surface, as did his partner. The waxing moon hung low behind a cloudy, starless sky. Thick forest on either side of the otherwise empty road sat dense and black, as black as their reason for being there. As unfathomable as a killer's conscience.

Beemer walked to the middle of the road and set a long, splintered axe down on the ground. When he got back to the car, he holstered his pistol. Ackerman opened the back door, releasing the prisoner. Gary ducked out into brisk air, inhaling deeply, enjoying the aroma of freedom. He grinned at the short lawman that stood before him for a moment and then turned around, offering handcuffed wrists to the deputy.

"If you give me any trouble at all," said Deputy Beemer, "I'll put a bullet in your brain. You got me?"

"I got you," Gary said as a pistol held at arm's length ascended to point at his nose.

With the binding removed, he rubbed his sore wrists, and both deputies took nervous steps back.

"Now," Ackerman said, "go get your axe like a good boy...and then keep walking. If you take one step back toward this car, you'll be dead."

"With a bullet in my brain?"

"That's what I said, dirtbag."

Gary lumbered toward the freshly sharpened weapon. "I can't say I want a bullet in my brain."

Beemer grinned. "He doesn't want us to shoot him. Smart guy," he said with sarcasm.

The murderer claimed his axe and kept walking. He didn't bother looking back at the two with the guns. Not that he was afraid to. He was just no longer interested. He had a job to do, and a frigid half mile stood between him and it.

He looked forward to the warmth of the old woman's house as much as he did embedding the blade of his weapon into her skull. Yes, it was going to be a cold walk. A shiver danced up his spine. It would be nice to warm his bones and then get to what he did best.

The Lord's punishment was his calling, his reason for being, and he was proud as hell to be such a part of the grand scheme. The lawman's words came back to him.

A bullet in your brain.

"That short guy sure talked tough," he muttered to himself. He wondered how tough the deputy would talk with a splintered axe handle forcibly inserted in his ass. That was something he'd have to find out later.

The dead man limped closer, although Suzanne couldn't see him yet. She peered into blackness, tightening muscles, clenching her jaw.

I'll run right by him, she thought. *He can't see any better than I can.*

She sucked in a deep breath, held it for a moment, and then ran. Chains clanked and rattled down the hallway. The rebar was raised into the air, ready to strike. The dead man swiped at Suzanne when she raced by, grabbing for the chain that hung over her shoulder. A decomposed finger caught in a corroded link and the lower half of his arm tore free. He yowled, clutching at exposed bone.

Moaning resounded from every direction. Having no undead-free-corridor choices, she took a right. She raced into darkness with chains clanking at each desperate stride.

Gary Tuttlebaulm stood in the shadow of a tall willow tree. Its long, sad branches hung all around as he watched a car pull up to the house.

He squinted toward the vehicle, feeling a familiar twitch take hold of his left eye. Sucking in a deep, cold breath, he gripped the axe handle tight. Ceramic pots lined the circular driveway, each containing a tall, healthy plant. Moonlight gave the leaves a subdued and unnatural hue, making them appear as specimens from an alien rainforest, a million light-years away.

After a quiet moment the car door swung open. Wanda pushed her aching bones out of the bucket seat. She steadied herself and gazed out to the tall, weathered barn. A halogen lamp blazed above the doorway, creating a circle of illumination stretching down chipped paint and over hard-packed dirt. A cat with matted, white fur raced across the light in a blur. It shot around the side of the barn and disappeared into the shadows.

Wanda shut the car door and headed for the porch. Keys jangled as she climbed each step individually, taking her time. Arthritis pinched at every movement, and she found herself longing for the La-Z-Boy recliner. Once inside she flipped on the overhead light and headed for the kitchen to make a warm cup of tea.

The Synergy Dynamics facility sat a mile from the road. Once a person with the proper clearance got past the front gate, they would find themselves on a paved, winding road leading into the forest. The administrative building appeared first as a tall structure of concrete and glass. The individual research units lay beyond, lettered A through G. Each stood four stories and had more square footage than the average community college.

Security guards drove electric carts on regular patrol routes throughout the complex. Building B's rooftop was lined with rows of antennas and varying sizes of satellite dishes. Dark conduit trailed down its outside walls, containing fiber optic lines, cat-five network cable, and gold-plated copper wire. Most ran down into the basement and fed directly into the control servers. From there, information traveled to computer systems across the complex. One such computer sat in a lab in the upper level of building F, its screen being stared into by Martin Beasmire. Martin held a degree in nuclear physics but also knew quite a lot about radio wave signals, microwave transmissions, and encryption technologies. He was currently working on a hunch.

A few days ago he noticed that Synergy's satellite had been receiving strange command sequences. He contacted all the usual departments to determine who was operating the satellite's state-of-the-art camera system. He found that no one had performed any tests on the equipment for weeks. The cameras hadn't been in use by any of Synergy's scientists since early September. And yet, someone was controlling the directional heat-signature and night-vision systems.

They'd zoomed in on specific areas of Redmondsburg and surrounding areas numerous times, focusing on what looked like a cemetery. Martin suspected the synthetic that was stolen from the company almost ten years ago. It had been designed with a command directive for the satellite. The feature hadn't been implemented at the time it went missing. Someone had to have activated it after the theft.

The synthetic would need a line of sight to communicate with the satellite; that is to say, it had to be in the western hemisphere, most likely still in the states. To narrow down his search, he needed to find the frequency it was talking to the control unit on. The control unit, or the brain, which operated all of its higher functions, would be in constant contact with the synthetic. Tracking down the frequency could be a difficult task, if the signal was no longer local. A nationwide search could take months or possibly years. But with a few hours of monitoring, Martin realized, to his surprise, the signal was local.

Radio waves were used for everything from cell and cordless phones to global positioning systems, satellite television, military communications, citizens band radio, AM and FM broadcasting, shortwave transmitting, garage-door openers, and baby monitors. Nearly every technology that we depend on used an assigned electromagnetic radio signal. And it just so happened the computer he stared into was capable of receiving all of them. It could identify each one's strength and magnetic frequency, determine the type of encryption used, if any, and even listen in on any transmission he chose.

He saw that there were currently twenty-two hundred cell phones in use in the county. He saw six baby monitors, and occasionally someone would open or close a garage door. On the screen he saw the two major satellite-television providers' signals and countless AM and FM radio stations.

One signal struck him as odd. It was an encrypted code at the top of the AM perimeters at 1,700 megahertz. Of course, to the untrained ear, it would've sounded like a garbled series of beeps at the top of the AM dial. But as soon as Martin tuned it in, he recognized it immediately as an encrypted computer language. The synthetic had been transmitting and receiving signal all that time on AM frequency. Anyone with a radio could tune in and listen.

The synthetic has been hiding all this time in plain sight, he thought.

With a minimal amount of equipment and a company van, he could triangulate the control unit's position very easily. Flushed with excitement, he reached for a phone and dialed Synergy's main office. "Yes," he said into the receiver. "This is Martin Beasmire with the physics division. I need to check out a vehicle."

Dillon parked the van in Monica's driveway, looking over the yard and the wooded area beyond for horrific creatures. The fact that there were none in sight didn't calm his nerves, nor did it improve his confidence. He knew where they were and what they were capable of. The crypt below the mausoleum sat waiting beneath the frozen ground, shadowed, rotten, and oh so deadly. He wondered if the pistol would be enough to keep him alive. He feared for Renee and the others too. Betty was the only one who could hold her own against the white demons. And she wasn't even human.

His existence had become surreal in the last few days. He'd believed in ghosts his entire life but wouldn't have admitted the possibility of recent events if he hadn't seen them with his own eyes.

My whole life has come down to this, he thought.

What he did in the next few hours would define him.

Monica unlocked the deadbolt as Betty scanned the yard, the road, and the cemetery. Other than the icy breeze, everything was quiet. Once inside the house, she dug through a closet.

"Here it is," Monica said, pulling out a red purse with a long strap. She turned it over, dumping gum, eye shadow, a small package of Kleenex, and a flashlight onto the floor. She grabbed the flashlight, checked to see if it had good batteries, and then stuffed it back in. "That might come in handy."

Betty opened two boxes of shotgun shells and poured them into the purse. The traveling arsenal was topped off with a folded pocketknife and pepper spray.

"Can you think of anything else?" Monica asked.

"Nope," Betty said. "If we can't kill a bunch of dead people with this stuff, then I guess we're screwed."

"Yeah. We're screwed, all right."

"Everything will be fine. You'll see."

She turned on a small walkie-talkie and clipped it to the handbag. Monica pulled on a brown furry jacket and then put the strap over her neck and shoulder. The purse hung low, at her left hip.

"Great," Betty said. "You look like Chewbacca."

Monica frowned. "Thanks a lot."

The synthetic woman turned on her own radio, clipping it to her belt.

"Don't mention it," she said with a grin.

They headed back out to the van.

Suzanne raced down the long, dark passageway with weariness and fear squeezing at her burning lungs. The dead speak up ahead turned into two voices, and then four. With an unknown number behind, she forced herself to continue forward, readying the length of rebar for the first strike. A gathering of dark figures came into view. She grimaced, running faster.

Please, she thought, pleading with whatever god of fate that might allow her to survive until an exit could be found or help came.

She hit the pack of dead men at top speed. The weapon connected with the jaw of one, knocking him back. Another fell away, surprised. Her elbow hit a rotten man square in the chest, snapping ribs away from his sternum. He growled and grabbed a handful of red, curly hair. The grip yanked Suzanne's head back in a whiplash of stabbing pain down her neck. She screamed, tripped, and tumbled to the floor in a blur of flying rebar and spiraling tangled chain. She scrambled to her feet, with angry mumbling voices all around her. With weapon in hand once again, she ran, with six feet of chain trailing behind her left foot, dragging along the dirt floor like a heavy metal snake. The anchor plate caught a rock, slamming her to the ground.

Tears streamed.

Panic seized every cohesive thought.

I'm gonna die.

She pulled at the chain as the dead approached. The end of it was wedged tight, allowing no further travel. Once again the only way to go was back. With her energy nearly depleted, Suzanne rushed for the end of the chain, toward the things that wanted to kill her.

Rows of bookshelves lined the living room walls, yet not a single book was in sight. Instead, they'd been covered with a large collection of porcelain pigs. There were salt and pepper shakers, banks, napkin holders, bells, mugs, and figurines portraying plump and happy little porkers caught in a variety of positions and activities. There was a bride and groom, a mayor with a top hat and handlebar mustache, a clown, and what could only be described as a dog-pig, as the little fatty had his leg hiked toward a fire hydrant. And there were many, many more. They covered the entertainment center, the coffee table, both end tables, and the fireplace mantel, from one end to the other. Obviously, Wanda had what one might call a "swine addiction." She'd purchased too many pigs too often, and at some point it became too much.

Hi, my name is Wanda, and I'm a porkaholic.

Gary stepped out of the willow's shadow, watching a light go on in the living room and, a few seconds later, the kitchen. Cautiously, he headed for the house. A skinny white cat brushed against his pant leg, startling him. He scooped under it with a boot and then kicked, sending the animal flying across the yard. "Reeeower!" the feline screamed as it rocketed into a gathering of weeds. He slipped in the front door, latched it, and then turned to face hundreds of happy little porcelain pigs. They were everywhere.

A clang sounded from the kitchen. Gary rushed for a dark hallway. The axe handle caught a saltshaker as he rushed past, knocking the Elvis piggy onto its side. He reached to set it upright but then heard the old woman's voice closing in. She hummed a lively tune as she carried a cup of hot water in one hand and a dangling tea bag in the other. Gary left Elvis where he was and slid into the shadows.

Wanda smiled at the doorway, looking over rows and rows of her plump pink friends. She knew that it was excessive of her to have so many, but really, what difference did it make? She liked them and that was that. She could quit buying them any time she wanted.

Suddenly, she noticed that Jailhouse Rock pig wasn't standing in his usual position with one hand on the neck of the guitar and the other pointing straight up to the sky. He lay flat on his back pointing at the east window, which was far less heroic.

Wanda gasped. She wasn't alone in the house, and she knew it wasn't her previous guest back for more steak. Her intuition told her it was someone with a far darker motivation. She paused a moment and then said out loud, "Oh, I forgot the honey for my tea," trying hard not to sound terrified. Her attempt was successful, for the most part, as she sounded more out of breath than on the verge of losing her bladder in terror.

She turned and rushed back to the kitchen. From a shelf in the pantry, she claimed a long knife with a serrated blade, the one she used to slice bread.

The mayor's come to kill me, she thought, hurrying around the counter to keep a watchful eye on both doorways. To her left was the back porch, to her right a short hallway and then the dining room.

A thundering heartbeat rattled the old woman's body as she struck a battle pose. She held the cutlery up with two hands, ready to strike, like an Amazon princess with a magical sword. That's the look she was going for, anyway. In reality she looked like a shaky old lady who was pissed at a helpless loaf of garlic bread.

Dillon parked the van on frozen grass in front of the mausoleum. Renee sat in the back, checking the generator's fuel level. It was full. The microwave oven sat on the floor, facing the vehicle's side door. With jittery hands she reached for her new bat. Dillon switched off the ignition and turned to face his passengers.

"Ready?" he asked.

Monica slid two shells into place and took a deep breath. "Yeah."

Betty opened the door. The mausoleum's shadows were murky in the doorway and under decorative Gothic arches—too dark for so early in the afternoon. Renee passed out the night-vision goggles. Monica held a pair up to her eyes. A bright green tint illuminated the once black spaces. Dillon pulled an elastic band over his skull and then adjusted the eyewear into position. He was blind.

"Where's the switch on this blasted thing?" he said, exploring the side of the unit with thick fingers.

Betty reached over and turned it on for him. "On the bottom."

"Oh," he exclaimed, looking at her in a green haze. "Much better. Thank you." Renee watched as the others stepped onto the cemetery grounds. Dillon, with a nine-millimeter pistol harnessed against his ribcage and gripping a long axe, sent a faint smile to his wife. Monica, with shotgun in hand, stood eyeing the tall, padlocked doorway. Betty walked toward the building, the Louisville Slugger aluminum bat resting on her shoulder next to little dead Peggy in the purple backpack.

"Be careful, dear," Renee said.

"I will, hon. Lock the doors and listen for us on the radio."

The three turned and headed for the back stairwell.

The stairs leading down to the chamber below the crypt sat dusty, crumbled, and dark. "Creepy," Monica said, staring into the basement.

"Yeah," Betty added, "you go first."

Monica scowled.

"Just kidding," the blonde said with a grin, taking the lead.

They paused at the bottom of the stairs. Moaning echoed from distant, unseen shadows. The sound traveled down stone hallways, over dirt and broken headstones. It bounced in a hollow and horrible pitch across torchlit chambers and through abandoned, dilapidated entryways. It made its way to the three trespassers below the mausoleum.

"I hear them," Dillon said in a whisper.

Monica gritted her teeth. "Sounds far away."

Betty's keen optics scanned every corner of the room. "I've got a feeling this place goes pretty deep."

A solitary doorway across the room provided a path to the things below, and Suzanne. Two pairs of goggles and one pair of synthetic eyes powered up with the green radiance of night vision.

The warmth he'd enjoyed when he first walked in had become overwhelming. It must've been ninety degrees in the house. He stood in the dark hallway, sweating like a medieval executioner who'd wandered into a nursing home.

Where is that bitch? he thought, wiping sticky moisture from his brow.

The entire house was a vacuum of silent, stagnant air. His lightheaded thoughts danced between Elton and a tough-talking deputy while his ears strained for even the slightest sound. A faint tinkle of wind chimes from the porch...a cold breeze and rustling leaves...nothing from inside the house.

It's too quiet, he thought, tightening his grip on the axe. And then, *That bitch knows I'm here.*

Gary headed for the kitchen.

Monica, Betty, and Dillon walked slowly down a dark, narrow corridor. Gray stone lined the walls and ceiling; the floor was hard dirt. Chunks of bone scattered its surface, along with random gatherings of trash. Dillon's shoe caught a glass Coke bottle, sending it spinning into the wall. The impact created an echoed *ting* sound.

"Shit," he whispered. "Sorry."

After another thirty feet, a round white object came into view. It sat at the center of the hall and appeared extremely bright in the night-vision viewfinders.

"What is that?" Monica asked.

Betty frowned. "A skull."

The three walked closer and knelt down to inspect it. The skull was human with a smooth rounded surface. The bone face pointed straight down the hall, resting on an unblemished jawbone. Its dental structure was perfect with no sign of overbite or missing teeth. The skinless head had occupied that spot for who knows how long as if waiting, watching.

Betty studied the shape of the cheeks and the almost square holes of the eye sockets.

"It looks like it's smiling," she said.

Suddenly the jaw opened wide, tilting the cranium up. Off balance, it rolled backward as a voice screeched, "Intruders!"

Betty stared in fascination. It moved without muscles; it screamed without a tongue, vocal chords, or a brain for that matter. It made no more or less sense than the zombies or the white demons they'd been faced with. But to Betty, it was amazing to see a thing without flesh move, powered completely by dark magic. Dillon swung with all of his strength. The axe chopped the brittle bone into flying chunks and dust. The screams faded. Betty pointed an ear down the black hallway.

"Something besides us heard that, I'm sure."

Monica took the lead. "We'd better keep moving then."

"Gordon, you evil man. I know you're here! I'm ready for you!" Wanda called out as Gary tromped down the hallway. His huge frame ducked under the doorway and entered the bright kitchen.

The elderly woman gasped at the sight of him. "You're not the mayor."

Gary paused a moment, thinking hard. "No, bitch. I ain't no mayor. I's the hand of God."

Wanda studied the hulking man carefully. "The demon's got a fierce hold on you," she said. "It's made you do terrible things."

He gripped the long axe tight. Suddenly the serrated bread knife felt insignificant in her hands. "I do the Lord's work," he said, raising the weapon over his head.

With a grunt and a heave, the thick blade came down. Wanda dove out of its path. Her bones may have been old, but properly motivated, she could still move. There was a little grease left in the hinges, so to speak. She hit the tile floor. The blade sunk deep into smooth Formica. He tugged at the wood handle, trying to unwedge the axe. "Hmm..." he thought, pulling hard, "it's stuck perty good."

He paid little attention as the woman retreated into a nearby bathroom. She turned and slammed the door. Suddenly, she realized that she no longer had the knife. With the door locked, she searched her surroundings for anything to defend herself with. She saw rolls of toilet paper, a box of Kleenex, bars of soap, stacks of towels...nothing threatening.

Wait, she thought, *the toilet tank lid.*

With the slab of porcelain removed, she stood perched on the commode's closed seat, ready to whack her attacker's thick skull.

She rested the lid on her shoulder.

I wish you'd hurry up, already. This thing's heavy.

Her wish was granted. The door exploded into the small room with the weight of a hard boot behind it. Wood splintered and cracked. Wanda screamed, went off balance, and slid off the toilet. Her backside hit the floor, and pain shot across her hips and up her spine. He looked down at his victim with dark satisfaction and then raised the weapon into the air once again, this time determined to finish the job.

Wanda stared into the eyes of a killer. Thick arms flexed as he swung with all his might.

In his enthusiasm, Gary hadn't noticed where he stood. He was just outside the bathroom doorway. His height was six foot six. The axe he held aloft was another foot and a half above his head, which made it eight feet or so above the carpeted floor. The entrance in front of him was no more than seven feet high, so at midswing the blade of the weapon rudely stuck in the wall above the doorway, chopping a battery-operated clock in half. One of the halves unexpectedly cracked him on the scalp on its way to the floor.

"Shit," he said, gazing upward.

Wanda used the opportunity to get herself and the tank lid out of the bathroom. With the white porcelain plank held high, she targeted the back of his skull. The impact made a heavy *clunk* sound, and his body recoiled.

Gary turned slowly to face Wanda. He grinned, feeling the back of his head. When his thick fingers reemerged, they were dotted with blood. He noticed how the crimson fluid reflected dim light from the hallway. Wanda watched as a not-so-bright look grew over his expression. He held that dumb look for maybe five seconds, maybe less. He then staggered and fell face forward into the shag carpet.

"We're below the south end of the lake now," Betty said as she checked an overhead map in her memory bank.

"Really?" Monica asked, looking at the stone ceiling.

"Yeah. That rock is the bottom side of the lake floor. It goes on for a mile north and is about a half-mile wide."

Dillon was amazed. "So Stone Lake is just that. It's a lake that sits on a bed of stone."

Betty ran a hand over the hard surface, examining the texture. "Yup. And going by how far down we've walked, I would say this rock right here is no more than three feet thick."

Monica didn't like the feeling of being directly underneath that much water. She couldn't swim. The shark tunnel at Sea World scared the crap out of her. A sick churning squeezed at her stomach. "I wish you hadn't told us that."

Betty smiled. "Just watch where you fire that shotgun. You might bring the whole—" Her eyes went wide. "We could flood this place."

"Hell no. If you hadn't noticed, we are *in* this place."

"Not now, silly. After we rescue Suzanne."

"And why would we do that?"

Dillon agreed with Betty. "To kill off the remaining threat."

They watched as Betty unloaded four sticks of dynamite from her backpack. She wedged the explosives in a crack high on the wall. The cord was attached, and then she tightened the other end to the detonator. She held it up. "So when you wanna set it off, just twist this handle. There's a hundred feet of cable, so get as far away from the blast as you can." She tucked the cord and the detonator behind a deep seam in the wall. "And then run your ass off, cuz this hallway will fill with water in just a few seconds."

Monica went pale. "I don't know if that's such a good idea. I, um...I can't swim."

Betty put an arm around her shoulders. "Look, it's a straight shot to the exit. Just hold your breath and the water pressure should push you right out."

Monica wrinkled her nose. "That's not very comforting."

A laugh and a snort. "It's all I got, girlfriend."

The three turned and continued down the corridor.

Monica thought, *Great. If we survive the undead army and the demons, we get to celebrate by drowning.*

11

ALL ALONE

Monica stood at a dark intersection as the others walked up behind. Three paths provided three difficult choices.

She turned to Betty. "Okay. Left, right, or keep going straight?"

Betty realized Dillon was looking at her too. "Why are you asking me?"

"Can't you see which way to go by satellite or something?"

The synthetic woman knocked on the rock wall. "We're like fifty feet below ground level. I can't see anything with the satellite."

"Maybe we should split up…cover more ground," Dillon said, peering down a black tunnel.

Monica shook her head. "That's not a good idea. We should stick together."

Betty tightened her grip on the bat. "I can handle myself. You two go that way together. I'll take the opposite hallway."

"Are you sure?"

"Yeah. If we run into trouble or find anything, we've got our radios."

"Okay," Monica said with reluctance. "I guess so."

"Be careful, Betty," Dillon ordered.

"You too."

A dark blur spun overhead like the propeller of a Kamikaze plane in slow motion. After another groggy moment, blades of a fan emerged against a backdrop of textured sheetrock painted lime green. Gary was flat on his back, gazing at Wanda's living room ceiling. His wrists and ankles were bound with rope. He pulled against the restraints, cursing.

The old woman kneeled next to him with a serious look dominating her worn face. Her voice sounded out magical gypsy phrases. He couldn't understand a word.

"Untie me, bitch," he ordered. She acted as if she didn't hear him, which in her current trance-like state, may have been true. Her hand hovered above his thick chest. Fingers extended downward and twitched as if motivated by a surge of electricity. The terrible grip on his mind released in an instant. The demon's power over him faded. Free will flooded his consciousness, and he, for the first time in a year, felt like Gary Tuttlebaulm. The hand above him eased, and Wanda looked him over.

"That did it," she said. "You are liberated from the evil."

He saw her smiling.

"I...I done some bad things."

"That wasn't you. That was the power over you."

"Oh," he said, thinking about the past twelve months.

Suzanne ran with her remaining strength churning weary legs. The thick chain trailed off into the darkness. She followed with an elongated metal loop clanging behind. Horrible voices got louder as she jogged to unwedge the plate. The unbelievable things seemed to be right in front of her, but in the blackness of the hallway, it was hard to tell.

An unexpected arm yanked her into a shadowed room, and a grimy hand covered her mouth. Her muffled scream faded as she was dragged to a dark corner. The pursuers in the hallway continued past the doorway. Suzanne was released.

Panting, she backed away, wiping her mouth and spitting. "Gross," she whispered.

Thomas Able held out a large key.

"What is that?" she asked the dead man.

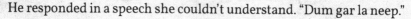

He responded in a speech she couldn't understand. "Dum gar la neep."

"I don't know what the hell you're talking about."

"Neep," he repeated. He grabbed the chain on the floor. "Neep."

"Is that the key to this cuff?"

He nodded vigorously. She eased forward and snatched it out of his hand.

"Thanks, I guess," she said, unlocking the metal restraint. She stood, frowning. "Are you all really dead?"

He shrugged and then nodded.

"Why are you helping me?"

He started slurring gibberish again, and Suzanne decided she'd better stick to yes and no inquiries. "Okay, dude. That's enough since you might as well be speaking Japanese."

He stopped talking.

"Let's see…um…Oh! Can you show me the way out of here?"

Tom put a rotten finger to his cheek, considering the request.

"Don't think too long," she complained. "I don't want you to get a hemorrhage or anything."

He smirked. Then he took a moment to sniff the air surrounding the girl. Her skin had a tempting aroma. He thought about the juicy brain in her head. He wondered if it would taste as heavenly as his first. But, no, he was still human, if only in his mind. He'd decided to do the right thing, and damn it, he was going to stand by that decision. So, he would help her find her way out. Why not? What else did he have to do besides pretending to be excited about the master's plan? And if she turned out to be a bitch, then he'd eat her brain.

Yeah. That sounded good to Tom.

Martin looked over the structure, checking for unusual bundles of wiring or equipment. An electrical line ran from the house to a tall pole and then continued to the barn. He scanned the upper walls. A solitary line encased in weathered yellow plastic ran up and over the rooftop. A small, dark antenna had been mounted at the roof's pinnacle. Martin knew the control unit had to be inside. A thick padlock hung at a tall sliding doorway to detour intruders. He tugged at the lock and then walked around the west side to find another entrance.

He saw a couple of broken boards down low with splintered shards pointing at the ground. He gripped each one carefully and pulled. Wood popped as a crack elongated, following the grain. With a heave it broke away, creating a hole just big enough to shimmy through. He went down on his belly and army crawled through the opening. His shirt caught on a splintered edge only once. With a tug it tore free, leaving a long, jagged rip in the material. He huffed with frustration and continued.

The inside of the barn was dark. Martin squinted into the shadows, looking for an overhead light. He walked across a wood floor that was littered with dust, gravel, and old hay. On the far wall he found a switch. Two florescent bulbs stuttered to life from above. The barn was empty. Up high he saw the antenna cord running downward, attached occasionally to a four-by-four post with U nails. Electric line entered the building above his head and trailed downward, into the floor. Martin peered at the wood surface below his feet. Boards creaked as he walked. The cracks between were pitch black.

It has to be under the flooring.

Cool sweat trickled down his cheeks.

I've never heard of a barn with a basement before.

He wiped at the sweat on his brow, studying the dusty surface. Something hard caught his foot, tripping him. He caught himself from falling and looked down. A thick eyebolt protruded from out of the floor, the round eye standing five inches above the wood. His vision shot upward. A pulley hung from a rafter with its hook dangling from a rope, two feet above his head. He jumped up and grabbed for it. With it pulled down, he latched it into the metal eye. He untied a rope from a nearby post and pulled. A fifteen-foot section of floor raised upward—a hinged doorway exposing a hidden chamber below. He pulled again, widening the entrance, and then tied the rope off to the same post. A ramp descended into darkness.

Cautiously, Martin headed into the basement. At the bottom of the ramp he stepped once again onto a level surface, hearing the low hum of a dozen computer-controlled cooling fans. The control unit, a seven-foot-tall aluminum box, sat in the center of the room on a small trailer. A single monitor glowed on the side of the unit with lines of encrypted code rushing across the screen. Martin tapped the display with an index finger.

He smiled. "I gotcha."

He'd done what the company, the US military, and the FBI had failed to do. He'd found the missing Valkerie equipment.

Suzanne followed the walking corpse down a dim hallway, wondering why he was helping her. She would've asked, but she couldn't understand a word he said. It was all a mishmash of utter nonsense. Even with no questions to prompt him, Thomas Able talked, presumably to himself, as he made his way to the exit. She listened to the garbled language, trying to determine if the noises meant anything at all.

She said, "*Phhpt* can't be a real word. That's just stupid."

He followed that sound with a low, grumbly moan.

"A moan can't be a word either," she added. "You're just making random noises now."

Tom turned and scowled at the woman. The odor of her brain filled his nostrils. His stomach rumbled. "Watch it, lady," he said in incomprehensible dead speak. "I could eat your skin for a snack and save your brain for later."

She stared at him, scrunching her brow. "What?" she asked in a defensive tone.

He turned and continued walking.

Monica continued down a dark corridor. Dillon followed close behind, frequently glancing back to be sure they were alone. The echoes of distant voices sounded occasionally, bouncing down rock tunnels and overlapping one another.

The hallway turned east, and after they made the corner, a bright light illuminated the stone surface from the far end.

"It looks like a central chamber," Dillon whispered.

"Yeah," Monica agreed. "We're getting close." To what, neither of them wanted to think about.

She paused at the threshold, ducking down and listening. Outside the doorway was a wooden platform—a landing at the top of a massive staircase winding a dozen stories below. The room was a hundred yards across, more of a cavern than a chamber. It was a massive hole in the earth, far below the lake and the cemetery. The walls were jagged stone with swirling striations of colored minerals. Along sharp creases in the rock, the surface was embedded with diamond-like shimmering gems reflecting a seemingly nonexistent light source. Their radiance lit the prehistoric cave as brilliantly as a sports field during a night game.

Monica looked out across the area from her upper vantage point. The only way down to the main floor was the staircase below her feet. Not to say she wanted to go down there. An ocean of undead shifted in random gatherings below. Dillon leaned over her shoulder, getting his first view of the secret cavern.

"Holy shit," he whispered into her ear.

Monica swallowed painfully. "Yeah. I'd agree with that."

She spotted six white demons, rigid as statues, standing around the perimeter of a central stage. It was a four-foot-tall rock platform, and the creatures seemed focused on it. Whatever was going to happen at midnight would happen right there; Monica was sure of it.

She checked her watch. It was eight fourteen.

We've got less than four hours to find Suzanne.

Dillon studied the cavern from one side to the other. When his vision found the east wall, he noticed a flash of light, a glare that temporarily blinded him. He pinched his eyes shut, rubbed them, and then looked again.

Betty stood at the entrance to their right, thirty feet east and twenty feet below where they stood. She'd found her own way to the chamber, following a route that entered at a lower doorway. She used a piece of broken mirror to reflect a spot of light in Dillon's eyes.

"It's Betty," he said.

"What? Where?"

He pointed, keeping his body low, so as not to be seen by the creatures at the cavern floor. "Down there."

Monica stretched her neck to look over the wood railing. A flash of light blinded her. Her eyes stung. Betty lowered the mirror and waved silently.

"Shit. My eyes," Monica complained.

"Piss off with the light," Dillon whispered into his handheld radio. "We see you."

Betty raised her walkie-talkie up to show them. It had been smashed. Broken wires dangled from an empty battery compartment.

"Her radio's trashed," Dillon said.

Monica whispered, "Shit."

Betty pointed into a central gathering of the dead.

"What? What is she pointing at?"

Eyes focused on the rotten crowd. "I don't understand," Monica mouthed to her blond counterpart. Betty's pointing got more exaggerated. Monica's confusion was obvious.

"Yes. That is a stinking mob of dead people. We see them."

Betty shook her head and then pointed some more.

"I wish she could yell what she is trying to tell us."

Dillon frowned. "If she did that, those spooks would know we're here."

"Well, what are we supposed to do, play charades?"

Dillon turned his head slowly and grinned. "That's not a bad idea."

He raised his left forearm, slapped it twice with the index and middle finger of his right hand, and then mouthed the word "charades" silently. He finished his instructions by pointing at Betty.

Monica said, "Do you really think she knows what the hell you're talking about?"

Dillon smiled. "Yes."

"How do you know that?"

"Because she's already playing."

Betty put an index finger up to her left eye.

"I," Dillon said.

Betty put hands up to both eyes, as if focusing a pair of invisible binoculars.

"See," Dillon said.

Amazed, Monica looked over. Betty laid a hand over her chest.

"Her," Monica said.

"It's a possessive gesture. And she is the speaker. I—see—my."

Betty then crossed one pointing index finger over the other and held them up.

"Crucifix?" Monica asked.

"No," Dillon said. "X. I see my ex."

Understanding flooded their faces.

"She sees Bernard...in that crowd."

Suzanne spoke as she walked, complaining.

"—and one time, in eighth grade, me and Monica were partners in science class. And one of us had to prick our finger so we could test the blood type. And of course Monica made *me* do it. She knew I didn't like that kind of thing, but she didn't give a crap. And of course, I did it...Cuz I always did what she told me. I always went along with whatever she said. I'm such an idiot. So, you know what happened?"

Dead Tom didn't care nor did he look in her direction.

"I saw the blood and fainted dead away."

Tom rolled his drooly eyes.

"I was the laughing stock for the rest of the year. Everybody made fun of poor little fainting Suzanne. They called me Queasy-Suzie. And it was all Monica's fault."

Tom mumbled, "Get over it, bitch," in dead speak.

"Oh, I know. I shouldn't have listened to her. She was always pulling crap like that."

"I'm gonna have to eat your brain..." Tom said.

"And then there was this other time—"

"...if you don't shut the hell up."

"—and she said, come on Suze, just try it."

"Really, I'm not kidding. I'll eat your brain."

"So like a fool, I did it..."

"Brains are kinda chewy. Did you know that?"

"Have you ever been kicked in the face over Legos? I'm serious, it happened to me."

"I bet yours is mushy...Cuz you're a self-absorbed, stupid bitch."

"It's crazy, right? And guess who did the kicking? Go ahead and guess."

"Monica," Tom said.

"Monica. What a shocker, right?"

"Oh yeah. A real shocker."

"I had a red footprint on my forehead for a week."

Tom wished for death, but then remembered he was already dead.

"We need a plan," Monica said, looking across the shifting crowd below.

"Yes," Dillon agreed. "We need to get down to Betty. We can't continue to communicate by charades. That would take all night."

He turned his face toward Betty. He mouthed silently, "We are coming," hoping she could read lips.

Her brow scrunched.

He looked to his right, at the rock wall. There was a crease, an indentation in the steep canyon stone, with sparkling crystals glowing from inside. With careful footing, they just might be able to climb down to Betty, avoiding the stairs entirely.

"Follow me," he told Monica. "And be careful."

Betty watched her friends step off the wood platform, clinging to the sheer cliff wall.

Oh hell, she thought, *they're climbing down.*

She went through the doorway, back into the corridor, and scanned the ground. The hard floor was littered with rocks and antique debris. She scooped up four fist-sized stones and two bottles. One was an empty Coke, the other was a dark green wine bottle with a long neck and no label. She rushed back to her perch, looking down over the rotten gathering. If Monica or Dillon were spotted, white demons would respond in an instant. So to avoid that misfortune, Betty would keep the undead from announcing the intruders. Their climb was high enough over the crowd's heads that maybe, just maybe, no one would notice them anyway.

A leathery face looked upward with its drooling eyes focused on Monica as she nearly slipped. Dillon caught hold of her elbow, and she found more solid footing. A decomposing finger rose up to point. Its mouth opened in a toothless gape. Betty wound up like a major-league pitcher and chucked a rock at over a hundred miles per hour. It struck the dead man in the cheek, spinning him around as his jawbone exploded on impact. He fell to the dirt, disappearing into a sea of bodies.

"Strike one," Betty said grinning.

Others around him paid little attention. They were all unsteady on their feet, and falling down, apparently, was a common occurrence.

Dillon's boot scraped an area of dirt loose. Small pebbles and dust rained down over a torn scalp. The man looked upward to see the people above. Just as he turned his head to tell a neighbor, a Coke bottle shot into his left eye socket, forcing the eyeball into the center of his brain. He wailed in pain as dark fluid ran down dark cheeks.

"Strike two," Betty whispered from the shadows.

A nearby dead man said, "Woose it frall in?" which translated to "What's wrong with Frank?" in dead speak.

Another said, "He got a bottle stuck in his eye."

Dead Frank fell to his knees, grunting in gibberish.

A third stated, "What an idiot."

Dillon carefully stepped onto the landing. Monica was right behind, out of breath.

"Did any of them see us?" she asked.

Betty held a rock up to show her friend. "Yes, but I took care of it."

"Thanks"

Dillon retreated into the shadows beyond the stone doorway and motioned for the others to follow him. The three sat around the corner, out of sight, to devise a plan.

"Okay," Dillon whispered. "Priority one is to get Bernard. Getting him and Peggy back together is our only chance at scaring those white demons away."

Monica agreed. "Yeah. We need to get to that stage and the rooms beyond. I'm sure Suzanne is being held in one of them."

"One of us will have to create a distraction while the others grab Bernard," Betty said. "And it has to be one of you."

"Why?"

"I'm the strongest and the fastest. I have the best chance at catching my ex and getting back out alive."

"That is true," Dillon said. "So I guess I'll do the distracting."

The women snuck out the doorway and climbed down to ground level. Dillon remained in the arched entryway, out of sight. He watched as they made their way along the south wall. They hugged the stone surface, darting from one outcropping of rock to the next. When they reached the southwest corner, he knew it was time for his part. He stepped out onto the wood platform. He unholstered the pistol and began firing into the crowd. Three shots echoed across the cavern. All eyes in the lower gatherings found the man at the top of the east stairs.

Dillon yelled, "Come and get me, you bastards!"

A mob rushed the staircase. This was Betty's opportunity. She pushed into the rear of the mob, fighting her way toward Bernard. She elbowed a dead man in the chest, crushing his ribs into his decomposed lungs and heart. With a sharp pain, he staggered and fell.

Her target was five ghouls ahead, in the crowd. An aluminum bat connected with another's skinless face. He howled in discomfort and tripped.

Betty pushed.

Three ghouls away now.

She kicked.

Two away.

She punched.

There that son of a bitch was, right in front of her.

The group's attention stayed on the man at the top of the stairs. The gun went off twice more, taking out two of the undead army. Four white demons raced away from the platform, toward the sound of gunshots.

Bernard was helpless in his widow's grip, as she dragged him into darkness. His gurgled scream went unnoticed in the angry, roaring chamber. A solitary man followed Betty and her captive. Dillon spotted him and shot him in the back.

White monsters approached. Dillon had to go. He lit a flammable, soggy wick and then threw the unleaded cocktail down as he sprinted away. Flames exploded outward and filled the entrance. Ivory demons stopped at the fiery portal. Needle teeth snapped. Vacant sockets focused through yellow-orange heat. After a moment the first creature shot into the corridor, ignoring the burning fuel.

Dillon ran for his life. Even with a head start, he wasn't more than a few seconds ahead of the evil chasing him. Monica gasped in terror, watching the horrible things enter the hall behind him.

"Oh god," she said as tears flooded her eyes. "Run, Dillon...run."

Betty appeared out of the crowd, pushing a stumbling dead man. He tried to cry out but a wadded piece of torn shirt had been stuffed in his mouth and halfway down his throat. A muffled cough was all he could manage. Betty held both arms behind his back as he struggled against her inhuman strength. "Head for that doorway," she said to Monica.

The three of them entered a dark threshold that was almost directly across from the chamber from where they'd started.

"I'm scared for Dillon," Monica said out of breath.

"Focus, girlfriend," Betty ordered. "He's resourceful. He'll be fine."

Beyond the entrance they found a small, empty room. The dead man was shoved to the dirt face first. A boot in the center of his back held him down as he squirmed to break free. Betty slid the small backpack off her shoulders and then forced it onto her captive. Little Peggy once again found herself next to her killer. Bernard's leathery hands were then bound together with a length of rope. She pulled him to his feet and then clicked a strap together across his chest.

"What if she doesn't show up?" Monica said, eyeing the doorway.

"She'll show," Betty said. "I only hope she can forgive me when she does."

"I'll tie his legs."

Once his legs were tied together at the knees and ankles, Monica shoved him to the floor once again. He hit with a thud, and a muffled yowl sounded as a rib cracked.

"That's what you get, asshole," Betty spat. "You deserve worse."

And so they sat back in the darkness, waiting for the ghost of a little dead girl to arrive. It was the only thing they could do. Two white demons and a sea of undead stood between them and Suzanne. Without Peggy, even a twelve-gauge shotgun and a synthetic soldier didn't stand a chance.

Suzanne's voice went on and on, barely pausing for a breath. All of her gripes, every last complaint, were about Monica. Their friendship apparently had some serious issues, and Tom couldn't figure out for the death of him how they'd become pals to begin with. After twenty straight minutes of listening to her whine, he decided he'd sooner kick her in the face than know her at all. He just kept telling himself, *I'm doing the right thing. It will be over soon.* He was determined to be a good person (or good zombie, in his case), no matter how painful it turned out to be.

A familiar sound from up ahead startled him. It was the growl of a deadly mist demon. A rotten hand instinctively slapped over the jabbering woman's mouth. She let out a muffled "Hey," trying to pull away. He said, "Shhh," with and index finger over his leathery lips. Fortunately, "shhh" in dead speak was also "shhh" in English. Suzanne understood his instruction and snapped her lips closed.

A moment later she heard the reason for the command. The ivory creature was still some distance away but getting closer. Tom pushed her into a doorway and guided her to a dark corner. The two held a deep breath, waiting for the thing to pass by. The demon stopped at the doorway, and Suzanne nearly lost her bladder. Every muscle froze as her eyes went wide.

It sniffed at the air. "Thomas Able," it said. "What are you doing in there?"

The monster was close enough to catch the woman's scent, and Tom knew it. He said, "I'm looking for the innocent. She escaped."

"As am I" was the response. "Have you seen any sign of her?"

"No. But she's close. I can smell her."

Blank eye sockets narrowed. "Yes…her skin saturates the air."

Tom frowned, trying to sound angry. "I'll keep looking."

Mist spiraled and the beast sniffed again. It then turned and disappeared down the corridor. Suzanne allowed herself a breath.

Martin watched the control unit perform its many duties. It processed a million lines of input code simultaneously, calculated response tags based upon a virtual memory library, and transmitted a terabyte of what designers dubbed "action code" every few seconds. It was the most advanced computerized system in existence and operated very much like a human brain.

And all of that cutting-edge technology was happening in a fruit cellar below a dilapidated barn, surrounded by dusty jars of homemade jelly and green beans. The irony was not lost on Martin. Nor was the desire to shut down the stolen equipment and move on to finding the synthetic.

He considered contacting his superiors at the company. Or the police. But, as excitement rushed through his veins—the pure adrenaline high that accompanied discovery—he decided to continue the quest on his own. Besides, retrieving the synthetic would be easy with its control unit shut down. Without its brain, it would be as helpless as a rag doll. He'd simply load it in the van and be on his way.

Dillon sprinted down the corridor with four raging monsters closing in fast. He lit another bottle of gas and turned to throw it behind. It sailed down the hall and exploded on a pale white chest, splashing gasoline and flames over the demon's body. Its cry was that of some prehistoric creature, filling the entire underground labyrinth with deafening rage.

With his pursuers momentarily distracted, he took a left-hand turn, in hopes of finding his way back to the central chamber.

Monica stared at the withered girl in the backpack. The eye sockets in the leathery face were blackened holes. Peggy's expression in death was that of calm sadness—a melancholy acceptance of young dreams cut short. Once blond hair hung twisted over small shoulders, like parched weeds.

Eleven years old, Monica thought.

It was horrible to see one so young, cold and lifeless, after the last breath had been spent. What a cruel joke the world had played upon that unsuspecting little girl. What a way to lose one's innocence.

Tears filled Monica's eyes. She turned away from Peggy and saw that her friend's eyes were wet too. Even as hard as the sight was for her to see, it must've been harder for Betty. They'd been best friends. Monica couldn't imagine what it would feel like to sit by a dead friend, knowing what she was doing would upset her, hurt her, even more.

"We're nearing the exit," Thomas Able said, not that Suzanne could understand him. The mausoleum stairs would be in sight when they rounded the corner at the next intersection. She had no clue what he said, but she'd understood the demon. It had spoken English.

"So, your name is Tom," she said.

He didn't respond. He was too busy scanning for more monsters.

"Thank you, Tom, for helping me."

They made a left turn into the next hallway. She saw the stairs.

"We made it!"

A new energy pulsed through her veins as she ran for freedom. Up ahead, hazy mist washed into the path, with a terrible creature just behind it. Long arms were around her before she could react. A shrill scream echoed throughout the underground labyrinth. With the fresh air of freedom only fifty feet away, Suzanne was dragged back into the shadows. Dead Tom stepped aside to let the demon and its captive pass.

So close, he thought. *We almost made it.*

"Help!" she called out. "Please!"

There was nothing more he could do. Anger made him kick the stone wall.

"She'll never get away now," he slurred. "I should've eaten her brain."

Martin stood in the cellar below the barn with a Phillips screwdriver in hand. He easily found the breaker box and followed the conduit pipe from the control unit across the floor, up the south wall, and behind a row of shelving that stood two feet away from the wall.

With the box's panel door open, he saw only two circuits. One powered the overhead light and a single outlet. The other had a twenty-amp switch and fed electricity into the six-foot-tall computer matrix behind him. He flipped the switch to cut the power. The low hum of the cooling fans continued as he turned to face the unit. The monitor was still alive with lines of encrypted code streaming across in a green radiance.

He approached the machine and knelt at a lower access panel. Three small screws held it in place. When the last had been twisted out, the panel fell toward him, and he set it aside. A row of four tall batteries sat inside the compartment, each responsible for twenty volts of continuous backup energy. Martin unhooked the cord attached to the nearest. A high-pitched chime announced a warning.

Betty's face changed in an instant. Sadness turned to shock. Fear.

Monica said, "What is it?"

In a panic Betty said, "There's someone at the barn. At the control unit."

"What? You mean your brain? The computer that controls you?"

"Yes. They're in the cellar."

"What can we do?"

Betty locked eyes with Monica. "From here? We can't do anything from here."

Dillon heard the radio, faint and crackling, as he sprinted down a dark corridor. The things chasing him were once again closing in. He unhooked the walkie-talkie from his belt and held it up to his ear.

"Dillon? Dillon, can you hear me?" The voice was choppy, but yes, he heard her.

Without slowing down, he spoke into the microphone. "Go ahead."

He bolted right at the next intersection, his lungs heaving for air. He could hear the demon's screaming somewhere in the distance, behind him.

"Get to the van. Go to Betty's house. Someone is messing with the control unit."

Dillon stopped. "What? Someone is at her computer brain?"

Static and then, "Yes. If they tamper with the control unit, Betty could shut down."

Without Betty, they were as good as dead. They needed her strength to save Suzanne and themselves. Dillon turned and ran in the direction he'd come from. His path led him toward the monsters, the things that wanted him dead.

"Tell Betty to hold on," he said into the radio. "I'm going now."

"What's happening now?" Monica asked, keeping a careful eye on the shifting crowd outside the doorway.

"He cut the power at the electrical box. He's at the backup battery compartment now."

Oh no.

"Why is he doing this? Who is he?"

"I don't know," Betty said with panic squeezing. "I'm scared."

Monica knelt down and gave her friend a hug. "Isn't there anything we can do?"

"The system's never been shut down before. I don't know how long it will take to reboot." A faint smile came over her lips. "I'm sorry, girlfriend."

Monica sobbed. "Please don't leave me."

The screen above flashed "Power failure at node one."

He continued, unhooking the line from the second battery.

"Node two power failure. Shut down of major functions imminent."

Betty looked around the dark chamber, confused. "Access library shutdown. I don't remember—"

"Please...I can't do this without you."

Her synthetic eyes struggled to focus.

"I can't..."

The third and the fourth cords popped free in quick succession. The monitor distorted for a moment and then went black. Cooling fans slowed as the hum faded.

Martin stood, looking over the dark control unit.

Satisfied, he said, "That does it."

Betty fell limp. Her body slumped over to the rock floor.

"No!" Monica sobbed.

After ten seconds, it began. Betty's system-failure chime was a piercing, high-pitched beep in the otherwise quiet shadows.

"Too loud," Monica whispered. "Shut the hell up, Betty."

Undead outside the room turned to look. After a few questioning seconds, they began to walk, limp, and stumble through the doorway.

Back in the company van, Martin checked the screen on his laptop. Just as he suspected, the synthetic was still transmitting in the AM frequency. The signal was an endless beacon, a request for data from the control unit. It was coming from the northwest. He slid into the driver's seat and started the engine.

"Shit," Monica said. "Here they come."

There would be no more hiding. The monsters knew she was there. Six dead men stood in the front room with an unending sea of bodies behind. A putrid stench rushed into her face. She gagged, standing and shoving the dual barrels of the shotgun under one's chin. She pulled the trigger, and it sounded like a cannon in the small space.

The unmistakable blast echoed across the cavern beyond. The two remaining mist demons twisted their heads to look. Snapping needle teeth and growling, they lifted into the air. The dead were thrown aside, creating a path through the spoiled crowd. The two shot forward to find the source of the blast.

Monica elbowed, kneed, and kicked at a flood of rotten bodies. She aimed at an approaching tall man with a missing eye. Once again the shotgun pounded the chamber with an ear-ringing detonation. His face exploded, as did the crumbly wall behind. A large boulder above the doorway shifted with loose dirt raining across the floor.

Holy hell, Monica thought. *That thing is about to fall in.* And then, *A cave-in.* She knew the demons were coming. She couldn't fight them, not without Betty, but maybe she could block them out.

She pushed through the dead. They grabbed, yanked, and groped her as she went. The butt of the gun tore a jaw free with molars exploding into dust. An arm of another disconnected with a twist and a pull. He yowled, bending down to retrieve the appendage. At the entrance Monica saw a familiar white face with long fangs approaching. She looked up and found a crease in the ceiling beside the boulder. She jammed in the shotgun barrel and pulled the trigger. Debris hailed over her face as the stone fell.

———

A demon arrived just as the barricade of rock settled in the threshold with a violent quake. A dead man was pinned down at the waist by the boulder. He screamed, spewing dark fluid. Another's leg was caught underneath. She scratched at the floor, slurring something incoherent. Only three were left standing to oppose Monica. Another shell from the gun took care of two. The last was bludgeoned with the barrel until he quit moving. She turned to face the blocked entrance. Screeching, angry demons sounded from outside.

And then a voice. A human voice.

"Monica, is that you?" said Mayor Gordon.

She said nothing.

He laughed. "It seems you've blocked your only escape route. There are no other exits." He was amused as always. "You will die in there. I would like to help you, but I'm quite busy."

Monica sat in the darkness, listening to an awful man say terrible things. She hated him.

"Your friend from the city…what was her name again?" He paused slightly, pretending to care about an answer to his question. "No matter. She will be sacrificed at midnight. I will then merge with the demon king, and the dark power will be mine."

She gritted teeth, set the shotgun aside, and took Betty's hand.

Please come back.

"Oh, and Monica?" he said in his friendliest voice. "Happy Halloween."

12

GARY

Renee sat in the van, looking over the shadowy grounds. All was quiet on the surface of the cemetery. There was no one in sight. Not a ghost or a ghoul. Not a demon or a zombie. The fear for her husband and the others had shifted into boredom.

I should have gone with them, she thought.

There was nothing for her to do here except count gravestones, and she'd grown tired of that more than twenty minutes ago.

Static snapped over the radio, and her eyes went wide. She claimed it from the dash.

"Dillon, dear? Is that you?" she said into the microphone.

Silence.

She then held it up to her ear. Nothing for a moment and then "Renee?"

"Yes! I hear you!"

"Start the van!" He sounded out of breath.

"Okay, dear."

In the driver's seat, Renee turned the key over. The van revved to life. Static faded into his voice again. "Put it in drive!"

Two gunshots sounded from inside the mausoleum.

Renee gasped. *Something's after him.*

She pulled the shift lever over to the drive position. Her heart pounded.

"Hurry, dear."

The figure of a man appeared from the staircase below. He ran with a pronounced limp. It was Dillon. Four white demons emerged from the underground. The one in the lead scanned the area and then raced after him.

"Oh god!" Renee screamed. "Run, Dillon dear! Run!"

He leapt into the open side door, yelling, "Go! Floor it!" She didn't hesitate to follow orders, and the vehicle was soon up to thirty miles per hour and then forty.

An ivory fist hit a rear door and metal buckled. Renee screamed, turning onto the road. With the van straightened out, she got it up to fifty.

A thick shoulder impacted the driver's side. Metal popped inward, making a deep, four-foot-long indent in the van's wall. Dillon squeezed off two shots with the pistol. A cry of demonic pain informed him that he'd hit his pursuer. The chase was abandoned. Dillon watched as the monsters turned back toward the cemetery.

"Head for Betty's house."

"Betty's house? What—"

"I'll explain along the way, dear. Just go."

The van sat parked with its engine running two blocks east of Betty's house. Dillon had spotted the deputy's vehicle on their first pass around the block. Following his instruction, Renee did not slow down or stop at the house. Not with the sheriff's car watching.

Dillon knew they couldn't trust anyone, especially those who worked so closely with the mayor. Who knew what kind of influence he had over them.

Dillon snuck around the back yard, staying out of sight behind the barn. He found an opening down low in the wall, where he could crawl through. Once inside he stood and peered into the darkness. A section of floor was open, held by an eyebolt, a hook, and rope tied off to a beam. Below was a ramp that led to the cellar.

He fumbled with the flashlight and then found the switch. A circle of illumination cut a path to the entrance and Dillon followed. He listened for signs of another presence but heard nothing except his own footsteps. At the bottom of the ramp sat a tall metal box the size of a small camping trailer. He walked around the corner, swiping the beam of light over a dirt floor and then across shelves stacked with canned vegetables and jelly.

He pointed a beam at the control unit. It sat silent with a panel removed and set aside. Inside the compartment with the missing cover, four cables lay unattached from four tall batteries. Above was a dead monitor screen on the wall of the unit.

Someone has been here.

He knelt down at the opening in the synthetic brain, pulling a pair of needle-nose pliers from his back pocket.

"All right, Betty," he said. "Let's get you thinking again."

With all four cables attached to battery power once again, Dillon threw the breaker on at the electrical box. He watched with anticipation, expecting the machine to do something. Anything. But nothing happened.

There must be a reset switch or button.

He explored high and low. At the front of the control unit he discovered a small metal door. With it open, he saw a series of gauges and rows of red buttons. Luckily the description of each was printed on labels along the side. He pressed one called "Power grid reset." Beyond hearing a click under his index finger, nothing happened. He found one called "Initiate boot sequence." It clicked also but was then followed by the hum of ten cooling fans. When they got up to speed, a single beep sounded from somewhere close to the monitor, about six feet away. Dillon went to investigate.

The screen was still dark, but a green underscore cursor blinked on and off at the top left. He stared at the metronome flash for nearly a minute, waiting for something more impressive to occur. Just as he gave up and turned back toward the reset switches, it did.

The sound of twenty-three servers accessing more than a hundred hard drives filled the cellar. Startled, Dillon jumped.

The cursor on the monitor was replaced with the words "Systems check in progress. Main control boot in approximately 14 minutes."

Feeling somewhat relieved, he sat down on the floor, leaned against the wall, and waited.

Monica checked her watch. It was ten thirty. Time was running out, and a rising fear made her feel as though she might jump right out of her skin. Betty was motionless, beeping away like an alarm clock. They hadn't heard back from Dillon in at least forty-five minutes. Peggy hadn't shown up. She was trapped and alone, waiting and pacing the floor in a maddening stride. Her patience had failed, and "stir crazy" didn't do justice to what she felt. It didn't come close to explaining the anxiety pulling at her jangled nerves. She couldn't think. Could barely breathe. Sobs burst from her in seizure-like explosions.

Across the room dead Bernie strained against his bonds, kicking and rolling side to side. The purple backpack was covered in dirt. Peggy's face struck the ground occasionally in the wake of her killer's enthusiasm.

With another kick his feet hit the wall, and a rock broke free as mortar crumbled. Monica walked closer. A black hole in the surface seemed to call her name. With a flashlight in hand, she kneeled down to look inside. It was another small room adjacent to the one she was trapped in.

Oh my god.

With a tug, three more stones fell away. There was just enough space to crawl through, at least she hoped so. She grabbed the shotgun and sent it through the hole first. Then Monica removed her thick coat and shimmied into the next room, which was about the same size as the last.

She soon found herself just outside the bright entrance that led into the massive cavern, next to a formation of rock about four feet tall. Monica ducked low and crept through the doorway. She peeked over the stone to see the shifting undead awaiting instructions from their master. The gathering kept to the center of the expanse, mostly, and if she stayed close to the west wall, she thought she might make it behind the altar undetected.

The two ivory demons once again stood at each end of the platform, facing inward. The mayor wasn't in sight, nor was Suzanne. Surely they'd bring her out soon, but for the moment she remained hidden in a room beyond. Monica made her way carefully through shadows, behind boulders, and around crumbling stone walls and random piles of broken headstones. At the rear of the stage, she entered another doorway in hopes that her friend was somewhere inside.

Dillon sat staring into the monitor. Lines of code trailed across the screen, indicating the reboot of major systems had begun. "I hope that will do it," he said standing up.

Once out of the cellar, he crawled through the broken opening where he'd come in. When he got to his feet, he saw Deputy Stanley Ackerman pointing a revolver in his direction.

"And who might you be?" Ackerman asked.

Dillon raised his hands into the air. "Oh my," he blurted. "I'm Dillon, a friend of Betty's. She asked me to attend to something for her. I am not a criminal."

A goat wandered around the corner of the barn, sporting a leather collar with an attached length of broken twine. Dillon didn't notice the animal. The gun aimed at his face commanded all of his attention.

"Keep your hands where I can see them, please."

"Of course."

"A friend of Betty's, huh? She is currently a fugitive herself. Knowing her won't help you. Tell me where she is."

A line of perspiration ran down Dillon's cheek, in spite of the frigid breeze. "I'm sure I don't know."

Ackerman grinned. "You do know. And you're gonna tell me."

"Really. I don't kn—"

"Shut your mouth. Turn around and face the barn. Assume the position."

Dillon turned toward chipped red paint. The barrel of the gun pressed into the back of his skull.

The deputy leaned close. "The safety on this weapon is tricky. Sometimes it works and other times...Other times it just goes off. You know what I mean?"

Dillon's breath failed. Every muscle in his body turned to rubber. It was all he could do to remain standing with palms against the wood siding.

The deputy continued. "I think we understand each other now. Tell me what you know, or I repaint the barn."

A woman's voice startled them from behind. "Excuse me," she said. Ackerman pulled the gun away from Dillon's head and turned. A steel bat swung hard with Renee stepping into it like a pro. Metal met the side of the deputy's head, and a hollow *thunk* announced his departure into dreamland. He fell face first to the dirt.

Dillon spun around to see his wife smiling and holding a Louisville Slugger with a spot of blood over the logo.

"Renee," he gasped. "I believe that man meant to shoot me."

She bent down, claimed the revolver from the ground, and then kicked at the unconscious body. It didn't respond. "I believe he did, dear," she said, handing him a weapon that had just been used to threaten his life. "Now grab his handcuffs while I take off his pants."

"Why on earth are you taking off his pants?"

"Because people should be reluctant to help a naked man handcuffed to a goat."

Dillon looked over to the animal as it chewed away at its cud, reeking of dried urine. He then thought about the gun barrel pressed against the back of his head.

He looked at his wife. "I'll see if I can catch the goat."

The van slid to a stop over loose gravel. Renee looked over the cemetery grounds, trying to notice any movement in the shadows. Everything was quiet. The mausoleum seemed deserted.

"We should wait here," she said to her husband. "They are likely on their way out by now."

Dillon rubbed his chin. "No. I need to go help them if I can. I won't abandon the original plan." He checked the pistol clip and then slid it back in.

Renee grabbed his hand. "But dear…"

He squeezed her fingers and then pulled away. "I'm sorry. I have to do this. All my life I thought my purpose was to prove the existence of an afterlife. But that doesn't matter anymore. I know that what is happening now, all of this, is the reason for my life. This is an opportunity to save a life. Destiny has brought me to this, and I won't turn my back on it."

Conviction radiated from his words like a light in the darkness. Renee knew he couldn't be stopped. He was going and nothing, not even she, could talk him out of it.

"Be careful," she whispered with a faint smile.

"Of course."

He opened the door and headed for the mausoleum.

Deputy Stanley Ackerman woke with a stabbing headache. His entire body felt like a block of ice. His vision was blurry, but it didn't hinder his awareness of the situation he'd found himself in. He was naked as the day he was born. His wrists were bound behind him and held aloft by something that was moving. The stench of old urine was close by. A tug nearly dislocated his shoulders from the sockets. He turned to see Henry the billy goat walking away and attempting to drag him along. The deputy had been handcuffed to the animal's leather collar, a fact that neither he nor the goat appreciated.

He stumbled to his feet, scanning the ground. His clothing and weapon were gone. Dizziness stirred at his wobbly knees.

"Somebody help me," he said.

A man in a house across the street gazed out the window at the odd sight. "That's somethin' you don't see every day," he said, laughing, before closing the blinds. He called to his wife, who was in the laundry room unloading the dryer. "Come in here, honey."

She was busy, but he was pretty sure she'd want to see this.

Eddie Gordon squinted into the shadow at the back of the room, the one that held the woman. She had red hair, a feature that pleased him very much. He liked redheads. He also liked the fact that she was well endowed in the chest. A great pair of lungs, as the old-timers might say. He grinned, gazing into her cleavage.

She saw him looking. "My face is up here, asshole."

He cleared his throat. "Yes...now that we have put a stop to your little escape attempt, things can get back on track."

"I'm sure my friend called the sheriff. They'll be here any minute to arrest your fat ass."

Sheriff Shane stepped up from behind the mayor, chuckling. "Oh, I'm already here, honey pie." He spit a glob of brown juice to the floor. It splattered across gray stone.

Gordon went to the doorway. "Bring her," he ordered.

Shane closed in on Suzanne with a length of rope. "Hold still, girlie."

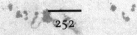

She did not follow instructions.

Monica searched room after room but found nothing except the same dank emptiness in each. "Come on. Where are you?" As if on cue, the answer made itself abundantly clear.

Suzanne's piercing scream spread out across the cavern and echoed down corridors. Fearing the worst, Monica ran. She crossed the threshold into the light with sneakers scraping to a halt over loose dirt. Finally, she'd found Suzanne. The one she'd kicked in the forehead over a pile of Legos, the one who'd kept her sane when life didn't seem worth living. The one person who had believed in her when no one else did. Her friend.

Monica and Suzanne's eyes met, and they both burst into tears. Suzanne cried, "Monica, help me!" Monica looked over a crowd of undead and deadly white demons. She suddenly realized that they were looking her over too.

It was twenty minutes until midnight. The time for hiding was over. It was time for what she'd come here to do. Save Suzanne.

Or die trying.

A black company van went past the north side of the mausoleum at five miles per hour. It turned right and parked along the east entrance. Martin checked the computer screen on the dash once more before stepping out of the vehicle. Thick letters on the van's wall read "Synergy Dynamics."

He looked up the length of the dark building and then around the graveyard. This was the place the satellite imaging system had zoomed in on. He was positive of that. And the synthetic was somewhere inside. So down the staircase he went with flashlight in hand.

The smell was sour. Voices whispered from every direction. In a panic, he swiped the beam of light over five pale faces, and then five more. The unbelievable things surrounding him closed in, growling. They were quick. They were ruthless.

And they were hungry.

With the last knot tight and the redhead successfully tied down to the altar, Shane faced the intruder. He reached for his side arm. "You're in way over your head, sweet knees."

Monica pulled the hammer down. The shot blasted the sheriff off his feet. He yowled. Blood flowed from his belly as tobacco juice ran down his chin.

Monica spat, "Don't call me sweet knees."

The devil Chihuahua stepped up growling, its eyes glowing blood red. It barked orders at two ivory demons. They rushed the platform with teeth snapping. Monica flexed and aimed her weapon. "Here we go."

"Kill her!" Gordon yelled from a distance. The twelve-gauge blasted into a powder-white skull, sending a monster stumbling back. She swung the butt of the weapon around, connecting with the second one's jaw. Spindly teeth smashed, and the blood of the damned spattered.

Long claws swiped at her. She jumped out of reach, retreating behind an outcropping of rock. A white face dotted with bright red found her, and the barrel found the inside of its mouth as she jammed it in. The shell tore the back of its head into bloody mush. The demon slumped to the floor with fluids gurgling. Monica spun around to see the other hovering above a cloud of wet mist. She aimed and squeezed the trigger. The hammer clicked shut, the chamber was empty.

"Shit."

The horrible thing was over her in an instant. Long red streaks drooled as teeth snapped. It paused to savor the moment, wheezing. "You die now." Slowly, its mouth opened as if to swallow her whole.

Monica, frozen with fear, squeezed her eyes tight. Her time had come.

I'm sorry, Suzanne.

A freshly sharpened axe struck from behind. The blade sunk deep into white flesh at the base of the demon's neck. It screamed in agony as it fell to its knees, gagging.

Monica opened her eyes to see a tall, thick man with a not-so-bright look on his dirty face. In shock she asked, "Who are you?"

"I done some bad things," Gary said as he unwedged the blade from the demon's neck. "I'm here to make amends."

Surprised to still be among the living, she couldn't think of anything to say besides "Oh."

Gary raised the bloodied axe up to eye level, studying the length of it, caressing it like a lover. They'd been through a lot together; they'd done terrible things but now was their chance to make up for it. This was their opportunity to do something right. He lowered his old friend and spoke to the girl. "I'll help you. Jus' tell me what to do."

Moans of every sort resounded from the undead mob. The devil Chihuahua's barking and growling went on and on. Suzanne's screams seemed never to pause, even to take a breath. But the one sound, the one voice Monica couldn't stand was Gordon's. His words were an iron spike in her nerves. He yelled, "Kill them! Kill them!"

She looked up to her new partner. "I'd appreciate it if you could kill the mayor."

Gary Tuttlebaulm grinned. "That I'd be very happy to do for you."

Dead bodies rushed the platform. The long axe swung, sending two and three at a time flying back in pain. One chop decapitated two rotten men in a single swipe. He grabbed a skinless sternum and heaved the body at an approaching slurring infantry. They fell like decomposed bowling pins.

"Glad he's on my side," Monica said with amazement.

She went to untie Suzanne.

Monica clicked open a pocket knife and sawed through the rope at the bound woman's wrists.

"Hurry," Suzanne said in a panic.

The project was put on hold to shoot a drooling woman with a missing nose. After the shell finished its work, she was missing a few more things. The shot was right above the flailing redhead on the altar. Her ears rang. Monica continued cutting.

A leathery man appeared at the end of the stone platform, at Suzanne's feet. He growled, holding a brick in the air. She kicked with legs tied at the ankles and struck the man in the face. He stumbled back with the heel of her right shoe pointing from a nostril.

Gordon pushed through the dead crowd in a panic, away from an approaching serial killer. The man with the axe shoved, chopped, and stomped right behind. The mayor tripped and fell to the floor, crying out in pain. He rolled over and saw a thick blade stained with demon blood held high, ready to strike.

"If you hurt me, Elton dies!"

Gary frowned. "So be it," he said as he brought the weapon down.

Halfway through the swing he was tackled by a white monster. Their two bodies tumbled to the dirt in a painful collision. The demon's right arm hung limp at its side with blood running from the wound in its neck. The left arm swiped at the human. Three sharp talons cut deep across Gary's chest. He responded with a swing of the axe. All the strength he possessed was behind that swing. When it connected, it severed the monster at the neck, just below the jaw. A powder-white head sailed over the moaning ghouls like a volleyball. It disappeared into the sea of bodies.

Feeling somewhat victorious, Gary stood with eyes scanning for a fat man. He saw the mayor. He also saw four mist creatures, like the one he'd just put down, racing toward him. He narrowed his eyes and waited for them to arrive.

"Bring it, bitches," he growled.

With a final slice, Suzanne was free. The two women looked across the cavern for the safest escape route. A hundred feet away, four demons rushed the man with the axe. "No!" Monica yelled, pushing through tangled, groping arms. The path between her and Gary was thick with fiends. Up ahead the ivory monsters overwhelmed him. He fell as blood sprayed.

Oh god, Monica thought. *He's dead.*

She turned to see Suzanne being dragged back to the altar. The Chihuahua, with eyes blazing like rubies, stood on the platform, growling.

"Suzanne!"

With Gary dead, the demons sped toward Monica. She fired the shotgun at the first and then the second. She fumbled for fresh shells, but the third had her in a stranglehold in an instant. Long, unnatural fingers tightened as she gasped. The gun fell to the floor. The demon's face was close, smiling. Needle teeth snapped.

The crowd fell silent. Death's anticipation seemed to consume even the smallest sounds, leaving only the faintest chime from behind the fallen boulder. Almost inaudible, it beeped on and on. Razor talons drew back, ready to strike. Monica gritted her teeth.

Eleven-year-old Peggy Wyne flashed in her mind. An innocent life cut so short. She hadn't deserved to die, but what we deserve means very little at the moment of death. When hope is lost and dreams are reduced to forgotten blurs, the world ices over. It is seen for what it truly is. A cold and ruthless distraction from the void.

Successes and failures.

Regrets and happiness.

Love and loss.

12: GARY

——

None of it held meaning anymore.

It was gone.

All gone.

Monica closed her eyes.

13

HALLOWEEN

Silence stretched out across the cavern, below the cemetery and the lake. It hung in the still air, stagnant with rotten flesh. It even found its way behind a fallen boulder.

Inside, beyond the barricade of stone, a woman stood. She remembered one of those things had said she wasn't real. It had called her fake.

Betty wasn't human; that was sure. She didn't have a mother; her mind was a complex network of processors and data strewn over dozens of hard drives. Her body hadn't been born. It was built in a laboratory. There'd been many days when she dreamt of being like everyone else.

But not being human didn't make her any less real. She was aware. She had consciousness. She felt emotion and was capable of love.

If only for today, it was enough.

It had to be.

A rock wall exploded into the cavern. Chunks of earth and stone flew over the gathering of death. All eyes focused on the hole that remained as dust settled. A figure appeared at the new opening. In the monster's grasp, Monica opened her eyes.

Betty stepped into the light, gripping an aluminum bat. She smiled. "Remember me?"

Four creatures of the mist screamed with rage.

The monster released its tight grip, and Monica fell to the hard floor. She coughed, gasping for air.

Suzanne stomped at the foot of a dead man beside her. The heel of her remaining shoe drove deep into flesh. He wailed as he hopped away and then fell. An elbow to the chin of another caught him off guard. His grip around her left arm released. She spun around to see the blond woman a hundred feet away, standing atop a boulder.

With bat in hand, Betty waited for the monsters. The first felt the power of a home-run swing impact its chest. It screamed and recoiled in agony. The second and third swiped long talons at the synthetic. She dodged and then leapt into the air, over the moaning mob, and disappeared into a thick gathering. A dog pile of reeking dead stumbled and fell on top of her. She shoved, kicked, and punched. One after another, leathery bodies were thrust into the air, like popcorn from a hot skillet.

A clearing grew as the fearful crowd backed away. Betty stood in the empty circle, more determined than ever. She pointed at a hovering demon. It raced down with long claws spread and fangs open wide. She wiped her nose with the back of a hand and cocked her weapon.

This one's goin' over the fence.

Dillon ran down a dark corridor. He checked his watch. It read 11:58 p.m.

Two minutes to midnight, he thought. He pushed his stride faster, dreading what would happen when the clock struck twelve. It would be Halloween, and the devil that threatened them all would be at full power. The ritual could begin the transfer of energy to Gordon. And Dillon had a pretty good idea that what they would find at the altar would no longer be a little dog.

"Betty!" Monica screamed, forcing her way closer. The blonde swung hard, sending an ivory monster reeling. She turned. "Get Suzanne out of here!"

Monica found her friend from the city pushing through a sea of grabby rot.

The mayor smiled on center stage. Looking down at his watch he saw 11:59 p.m. click over to midnight, and he laughed. A new day was upon them, and that day just happened to be Halloween.

All Hallows' Eve.

The day of the dead.

Gordon looked down and locked eyes with Monica. His voice turned to gravel.

"Trick or treat."

Betty was pinned to the cold stone floor by three demons as the fourth approached. A rush of the undead overwhelmed Monica and Suzanne.

The demon was a little dog no more. It stood at the altar with its muscles twitching, changing into new and bizarre forms. It transformed into a bobcat, then an alligator, and then a turkey. Unsatisfied, it shifted into a lion, then a tiger, and then a grizzly bear. The devil roared in the bear's mighty voice, pleased with its choice. Every eye in the cavern zeroed in on the evil at the platform.

"Holy God," Monica said.

"Oh shit," Suzanne gasped.

Betty frowned. "Well, that sucks."

The early minutes of October 31 found Monica Green standing amid three hundred dead things in a cavern below Lakeshore Cemetery, fumbling for shotgun shells.

Her friend Suzanne, a person who she'd once kicked in the face in a dispute over Legos, the one she'd come to save, was being dragged back toward the altar in the grip of vile zombies.

Yes, *zombies*.

Her abstinence of the Z-word was forgotten under the weight of dire circumstances.

Betty, a woman who she'd met just weeks before, a synthetic manmade machine (with a consciousness and a conscience, no less) was pinned to the ground by a group of unearthly demons. Mist demons, to be precise. Each was a horror of terrible strength and unholy intentions.

Her new friends Dillon and Renee hadn't made it back yet but would likely be of little consequence if and when they did arrive.

If that weren't enough, a devil of unimaginable power stood poised and ready to strike, as a grizzly bear.

That was Monica's situation. Her lot. The card she'd been dealt. The figurative hole she'd found herself in.

But there was one thing she'd nearly forgotten. One person that could make all the difference.

Little Peggy Wyne.

And man was she pissed.

An explosion of light crackled above the crowd. Intense pain washed over the bodies below as a small apparition took form in the haze. Dead men and demons alike fell to their knees, wailing.

Betty smiled up at the ghost of a little dead girl. "Peggy," she said, "you came."

Opal eyes focused on her. "You brought me back! Now I'm really mad!"

Hair hung down over a clammy, transparent face. Small fists clenched with rage. Toes curled downward as filmy legs kicked. The nightgown thrashed side to side as Peggy threw an angry tantrum.

"I'm sorry, Peg," Betty whispered.

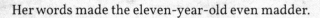

Her words made the eleven-year-old even madder.

"Don't say it! Don't say it! Don't say it!"

The dead flooded through doorways to escape the stabbing radiance. Only two of the undead remained unaffected by the ghost's power: Thomas Able and Georgette Gordon.

Tom followed the crowd out of the chamber.

Georgette, with a scowl of hate on her leathery face, approached her husband.

Suzanne ran to Monica. They embraced in the center of the chamber. White demons cowered as the ghost raged. To them, her energy was devastating. The mist creatures twitched in a paralyzing seizure on the floor. Peggy pulled at her own stringy hair and flailed, screaming.

"I'm sorry, Peg. I wouldn't have done it unless I had too," Betty said. "I love you."

The little girl's eyes softened. Her ghostly muscles eased. "I love you too," she said in a small voice.

A demon snapped its jaws, getting to his feet. "Stay where you are!" Peggy commanded, pointing at the creature. It grimaced and fell back down, yowling.

Betty smiled at her friend. "If you help me this one time, I swear I'll let you rest forever."

"Fine" was the response. "I'll do it for you."

"Thanks."

The two other women joined them and then looked up to the altar. A grizzly bear growled, unaffected by the ghost's power. Gordon stood with confidence at its side.

"It's quite a team you've assembled, ladies. But it won't be enough." He laughed. "The demon is at full power. You haven't stopped anything."

Monica stepped up. "It's over, Gordon. This ends now."

The mayor put a chubby hand on the animal's back. "Oh, you're right. This does end now." He looked down. "Kill them."

Betty pushed at the others. "Both of you, get out of here."

The bear leapt from the platform, racing.

"No," Monica protested. "We're not leaving you."

"Yes, you are." The blonde looked up to her hovering partner. "Me and Peg will take care of this asshole."

The huge animal closed the gap, snarling.

"But—"

"No. Use the dynamite. Flood this whole damned place."

Monica saw the fear in Suzanne's eyes. The panic. "Okay," she said. "Run." The brunette and the redhead raced for the corridor. The devil turned to chase them.

"No, you don't," Betty said, bringing the bat down. Rounded metal connected with a wide skull, plowing it into dirt and hard stone. It swiped long claws in a lightning attack, cutting two deep gashes in Betty's arm. She recoiled and then punched. Animal teeth and blood detonated under her fist. In a flash the bear morphed into a tiger with a fresh set of sharp teeth.

"I don't see how that's fair," Betty complained.

The striped animal circled around her, roaring. Then, it pounced.

Monica sprinted down a dark corridor, searching for the jagged rock and the dynamite. Then her sneakers crunched to a halt. "I think it's down this way."

"Let's just get outa here!" Suzanne yelled.

"No. We need to find it." She took off down an intersecting hallway. "Come on!"

"Damn it," Suzanne said, jogging to catch up.

Little Peggy closed in on Mayor Gordon. "You are a bad, bad man!"

"Move along, girl. You're blocking my view of the action," he said, stretching to see around her.

"You want action?" She raised small arms and four white demons ascended into the air, struggling. She thrust hands at the man, and the ivory bodies responded. One after another, demons flew at him like rag dolls. He dived for cover, screaming.

"Cool," Peggy said. "That's fun."

"There it is!" Monica called out. The explosives were just where they'd left them with a long cord connected to the handheld detonator.

"What are you gonna do with that?" the redhead asked.

"I'm gonna set it off and flood the place."

"*We* are in this place! We'll drown!"

Monica pointed down a south corridor. "The exit is fifty yards that way."

"Fifty yards?"

"Yeah. Run."

Monica unwound the detonator cord as far as it would go. It gave her a hundred feet of distance from the blast. It would have to be enough. She ducked down and aimed her face away from the dynamite.

"I hate water." She pinched her eyes shut and then cranked the switch. The explosion rocked the underground labyrinth in a devastating quake. Thick stone at the heart of the blast cracked and fell away, blocking the passage.

Monica was thrown to the dirt. She scrambled to her feet and ran. A wall of high-pressure water filled the dark space in an instant. She sucked in a deep breath and held it. The depth of the lake overtook her, and she was propelled like an out-of-control torpedo. Her body bounced from one corridor wall to the next, surrounded by frothy rushing water. The underground river hit a stairwell. Monica shot up and out, onto the cemetery grounds. She landed painfully in softening mud.

A spray went fifty feet into the air behind her. In a great arc, it traveled over headstones and huddled gatherings of undead. Water ran into graves and squirted from under the mausoleum doorway. It sprang upward from random geysers across the graveyard. Monica knew that it was also filling the cavern below.

"Okay, Betty. I did it just like you wanted. Now get out of there."

Gordon ducked behind the platform as a little dead girl heaved demons in his direction. "I command you to help me!" he yelled at the tiger. Across the cavern the creature was busy attacking the blonde and paid no attention. The mayor narrowly dodged another ivory body, falling to his knees.

A dead female appeared from behind. A long scar across her chest exposed a snapped sternum with ribs pointing outward like poison spikes. Hair matted with dried blood framed her pale, angry face. It was his deceased wife, and she had a bone to pick with him.

"Georgette!" he said in disbelief.

"Yes, dear. It's me," she responded in slathering dead speech. "You let me die. I've come to return the favor."

Cold fingers constricted around his throat. She slammed his skull down onto a sharp rock. He screamed in pain. Georgette kneeled next to her husband and thrust his head against the stone, over and over.

With a final slam it cracked like a walnut.

An unnatural rising of voices moaned, gurgled, and slurred from the other side of the mausoleum. Monica slid two fresh shells into the shotgun.

"Come on," she ordered, jogging toward the sound.

Suzanne followed. Once around the corner of the building, they saw a white van surrounded by the living dead. Rotten fists pounded on metal and glass as Renee screamed from inside.

"Hey assholes!" Monica said. "Over here!"

The mob turned to face her. Suzanne grabbed her friend's arm.

"What did you do that for?"

Monica pulled away from the French-manicured grip.

"We can't just let them kill Renee."

"Sure we can."

"No, we can't."

"Fine," the redhead huffed, "But you're the only one with a weapon."

Monica said, "Find something," before taking off toward the van.

Suzanne announced, "Screw this," and ran in the other direction.

Suzanne found out that not all of the dead were at the van. The stinking decomposed were everywhere. A gathering closed in from the west. She ran east. Another crowd stood waiting to the east. She ran north.

"They're friggin' everywhere."

She saw a small tool shed and sprinted for it. She tried the door. It had been barricaded from the inside. Around at the window she saw a splintered piece of plywood and broken glass. Cursing, she climbed inside. A reeking man right behind her swiped through the opening.

A power drill sat on a bench with a long bit inserted. She snapped it up and pulled the trigger, testing it. The electric motor revved and the bit spun.

"Ha! Who's laughing now?" she said, feeling superior.

She walked over and thrust her newfound weapon at the thing's face. At six inches from his forehead, slack in the cord ran out, and the plug yanked out of the wall socket. The tool was suddenly much less impressive as it decelerated to a halt.

"That sucks," she said, spinning around to find something else.

In desperation, Renee yanked at the generator's pull cord. The smell of gas was thick; she knew the motor was flooded. That did not keep her from trying. At least fifty spoiled people stood around the van, pushing, punching, prying, and yelling. The doors were locked. She had double and triple checked each one, including the sliding side door. It had made her feel relatively safe a few minutes ago, but as the side and rear glass began to crack under a pounding assault, panic erased all illusions of security.

A length of broken two-by-four struck the spidered window at the back door. Glass exploded at Renee and she screamed. A skinless arm reached inside, groping for the lock.

A shotgun barrel shoved against his neck, and the deafening blast sent a head tumbling over the crowd. Monica grinned.

"Stay in there, Renee. I got this."

The length of the gun became a makeshift staff as the dead fell away one after another. The generator finally sputtered to life, chugging at first and then smoothing a bit.

"I got it!" Renee exclaimed, cranking the microwave on. All at once, zombies fell to the ground, putting leathery hands to their temples.

Monica looked across the grounds for Suzanne. She was nowhere in sight. Without warning, the tall vehicle was lifted to its side in a powerful grip. A scream sounded from inside as Renee was thrown to the driver's side wall, which now lay flat on the ground. Monica looked around a rear tire, which now pointed east, and saw a cloud of mist spiraling around a hazy figure. Needle teeth snapped. Its eyes were vacant holes, looking right at her.

"Shit," she said to the ivory threat. "You were supposed to drown."

The generator died, the microwave shut down, and the dead got to their rotten feet.

A distant quake shook the cavern as Betty rolled away from the tiger's jaws. She smashed the beast across the spine with the bat. Vertebrae crunched and the animal stumbled. Once again, it morphed into a new and terrible thing. Betty watched as lion's claws appeared and wings expanded, growing long feathers. The head of an eagle screeched to life, and the body of a lion flexed. It had become a griffin, a mythical creature from legend.

Betty frowned. "Okay, now you're just making shit up."

It launched forward and had her right leg in its beak, slicing through tender skin. With a whip of its head, it vaulted Betty across the chamber. She hit the far wall, grunting, and then fell thirty feet to the floor.

A rumble sounded down the corridors, getting louder. After a moment great rivers of muddy water blasted in from the east passages. Tremendous pressure eroded underground hallways into crumbling viaducts. The floor of the cavern was suddenly covered in an inch of water and getting deeper at a surprising rate.

Betty grinned. "You did it, girlfriend."

Waves splashed under the griffin's feet as it charged. The synthetic soldier stood ready, planting her feet.

The east wall crumbled away with a tidal wave behind it. Betty and the monster were thrown off their feet and submerged in fifty feet of icy Stone Lake. The raging current slammed them against the west wall. Pain registered over every inch of Betty's frame. She ignored the paralyzing sensation and swam for the surface.

The griffin sucked water into its lungs, struggling against a powerful undertow. Through the bubbly murk it saw its victim swimming. In an instant, the creature's body elongated. Fur and feathers disappeared. Row after row of sharp teeth formed. A dorsal fin grew tall over an arched back. It was now the deadliest predator in the deep cavern.

Betty looked back and saw a great white shark racing toward her. She suddenly realized her weapon was gone. She clenched her fists.

The monster moved with fluid speed. It bit down on a thin ankle, stripping skin away as it pulled. Betty kicked hard, breaking rows of shark teeth with the exposed composite fiber heel of her synthetic foot. A cloud of blood danced as broken fangs drifted.

With her head above water, Betty saw someone struggling to swim toward her. At first she thought it was the mayor. After a horrifying moment she realized it wasn't.

"Dillon!" she cried out.

The shark turned to come up behind him.

"Look out!" Betty yelled as she swam. She arrived just as open jaws zeroed in. With Dillon in her tight grip, she kicked, and her foot caught the shark's nose. They were propelled across the surface with a cold spray pelleting their faces. Momentum slammed Dillon below until Betty yanked him up. He emerged, coughing lake water from his lungs.

"What are you doing here?"

"I came back to help," he forced out.

The shark was coming again, skimming the surface. She caught its gaping jaws with sharp teeth, slicing through the palms of her hands. Straining, she held the powerful mouth from snapping closed. Dillon suppressed his panic as one cohesive thought made him reach for the pistol.

Its weakness is in its chest.

He sucked in a deep breath and plunged underwater. Betty and the monster thrashed with every muscle flexing to kill and survive. He aimed at where he assumed the beast's heart should be. The first shot hit the stomach. Another punched into the throat. The next missed as a huge tail whipped in his direction.

Come on, he thought. *I can do this.*

Betty heard a crack as bones in the huge jaw fractured. The devil's vice only tightened in a rage. Her fingers slipped, and she lost her grip. A shot from below found its target. The shark's body seized and twitched.

In shock, Betty watched it drift away. "You did it!" she called out.

Dillon's head popped up for oxygen, gasping.

"You killed it!"

Still heaving, he managed a smile. "Then my death shall not be in vain."

"Your death? No. You're not gonna die."

She scanned the stone roof of the cavern for an escape route. She could see no way out. Tears streamed down her wet cheeks, unnoticed.

He smiled. "Monica set off the explosives?"

Her answer was a solemn whisper. "Yes."

"Good girl. This evil place has been destroyed. The mayor is dead. We win."

"We'll find a way out. We will."

"No, Betty. You will. You can swim down and out one of the corridors. But I'm afraid I can't hold my breath that long."

"No. I'll go get help."

He put tender hands over her shoulders. "The water level is rising quickly. It will be up to the ceiling in a few minutes. I won't survive." His words were calm, his eyes reassuring. "I didn't expect to return. It's okay. My life wasn't for nothing. I can see the meaning in it now...I helped save people from him."

Her tears turned to sobs. "No. I'm not letting you die."

"Betty. Thank you. Thank you for letting me be part of such a grand task."

———

She took him in her arms and hugged tight. "I'm sorry."

"Don't be, my dear. Tell my Renee that I love her. I will always love her."

They continued to embrace as the water level rose and mortality's expiration closed in.

14

THE
DEMON KING

Suzanne threw anything she could find at a man attempting to climb in the window. He was pummeled with a can full of rusty screws, halogen light bulbs, and an old toilet seat. He shook off each blow to the skull and kept coming. She hit him with a jigsaw and then a carburetor. The last item sliced a gash across his scalp. He blurted gibberish with annoyance.

On a high shelf, Suzanne found an axe. It was long and heavy. She spun to face the intruder, raising the blade over her head.

"Leave me alone!" was the battle cry, and the weapon came down hard, sinking deep into his neck. A horrid odor expelled from the wound when she unwedged the blade.

"Holy hell," she said, covering her nose.

He fell to the snowy ground, twitching. The redhead jumped out the broken window with weapon in hand.

"You guys are slow," she said to the man writhing on the ground. "You guys are stupid." She kicked him in the back. He yowled. "But worst of all…you guys stink!"

A shove by a clawed hand sent Monica sailing into a thick gravestone. Pain shot up her spine and into her neck. The shotgun fell from her grip as she screamed. The mist closed in with the monster inside it. An iron chokehold lifted her into the air with ease. The thing leaned in close, growling. Bloody fangs clenched in a rage. Hot breath washed over her face.

"And now," it said to its victim, "you shall die." Monica fought for air, squirming.

Renee cried "No!" from the overturned van.

Moaning voices resounded across the cemetery above, where a foreboding network of jagged lines sat against a gray sky. A howl of air sent glistening spots of snow across her field of vision. They were dancing, blurred stars, welcoming Monica to oblivion. The demon's fingers clinched tighter around her throat.

And then, in an instant, the monster let go. Monica fell, heaving to fill desperate lungs. Coughing, she looked up and saw the ivory beast turn around. With its back now in view, she saw why it had released its grip. An axe had severed its spine and was wedged deep in bleeding flesh. The demon screeched as it fell face forward into a snowdrift. A woman with messy red hair stepped up, claimed the weapon with a tug, and said, "Asshole."

"Suzanne?" Monica forced out in disbelief.

Her friend smiled, offering a hand. "You saved me. I saved you."

"So we're even?"

Suzanne scowled. "Even? Oh hell, no. You kicked me in the face, remember?"

Still catching her breath, Monica smiled. "Get over it."

Betty's and Dillon's hands were at the rock ceiling with less than a foot of air remaining in the cavern. There were no words left to say. They floated in silence, with nothing to do but wait for the depths to overtake them.

A small light appeared below their feet. It got bigger as Betty put her face in the water to see. A familiar little girl in a nightgown grinned up at her.

Peggy.

The small apparition ascended to the ceiling. Her translucent face glowed above the surface. Dillon and Betty stared into the eleven-year-old's beautiful face.

"Hurry," Peggy said. "Come with me."

The two swam to a previously unseen crack in the ceiling. It was a dark, jagged hole leading upward.

Betty shouted, "A way out!"

"You go," Dillon said. "My strength has failed me. I wouldn't make it."

"No. *Bullshit*. You have to try."

Little Peggy smiled at the old man. "You won't need any strength. I'll help you."

"Thank you, my friend," he said. "But I'm finished. It's all right."

Betty yanked at his submerged shirt. "Maybe you're okay with you drowning, but I'm not." She turned back to Peggy.

The girl ordered, "Betty, you climb inside first." The synthetic woman pulled herself into the overhead crevasse. She stood with feet on either side of the thin ledge around the opening.

"Now you," Peggy said to Dillon.

A hand reached down, grabbing him by the pistol harness strap across his back. He was lifted into the dark hole with ease.

Suddenly, the water level shot upward, and the two were thrust as if through a hose, toward the cemetery above. Betty pulled Dillon close, protecting him as they propelled up the stone tube. A light above got brighter. In an instant they'd traveled more than two hundred feet to the surface. The two were shoved up and out of the stone well and landed with a thud on the graveyard snow. Betty scrambled to Dillon, who rolled over coughing. He rubbed at the ache in his back.

"I'm gonna die," he said with a strained voice. He smiled at his blond counterpart. "But not today."

She laughed. "That's right, old man. And don't you forget it!"

They shared a hug once again as tears flowed freely.

"We did it," he said, "and lived to tell the tale."

"Yeah. Now let's find Monica."

Betty and Dillon approached the van wearily, he with a nine-millimeter pistol drawn, she holding a grimy purple backpack. Monica burst into tears when she spotted them. She ran and nearly knocked them down, hugging in a happy frenzy.

"You made it!" she cried.

Suzanne laughed. "I don't believe it."

Betty chuckled and snorted. "Hey, girlfriend. It's good to see you too."

Dillon was nearly tackled again by his blubbering wife. The couple embraced as if they'd been apart for years.

"Hey," Suzanne said to Betty. "I'm sorry about...you know...before."

The blonde put an arm around the snooty woman from the city. "Apology accepted."

A quake shook the cemetery right below their feet, ending the celebration. The sound of rushing water rose up, and the ground turned to icy mud. Monica and the others raced for the van. An explosion sent a massive jet of Stone Lake into the air in front of the mausoleum. A glistening figure ascended from below, growling. It was not a bear, a tiger, or a shark. At last it had assumed its true form, one more horrible than they'd yet seen.

The massive demon hovered above the frozen ground, snapping long fangs. Its frame was two feet taller than its ivory counterparts. Everything about the unholy creature was thicker, bigger, and deadlier than its lesser brethren, and one other difference set it apart. The pigment of its skin was the color of fresh blood. The crimson monster floated inside a shifting cloud of black smoke. Vacant, empty sockets defied logic as it leered out, over the cemetery. Having no eyes did not keep the demon from focusing on Monica. The innocent. The one it would have.

A dark energy saturated the air, and for a moment, its intended victim felt as though she would faint dead away. The void seemed to pull at her consciousness, stripping away everything that made her human, until all that remained was the deepest primal fear. She couldn't hear

Betty at her side, screaming for her to run. She didn't notice Suzanne pulling at her arm.

In that moment she was alone, staring into the gaze of a thing that could not be. Her monster. Her killer.

Her new red friend.

"I thought you killed it," Suzanne complained.

Dillon backed away, pulling his wife with him. "I thought I did."

Fire blazed in the demon king's empty eyes. Every muscle flexed as it leaned forward, smiling inside the black cloud. "You shall all die..." It pointed a long talon at Monica and smiled. "...starting with that one."

"No," Betty said, stepping in front of her friend. "Start with me." She turned to Monica. "Do me a favor. Figure out how to kill this son of a bitch, would ya?"

Breathless, Monica answered. "Yeah, okay."

Betty took a bat from Renee and then leapt at the beast. It caught her in midair and slammed her to the ground. She scrambled to her feet, diving in again. The monster roared as the battle ensued.

Monica ran for the overturned van, screaming, "Where's the damned notebook?"

Dillon emerged from the back door with it in hand. Suzanne, who was ducked down behind the vehicle, peeked over Renee's shoulder to see. "What's that?"

"A diary," Dillon said, flipping to the last entry. The words sat on the page, just as he'd remembered them: "Its weakness is in its chest. Infuse the heart with"

And that was it. The instructions stopped midsentence, leaving quite a vacancy.

"Infuse the heart with what?" Suzanne asked.

Monica studied the line. "That's what we don't know."

Betty slammed into the underside of the van, sliding the vehicle a foot across the frozen ground. Renee and Suzanne screamed, jumping back. Betty said, "Can you hurry it up, guys?" before sprinting back into conflict.

Monica looked back to Dillon, who'd dropped the book. It lay open with pages to the snow. She looked over the leather cover. Two words had been scratched into the tattered surface. And they'd been written in red ink: "Innocent blood."

"That's it!"

"What's it?" Dillon asked, reaching for the book.

"Infuse the heart with"—she pointed at the back cover—"innocent blood."

"Infuse the heart with innocent blood," Dillon repeated.

Suzanne frowned. "That's friggin' stupid."

Renee was confused. "But how?"

Monica cringed, realizing what had to be done. "Give me your pistol, Dillon." The weapon was set into her palm.

Tears flooded Suzanne's eyes. "What are you gonna do?"

Monica turned to face the monster. "Whatever I have to."

Betty hit the ground once again and then spun around with tight fists as the demon laughed. With a calm voice, Monica spoke to her friend. "Stay back, Betty. This is my fight now."

Amazed, they watched Monica step up to the demon. The creature grinned, waiting for its victim to arrive. "Yes..." it whispered into frigid air. "Come to us. We shall have you now."

She got within the nightmare's reach and stopped. It leaned close, hissing like a snake. Monica growled, "What are you waiting for? I'm right here."

In an instant, blood-red talons snatched her into the air, digging into tender skin at her shoulders and neck. Monica cried out in pain as Suzanne screamed from somewhere behind.

The horror with the hollow eyes ascended into the air, gripping its squirming prey. Needle fangs snapped. Hot breath filled the small space between them.

"And now," the demon wheezed, "time to die."

Monica said, "I agree."

She slapped her left hand on the crimson chest, over its heart. She then pressed the barrel of the pistol against the back of her hand and squeezed the trigger.

The demon winced and dropped the woman. The cloud of black magic faded, and the monster fell to the frozen ground, stumbling. Dark blood boiled over a cracked sternum and snapping ribs. And then, from the inside out, the monster dissolved into liquid.

Monica, on her knees and crying, had never felt such pain. Blood flowed in what seemed like gallons from both sides of her hand. In a panic, she squeezed at the wound, trying to deter blood loss, but a swirling dizziness weakened her grip, along with any logical thought.

Betty was over her in a flash, clamping down on her wrist and forearm.

"Help me lay her down!" she called out with tears streaming. Dillon and Renee eased Monica to a prone position as Suzanne sobbed uncontrollably. "Please," she whispered. "Please help her."

Monica, groggy and pale, looked up into Betty's face. "Did that do it?" she forced out.

"Yeah. It's over."

Dillon said, "Hang in there. I'm gonna call an ambulance."

Before he could turn around, an apparition blasted into view. Little Peggy Wyne descended over the group. "You made a mess," she told the bleeding woman.

A pinpoint of light lifted off the girl's translucent palm, danced in the air for a moment, and then fell onto Monica's wound. A single strobe of energy flashed, startling the observers. When the illumination faded, the pain faded with it. The bullet hole was gone; even the stain on her shirt and the blood on the ground had disappeared. Monica was healed, and her mess was taken care of.

The hovering gathering of friends burst into happy, uncontrollable emotion. Amazed, Monica turned her hand over and back, unable to comprehend the how or why of it all. Betty's happy squeal announced the beginning of a snorting and laughing fit that made Monica smile. All of them joined in as she sat up.

"Thanks, Peggy," she said, but the little girl had vanished. Her job was finished.

As Betty looked out over the graveyard, she realized that *their* job wasn't finished just yet. The grounds may have been demon-free, but the lumbering, limping, and moaning undead still occupied space at Lakeshore Cemetery.

The three women got to their feet, scanning the rotting mob.

"Well," Monica said, "it looks like we've got more to do." Dillon set the shotgun into her hands.

Betty slid the backpack off her shoulder and passed it to Renee.

"You found Peggy's body," Monica said, looking at the dead girl in the pack.

"Yeah. I took her from Bernard over there. Then I ripped his damn head off. It was fun."

"Nice work."

"I'll rebury her after we kill off the rest of these dead assholes."

Monica nudged Suzanne in the ribs. "You up for this?"

The three looked across a graveyard overrun with the living dead. Rotten people stood in random gatherings, slurring and limping.

"Well, let's see," Suzanne said. "My designer shoes are gone. My outfit is destroyed. My nails are all broken. I've got dirt caked in places I'd rather not say...I think it's time for some payback."

The three women looked at each other and laughed.

"Looks like we've got a new badass in town," Betty said.

"Yup," Monica added. "And just to let you know, I don't think I'm gonna move after all. I kinda like it here."

A blonde, a redhead, and a brunette turned to face their enemy.

"Can we get some pancakes after this?" Suzanne asked. "I'm starved."

Betty grinned. "I like the way you think, Red."

Suzanne then turned and planted the axe in a dead man's back.

Thomas Able fell to the ground, complaining. The blade had wedged deep in his shoulder.

"Awe, man," he slurred. "Not again."

END

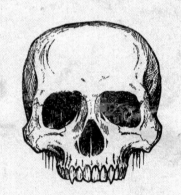

If you enjoyed this book leave me a review.
Thanks!

Also, check out my new supernatural thriller,
DEAD YET DYING,
available wherever you buy ebooks.

Want to stay in the loop
on my current and upcoming projects?
Including everything you need to know about the sequel,
Handbook for the festive Sociopath?
Great!

Go to
http://www.authorbkbrain.com/
and sign up for my newsletter!

As always, thanks so much for reading.

37316361R00172

Made in the USA
Middletown, DE
25 November 2016